Francesca Polini was born and grew up in Rome were she studied languages and politics. She then lived in France, Holland, Mexico and currently resides in London, where she graduated in Economics and obtained a MSc in Corporate Responsibility. She lives with her husband Rick and their children Gaia and Luca, and is the founder and CEO of a sustainability consultancy Wecare, and a canpaigning organisation, Adoption With Humanity.

To Devon with love

MEXICAN TAKEAWAY

FRANCESCA POLINI

Matador
5 Weir Road
Kibworth Beauchamp
Leicester LE8 0LQ, UK
Tel: 0116 279 2277
Email: books@troubador.co.uk
Web: www.troubador.co.uk/matador

ISBN 978-184876-627-3

British Library Cataloguing in Publication Data.
A catalogue record for this book is available from the British Library.

Printed in Great Britain by the MPG Books Group, Bodmin and King's Lynn

Matador is an imprint of Troubador Publishing Ltd

To Aurora

Contents

Acknowledgements

To my husband Rick for joining me on this journey and for his endless patience and calm when the walls seemed to be crumbling. To Anne Aylor who brought the joys of writing home to me through her writing course and made me believe I could write a book. However this book would not have made it had it not been for the hand-holding, coaching and inspiration of Lena Semaan, a talented writer who helped me turn my thoughts into beautiful sentences.

After my initial horror at his ruthless editing, I would also like to thank William Kovalski who kept the book fantastically on track. A big thank you also to Peter Chadwick for his brilliant work on the cover. Last but not least my kind and long suffering family and friends, particularly my parents and brothers, my soul sisters Lisa and Shannon, and finally Oscar who lived through every moment of the adoption process with me and helped me make it through. It is because of their love and support I have a story to tell.

Are you such a dreamer, to put the world to rights?
(Radiohead)

Prologue

I did not legally become a mother until the paperwork was signed and Gaia was ours. But I had become a mother in my heart the instant I made room for her there, long before we had even met.

I'd heard other women speak of that magical moment when their newborn baby was laid on their breast to nurse for the first time. They talked of a sense of recognition, and of forming an eternal bond in an instant. Of course, that instant was really the culmination of a nine-month-long journey, one that could be long, arduous, and fraught with uncertainty.

Our journey to Gaia was no different in that sense. It was a search that often felt like it would never end. More than once it threatened to tear apart my sanity and my marriage to Rick. In my case, though I had not carried Gaia in my body, I had carried her in my soul, dreaming of her with all my might, and like the belly of a pregnant woman my soul had expanded to fit her. I'd spoken to her in my darkest moments, asking her to be patient, to have faith that we were coming. We were meant to be together, I told her. I explained—for I was sure she was listening—that there were great hurdles to be overcome, and there were strong forces working to keep us apart. But I assured her that we would never give up—never.

And we did not. When I first saw my baby, I understood what those birth mothers were talking about. A piece of me that had been missing suddenly clicked into place. In that single moment, all the pain of the past year became worth it. Finally, we were a family. The dark energies that were trying to separate us had been vanquished... or so I thought.

This is the story of how we found our little girl and brought her home. In one way, it's a simple, small story, but I have several strong reasons for writing it.

I write to raise awareness of an issue, the one of adoption, that is both complex and convoluted and where the system is failing the very children it was set up to help. We weren't infertile, that wasn't the issue. We decided to follow our political principles and give love and a home to a child who would otherwise not have one. It was that simple. Or so we thought. In our quest we were judged every step of the way and had to contend with a system that needs reforming and has a long way to go before the choice of giving love to a child who needs it becomes as simple as it ought to be. We were forced to waste precious resources—time, money, energy—on dealing with redundant legal procedures and governmental incompetence, when we could have been lavishing these on our child instead. Every day hundreds of thousands of children are forced to live in dire circumstances or languish in care because the paperwork to adopt them either domestically or from abroad is simply too complicated.

While I understand adoption is not the only way to help them and vetting potential adopters to make sure they will be fit parents is crucial, the process is needlessly long and invasive and bureaucratic. It is quadrupled if you are the first from your own country attempting an international adoption in a certain place for the first time. In our case, we were the first people from the UK to adopt from Mexico, and judging by the reaction we received from adoption and immigration officials, one would think we had announced our intention to eat the child, rather than give her a good home. This is a state of affairs that needs to change, the sooner the better.

I write to give courage to those who feel that the best way for them to help this troubled world is to give a home to a child who otherwise wouldn't have one. Like us, you will sometimes encounter polite confusion at best and outright hostility at worst. Don't give up. Your child is out there waiting for you.

I write especially for the orphaned and abandoned children of the world, of whom there are millions. Many of them will die of starvation, disease, or neglect before reaching adulthood; others will never realise their full potential; and some will even grow into adults who perpetuate the very injustices that caused their own unfortunate circumstances. There are many children in need, but there are also many families who would give them a good home. By raising awareness to this issue and campaigning for a more humane adoption process, I hope less of them will grow up hungry, scared, or sick, with loving parents. It's a dream, I know, but I can think of no more worthy one to pursue.

I am writing also for more general reasons: to give support to those who feel they have a strong vision of how to make the world a better place, but who may feel overwhelmed by the obstacles put in their way by the prejudices of society or the pitfalls of bureaucracy. Two of my heroes are Martin Luther King, Jr., whose famous "I have a dream" speech continues to resonate throughout the world, and Mahatma Gandhi, who said, "Be the change you want to see in the world." Both these men accomplished feats that transformed things on a global level, but they started out small, in the face of tremendous odds, armed only with the belief that one person can make a difference. I believe that no matter what our personal mission or vision may be, following their examples will ultimately benefit all of humanity.

And finally, I am writing this as a gift for Gaia, so that our little girl may read this one day and know how much we always loved her.

Foreword

Common sense might suggest that the route to adoption should be as uncomplicated as possible but we now have a situation in the UK where there are thousands of children in need of a stable permanent home in spite of the increasing demand from potential adoptive parents. Yes, there need to be the necessary rules and checks, however the current experience is one that is exasperating, grueling and unintentionally inhumane. That description does not simply apply to potential parents but also to the children in waiting, and, frequently, the birth parents.

Today it is nearly impossible for a white family in the UK to adopt a black or dual-heritage child. Back in the sixties me and my four ethnically different foster siblings were raised by a single, white woman. Can you imagine that happening in today's climate? It wouldn't because political correctness and the attendant issues of colour and race would take precedence over the need to give a child a loving home. So we wouldn't have had a secure home, food, warmth and the inspiration of a wonderful woman who shaped the way we see the world today.

When I read *Mexican Takeaway*, I strongly felt Francesca's exasperation in her own attempts to navigate the system. While this is a personal book, she does not attempt to wring pity from the reader but rather to show that despite her and her husband's resources- along with her dogged Latin determination and sheer stubborness , it was still insanely difficult to adopt a child either in the UK or internationally.

It appears that our society has replaced basic human needs (especially those of children in care) with the kind of obsessive bureaucracy that has led to race, religion and class becoming key criteria for matching children and potential parents. As desirable as this looks on paper, it doesn't acknowledge the realities of the world we live in; a world where the majority of children looking for homes are black or of mixed race and the majority of parents willing or able to adopt are white. The system also fails to recognize that children *do* pass their sell-by date in the adoption stakes once they leave toddler-hood so it's ill-advised to let children languish in temporary care, waiting for all the boxes to be ticked in the search for a politically correct 'fit'.

This is as much a book about a life-changing journey as it is a story of a couple's attempts to adopt. My view is that even if you are not directly interested in the subject of adoption you will be gripped by this emotional, funny and observant road trip through Mexico.

At the same time *Mexican Takeaway* raises some key issues that I hope will inspire discussion and action. When tens of thousands of children, both here and abroad, languish in care until they are teenagers only to be thrown into the big wide world with no support, something isn't right.

A merry go round of multiple foster homes is simply not an alternative to a secure, permanent home for a child. In the end it is about love. Luckily today we live in a world where the concept of family is a diverse one. If there are people who will love and care for you, then you have a chance in life. In writing this book, Francesca wants to open up the debate so that ultimately more children can have that shot at a life. I hope so too.

Bruce Oldfield OBE

BRUCE OLDFIELD OBE

Bruce Oldfield was taken into care by Barnardo's as soon as he was born. He was brought up by a seamstress, which led to his love for designing and making clothes.

In 1975 the Bruce Oldfield label was born and throughout his long career Bruce's couture clients have included celebrities, aristocracy and royalty, most notably the late Diana, Princess of Wales. His couture and bridal boutiques in Beauchamp Place, London SW3 continue to offer a couture and custom made service that is second to none.

In 1990 Bruce was awarded Officer of the British Empire (OBE) for services to The British Fashion Industry. He actively supports Barnardo's and has been one of its Vice Presidents since 1998.

www.bruceoldfield.com

1

Too White To Adopt

June 5th, 2008

The queue in the customs hall at Heathrow was long, full of weary and bad-tempered travellers, but I didn't care. I was just happy to be home. We stood behind the yellow line, waiting our turn to be called to the desk.

"Next, please."

Rick went ahead and put our three passports triumphantly on the counter.

The agent, her skin pallid, her brows wrinkled, peered at us over her spectacles with suspicion. I wondered if it was because our passports were each of a different nationality; his British, mine Italian, and Gaia's Mexican.

She looked down and then looked up again, this time with a stony visage.

"Where have you been?"

"Mexico," I said happily.

"For how long?"

"Five months."

"Why were you there for five months? What were you doing?"

"We were adopting our daughter. This is her," Rick said.

"Adopting, were you?"

I sensed she was angling for something.

"Yes, we went especially to adopt a child."

"Is she yours then?"

What a strange question, I thought.

"Of course she is ours," Rick said proudly. "See? There's our surnames on her passport"

She shot him a glare, then fixed us with a look that said: *Here is another couple trying to cheat me.*

"Did you visit the Embassy before travelling?"

"Of course we did." Rick's reply was clipped. The poor guy had been suffering food poisoning for weeks and barely had the energy to stand, let alone put up with an inquisition.

"We have all our documents here in case you wish to see them," I said helpfully. She ignored me and looked hard at Rick.

"Mr Bowden, I will have to detain this baby and yourselves."

I gripped Rick's hand. He looked at me as if to say, "I'll talk."

"What are you talking about? This is nonsense."

The agent wrote something on a piece of paper.

Gaia, who was unsurprisingly exhausted after thirty-six hours of bus and plane travel, began to scream. I ground my teeth and tried not to cry.

"Didn't you hear? I am detaining your daughter." She handed Rick the piece of paper. "Follow me," she said.

We followed her to a tiny cubicle, where two Mexican girls had already taken up involuntary residence in one corner. They both looked scared. One of them was sobbing. We looked at the paper where she had written Gaia's name. It read:

Gaia Polini, I am detaining you. I am also confiscating your passport.

"How can you arrest a baby?" I asked. She shot me a look of pure poison, then turned to Rick.

"Listen to me. There are a lot of things you are supposed to have done before you brought that baby into *this* country. You are supposed to have interviews with social workers, and something called a Home Study…"

I jumped up.

"But we did all that. I can tell you the name of our social worker, and even the name of the person we met today at the embassy before leaving!"

"I am not talking to you. You are not even British."

This woman was pure bile. I wanted to scream at her, to shake her, to say, "Don't you understand what we have gone through to bring this child here?"

She ignored the question and then began to address Rick as if he was intellectually challenged.

"Now, Richard. Let me tell you why I have put you in this little room. We are here to protect the welfare of the children, and you clearly haven't followed the legal steps to get you here. There are many people like you who try and bring babies illegally into the country."

God, did she think we were child traffickers? I had to put her right.

"But... but..." I said.

Rick shot me a look that said, *Please keep your mouth shut.*

Gaia, meanwhile, was yelling at the top of her lungs, despite my best efforts to rock her to sleep. Her nappy was wet, and she was hungry, but I was too scared to say or do anything, I had run out of boiled water to mix with the formula milk, so I couldn't even comfort her with her bottle.

"Now, what documents, if any, do you have with you?" she asked Rick.

"We have them all," I said to Rick.

I started pulling them out of the trolley suitcase.

"Home Study..." I was spelling them out one by one to him as I was getting them out, knowing she would hear and realise she was wrong.

"References, CRB checks, finance checks, birth certificates, marriage certificate, psychology report, doctor's report, certificate of eligibility, Gaia's birth certificate, adoption order from the court of Colima, ticket of meeting with the British embassy."

As I finished emptying the bag, a look of surprise appeared on her face. Then she turned to me and said: "I need your passport too. I am confiscating that also."

🐖

There's a name for people like us who can have children but choose to adopt instead. We are called preferential adopters.

How we got to that point is a result of my family background and political beliefs, Rick's own beliefs about society, the desire to share our lives with a little one, and a hell of a lot of debate.

Rick and I had been married for two years, but we'd been together for six. We were happy and childless by choice. We were the stereotypical high-flying couple with dream jobs that took us around the world, often in different directions. We commuted regularly to exotic cities, and for both of us the lifestyle was addictive... for a time. But the novelty had worn off. We began to feel like it just wasn't quite enough. We had so much to give that it didn't feel right to keep it all to ourselves.

We had gone back and forth with the thought of starting a family. Yet something about having a baby just didn't seem 'real'. Our conversations fluctuated wildly between for and against. We'd talk about how exciting our life was compared to that of our friends with children, but how uninspiring, exhausting, and empty it could be. Relationships need to move forward, and frankly there are only so many weekend breaks you can have before you think: *I've done this all before. There has to be more.*

That 'more' was a family.

Falling in love had happened relatively late for us, and we knew better than to take it for granted. We both felt we had been able to put the 'soul' in our soulmate relationship. We didn't just like each other; we each thought the other would make a great parent.

When I hit thirty-five, I realised that I didn't want young teenagers when I was heading towards sixty. For Rick, this appeared to be the signal he was waiting for. We began to discuss the possibility of children in earnest. For most people, that discussion would usually revolve around the woman taking folic acid, keeping track of exactly when her period came, and ensuring they had sex on the 'right' days.

"We are trying for a baby," they would then announce to their friends.

Our methodology was more unorthodox. For a start, I had strong social and political beliefs, borne of the teachings of an intellectual trade union leader father and a savvy mother.

My parents gave me a biological brother, but also an adopted one. Growing up with Francesco taught me that not everyone in the world was as lucky as we were. I am sure there are many middle-class children in the Western World who would not consider having to share the sofa bed in the lounge with a little brother as 'lucky'. We lived in a tiny flat, and we had hardly any toys. But we had a family, and we had love, which my parents felt we could share with another, less fortunate person. They taught us that love is something you give away. The more you give, the more it grows, and this is how we help create a better world. They also taught us that a home is not a gigantic house or a bedroom to yourself, but a roof over your head, a nourishing meal, and plenty of cuddles. My views on social justice and opportunity were established well before I became a news journalist and saw the world in all its beautiful humanity and ugly despair.

Rick had also come from a very socially aware family. He grew up in a council flat in Scotland, with parents whose flower power ethics stayed with them throughout adulthood and influenced their teaching careers. He shared my views on home, family, and love. We were in perfect agreement: love makes the world a better place.

One lazy, rainy November weekend, after making love, I lay on my back while Rick lazily stroked my stomach.

"You'd look stunning as a pregnant woman," he said.

"What?" I smiled.

"You heard me."

"Really… I wasn't necessarily thinking that's how we would start our family."

"What do you mean?"

"There are already so many children in the world with no love in their lives. You know I've always felt we would do more good by opening our hearts to a child who's already here, whose life would be miserable otherwise."

"So no baby with my eyes and your hair?"

"Is it so important to you to have a little mini-me? You men and your egos!"

"Fra," he said. "You can't simplify it like that. Humans have a biological and emotional need to procreate. You can't just say that has to be put aside in order to help suffering children. You're opening up a big Pandora's box on the whole business of existence if you do that."

But the more we talked about it, the more he became open to thinking beyond having a child in his own image. He was more curious about adoption than afraid of it. Initially our deliberations were abstract, but over a period of months they became more serious and specific.

♠

"I am in two minds about it, really," he said one night over dinner in our favourite local restaurant.

"I know you are. But don't you agree that there are so many children in need in this world that we don't need to necessarily procreate? Plus we have limited resources, and there are too many people on our suffering planet, right?"

Silence, while he pretended to read the menu.

I turned to the waiter, who'd been waiting.

"What do you think? Do you have children?"

The poor guy had nowhere to go.

"Er, no, I don't, but… I think adoption is a good thing to do if you feel that strongly. Can I take your order?"

I wasn't listening. I was on my soapbox.

"It's upsetting how in today's supposed 'developed world' we just *want, want, want*. We *want* children, we *want* a boy or a girl, we *want* two or three or just one, we *want* them white, black or a nice mixture of the two. We *want* them to look like us. I guess I am no better as what I am really saying is that I *want* to adopt! Oh, it's so complicated."

Rick tried to change the subject.

"Fra, they've got your favourite risotto on again. Look, wild mushroom. Come on. We'd better order."

"I just know…in my heart that it's… right… at least for me… for us…"

Rick interrupted.

"Francesca is having mushroom risotto. I'll have the halibut, thanks."

He'd had enough for now. But I knew he was thinking about it.

◆

Pretty soon everything we did seemed to lead to the question of having a family and how we should do it. Watching documentaries about disaster or famine, seeing the faces of children who were starving or homeless or orphaned by war, was a cue for me to put forward my views.

"There are just so many children out there reaching out to us. You are right," he would say.

"And?" I'd say, hoping for some definitive answer.

"Sometimes I want to take them all home with me. But we're still not going to solve the world's problems by adopting one of them, or even two or three."

"Look, I am sorry. I hope this hasn't become an obsession. I agree with you. It's just a very small way of giving something back.

But then, as Gandhi would say, you have to be the change you want to see in the world, right? And I think we can be that change."

"We can't jump to such a decision. It's just not that simple. Perhaps we should do both."

"What? Adopt and have a baby? One has to come first."

The reality was that the experience of pregnancy and natural birth did appeal to me too. But the need to adopt was overtaking my biological desires. I can't explain it any other way than to say it felt like the right thing for me to do.

One night, early in January of 2008, Rick asked me to take the next morning off work.

"Why?"

"I can't tell you. It's a surprise."

"Oh, sure. Tell me you have a surprise late at night and expect me to sleep. Come on, out with it."

I'd seen him hiding away in his study and being quite secretive. This just wasn't his way. I worried. I thought maybe he was ill, and was working out how to tell me. We got into bed, but every time he looked like he was about to fall asleep, I'd wake him up and beg him to tell me what was going on.

Finally he sat up.

"You always ruin surprises, don't you?"

"Sorry, it's just that I need to know. I can't sleep with this tension. I am worried about you." I sat up too.

"Well… we have an appointment with the council to discuss adoption. I figured that way we'll both know more about it, and we can get closer to deciding what to do. Call it my New Year resolution."

"Wow. Oh, Rick… I didn't think you were listening!"

"Ah, well, you don't know me as well as you think. The appointment is at nine o'clock, so you have four hours to get some sleep."

He drew me towards him, gently turned me so we were like perfect spoons, and wrapped his arms around me. I lay there most of the night with my eyes open.

In the morning, I was frantic.

"God, I can never get it right!" I yelled.

"What are you talking about?" he said, coming into the bathroom. I showed him my smudged and smeared fingernails. It was my third shot at painting them, and probably only the fifth time in my life I'd bothered doing it.

"You look great. You don't need nail varnish, and anyway it's not you. Let's get going, or we'll be late." He strode out and down the stairs.

I quickly removed the offending polish and ran after him.

It was an icy winter morning in London, which meant we were late to our appointment.

At the council office, we were met by a woman with a no-nonsense short haircut and just a trace of a smile. She was, however, wearing a pair of funky red spectacles. I wondered if this was a good sign. They were just the kind of glasses I would buy for myself.

"Good morning. I'm Anne, the adoption team leader. Please take a seat."

She wasted no time giving us our first reality check.

"You can't adopt in the UK, I am afraid. You are too white," she said.

I didn't know whether to laugh at such a ridiculous statement, or cry at its implications.

"Too white? What is that supposed to mean?" asked Rick, before I could.

Anne answered in the jaded tone of someone who'd done this many times before.

"Well, there is a cap on the number of white couples who can adopt in this area of the country, because most of the children for adoption are black. That's the way it works in our local council."

I was shocked.

"Surely it should be up to us to choose," I said.

"No, it isn't. Not much in this process is up to you, I'm afraid," she said, peering over her spectacles. "You could think about registering for international adoption."

"How?"

"You enroll in an introductory training course to learn about the mechanics of the process, so you can make an informed decision. At the same time it allows us to establish if you're suitable candidates for a Home Study. The next available spaces for training are not until April, I'm afraid. This is the number you need to ring to book yourselves in. The centre will contact you directly if you have been successful, so you don't need to contact me any more."

Then she checked her watch.

"Look, I'm sorry, I don't mean to be rude, but I have another matter to deal with right now. I wish you the best of luck with it all."

Seven minutes. Done. Now run along and take your hopefulness with you.

"Wow, that was quick and nasty," I said as we got to the car.

"And look at this! We have a parking fine, too!"

Rick grabbed a yellow plastic envelope from the windscreen and dangled it.

"By the way, did you realise you were wearing your recycled shoes? I couldn't stop looking at them."

I looked down. I was indeed wearing my prized recycled black trainers, made from car tire waste. I must've picked them up in the rush—they were pretty much a habit these days, and I was rarely without them.

"Oh, no. How embarrassing. Did they look really stupid with my dress?"

"Yep." Rick ran around to the back of the car and pretended to hide.

"Bastard."

That seven minutes had drained us, but had also provided a lot to think about. And call it luck or fate, but a vacancy for the initial adoption training suddenly became available at the end of January.

2

Does Your Cat Speak Spanish?

"Do I look OK?" Rick said as he came into the bedroom, wearing his cream suit and his best tie.

"Uh oh. Cream?"

"I don't want to wear a dark one. It doesn't seem friendly enough; too businesslike. They might think I don't have time for children if I wear that."

I'd never seen Rick this anxious. He was normally so calm and composed about absolutely everything.

"I think I want to marry you all over again. It means a lot that you're going along with me on this."

"Fra, I believe in adoption too. I am not going along with you just because you are stubborn, which you are! I can totally see the point, but I want to know more and see if it is for *us*. I'm our left brain, remember?"

I collapsed in giggles on the bed. Rick bounced over and gave me a huge hug.

"Careful, you'll crease the suit."

"Shut up, you."

We kissed, then lay there just holding each other close for a while.

I had opted for a more casual look than Rick. Smart jeans, a long blue cardigan, and a pair of boots instead of recycled shoes. It was freezing again. In the car, I asked him: "Where do you think you are in your heart, Rick?"

"I find it frustrating that they have to decide for us that we cannot adopt locally. It's not like there are no children who need a family here in London."

"I mean what about adoption? How do you feel about it now?"

"I think if we decide it's worth a shot, we should start the adoption and try to have natural children at the same time."

"And then let the Universe decide which one is right first."

"I knew you'd say that! You and your Universe!" There were times when Rick's pragmatism and my spiritual outlook clashed, but on the whole our combination worked.

🐟

We filed into a room with the other couples who were doing the training. There was tea, coffee and biscuits on offer. Everyone seemed very shy. This wasn't surprising, since for most couples choosing adoption is a public admission that they can't have children.

We were invited into a room and directed to a circle of chairs. I chose to sit next to a woman who appeared to be alone. Rick sat on the other side of me, munching a biscuit.

"This is what it must be like attending a twelve-step programme," he whispered.

"Sshh! Someone might hear you!"

The two trainers arrived and introduced themselves. They were both women, and they exuded warm energy. One had an endless mane of hair and wore a long hippie skirt. With her big eyes and enormous glasses, she reminded me of a cartoon character from *A Bug's Life*. The other woman wore a suit and smart flat shoes, and sported an elegant short bob.

"Hello everyone, and well done for arriving on time in such bad weather. It shows this means a lot to you. We are trainers for this course, and also we are both international adopters. I have two Bolivian children, and Susan has a Chinese girl as well as a natural one."

"Oh, good," I whispered to Rick. "They've actually done it."

"At the end of today you will have understood more about the process, and we will file a report for your council to say whether or not we feel you are ready to start the Home Study."

No pressure then.

We were asked to introduce ourselves and say a little about why we were there. I realised suddenly that we would be putting ourselves on show in public for the first time. Amongst the couples talking about their fertility problems, multiple miscarriages, and failed attempts at in vitro fertilization, we would stick out. God, what were we doing here? Did we have a right to be in that room? I felt slightly ashamed when it was my turn to speak.

"For all intents and purposes we can conceive, but we feel strongly that adoption should play a big part for various reasons."

It turned out the single woman next to me, who was a Spanish journalist, had also decided on adoption, even though she could have children. At the end of the introduction, one of the trainers gestured towards us and said:

"The three of you are called *preferential adopters*. This means that you have chosen to build your family via adoption and not because of fertility issues. The rest of you are traditional adopters."

"What if we wanted to adopt and try and have natural children too?" asked the Spanish lady.

Thank God she asked that one. I was dying to know but didn't want to appear too radical or anything.

The woman from *A Bug's Life* answered.

"You can't do that. If you happen to fall pregnant during the Home Study you will have to stop the adoption, have your baby, and wait until he or she is at least three years of age before you can start the process all over again. If you have a miscarriage, you will have to wait for two years to grieve and overcome the trauma."

Two years to overcome a miscarriage! How did they work that out?

"How do you even know if we are trying, anyway?" I joked.

"Your life will never be the same, my dear, once you say yes to the adoption process. Believe me, it'll feel like a crowd of people are watching you having sex."

Laughter from around the room.

"Seriously, guys, your entire life will be scrutinised every step of the way. Nothing will pass unnoticed."

Later, when we were let out for lunch, we sat with the Spanish woman and three other couples in a nearby deli, conducting a post-mortem on the morning's proceedings.

"So which country do you think you would like to adopt from?" asked the Spanish lady.

"We would like to adopt from Russia because my husband has blond hair and mine is dark, so we figured that whether the baby is from the eastern or western part of the country, it will look like one of us," said one woman.

"We're going for China, as we want a baby girl at any cost, and all babies for adoptions are girls," said another woman.

"Anyway, as if I'm going to stop trying in the meantime!" said Michelle. She and her husband Simon had already attempted I.V.F. a few times.

"What was that all about? What gives them the right to be all Stasi-like about sex?" I said.

"No disrespect to you guys," said the single Spanish lady, looking around the table, "but it seems almost as if adoption is an industry for infertile people. Unlike those of us who choose, often in your cases it's a second best, right?"

She may as well have thrown a hand grenade. It was clear that at least one couple were taking her comment personally. The table went quiet.

"Oh, look at the time," said Rick. "We'd better get back."

The rest of the day was spent in various exercises, scenarios, and conversations about the pitfalls and challenges of the adoption process. At the end of the day, one of the trainers looked around at us all and said:

"It won't be the same for all of you, and some will handle it better than others. But it's neither an easy ride nor a short one. You have anything from two to four years ahead of you from this moment. But I am sure you will all be fine. Good luck."

I felt like I do when my Chinese doctor sticks a million needles in my face, tummy, ears and neck, then calmly says, "You can sleep now till I am back."

Really?

🐖

The invasion into our lives, also known as the Home Study, began in the first week of February. I'd been up early making sure the house was in pristine condition, arranging biscuits artfully on a plate and trying to meditate to relax. Rick was wearing his cream suit again, as one does at 8:00 am on a Saturday.

I was at the window, peering through the slatted blinds, when an unfamiliar car pulled up across the road and stopped. The woman driver took something out of her bag.

"Do you think that's her?"

Rick looked.

"Yes, I'd say that's her. Why would you eat your breakfast in the car unless you were going to see people you didn't know?"

The doorbell rang. I opened the door as nonchalantly as I could.

"Hello, you must be Francesca. I'm Barbara. Lovely to meet you."

Barbara stepped inside. She was a tall, slim woman with a lovely disposition.

"Not a very good idea to have all these wine bottles on your shelves when your social worker is coming to visit," she laughed, looking around, "but as I'm half French, I love my wine and will forgive you because you have good taste."

"Then I hope you'll like my biscuits," I said, offering her the plate as Rick poured the tea. We all sat down.

"They look gorgeous, but I don't eat or drink during the visits, thank you." She opened her laptop. "Let's get started. How did you two meet?"

"We met at work. I had been admiring Francesca from afar for months, but had been too shy about approaching her."

"Did she have to use her Italian charm and ask you out then?" Barbara laughed again while she typed every single word we said on her small laptop. We found ourselves relaxing. This wasn't so bad.

But we soon came to realise that her questions were unbelievably intrusive. Over subsequent visits, they became even more so. Although it became easier to talk to Barbara and to see her as part of our team, we never let ourselves believe for one moment she was our friend. As nice as she was, she was there on behalf of the council to determine if we were fit to adopt. And that meant asking us a lot of questions that you don't get asked if you're carrying a baby in your tummy.

When you're pregnant, people don't ask if you have a sense of humor. Or where you will put the medicine cabinet when the baby is born. Barbara insisted on detailed descriptions of our grandparents, brothers, cousins, and even our neighbours. She wanted to know what we liked and disliked about each other, how many partners we'd been with before each other, why we liked them, why we finished with them, and if we were still in touch. Were we happy, were our parents happy, were we achievers, would we smack a child, were we racists, were our friends racist, were they supportive of us, what do we like doing with our friends and family, did we drink, how much, was it wine, beer or spirits, would I go back to work, would it be part-time, would we change the child's name, who would look after the child when we go back to work?

She even asked how our cat would react to a child in the house who doesn't speak English.

The illusion perpetuated by high-profile American celebrities—

that the adoption process is as simple as visiting a big global sweetshop and picking the flavour and colour you want—is just that, an illusion. For us mere mortals, you have to prove yourselves time and time again.

🐾

"You're lucky. At least you can start straight away," Michelle said over coffee, the Sunday after our first Home Invasion. "We've been told that we're not ready."

"What does that mean?"

"The trainers sent a report to the Council saying that I have not overcome the trauma of I.V.F. yet and am not ready to even start the Home Study."

"Oh, I'm so sorry!"

"It's upsetting. I have started learning Chinese, though. That will keep me busy for some time!"

I admired Michelle's spirit. She refused to let this setback get her down. Soon enough, I would need to call on her for her support, and this same determined energy would help sustain me as we suffered setbacks of our own.

🐾

"Today we have to discuss your choice of country. Let's first think about racial considerations," announced Barbara during one of our Home Invasions.

"We haven't really thought about it at length. We wouldn't mind a child who isn't white," said Rick.

"This is not about you, it's about the child. What shades of black would you be comfortable with? How many mixed raced families do you know?"

We didn't know many mixed race families. In fact, we knew just one. We had African and Asian friends and colleagues, but nobody who was really mixed.

"You see," she continued, "this is about walking around with

17

your adopted child and everyone knowing you are not his natural parents. You are white, they are black. Can you handle it? Can you handle the questions that he or she and *you* will be asked constantly at school, the taunts in the playground? Or the funny looks in the supermarket?"

We spent many nights thinking about this. In the end, we decided that we were probably not quite ready for a child of a different race. We opted for Russia, where many UK couples were adopting from. As usual, Rick was able to look at it logically.

"Look, Fra, we're both multilingual. You speak six languages. I speak three. So we have to choose a country where we can converse with the lawyers, the social workers, the staff from the children's home, and obviously with the kid."

I wasted no time. Thinking of Michelle and her Chinese lessons, I took out my old Russian books out and started reviewing.

🐾

Because there are no private adoption agencies in the UK, we had to find one in another country. But we didn't even know where to start looking. At that time, Rick lived and worked in London, while I rented an apartment in Geneva, where I worked most weekdays. These life-changing decisions were therefore taken at the weekend, or on the phone in between meetings.

SHOULD WE CHOOSE AN AGENCY IN THE US OR RUSSIA ITSELF? THE US ONES ARE MORE EXPENSIVE BUT MY RUSSIAN ISN'T GOOD ENOUGH TO DEAL WITH AUTHORITIES… I texted Rick one day.

YOUR CALL…was his answer.

I was restless for the rest of the day, waiting for the evening when we could speak on the phone. This was too important to be left to me. Cycling home, I reminded myself to stay calm. I should have been pleased that he was going along with it all and trusting me. But still I felt that I was doing all the work. Our 'paper pregnancy' was like any natural one. A woman's business. All Rick had to do was turn up at the Home Invasions. As I was locking the bike, another text:

STILL IN MEETINGS, THEN DINNER WITH BOSS. REALLY HAPPY FOR YOU TO DECIDE. MISS YOU. X

Yeah, miss me.

I went upstairs, opened the window, and sat there watching everything and nothing. Was he doing this just for me? Were we good enough to adopt? I felt lonely.

My best companions were my Tarot cards. I burnt some incense, sat on the bed, and took them out of their beautifully hand carved wooden box. I held the blue velvet pouch in my hands for a moment. Embroidered on the front was the eye of Horus, the ancient Egyptian symbol of strength. I closed my eyes, putting my left hand on the cards and my right on my heart, where I have the same symbol tattooed to protect me from evil. I asked the cards to tell me if I… if *we*… were doing the right thing.

I pulled a card and placed it face down. I opened my eyes and turned it. The Fool. My favourite card. It shows a garishly dressed young traveller, with his (or her) possessions wrapped in a small sack tied to a stick, skipping along an isolated mountain road under a bright sun and golden sky. The path is treacherous. But the Fool is looking blissfully above. He is walking perilously close to a cliff, and his only companion, a small dog, is energetically attempting to alert him to where he is headed. The Fool's impractical clothing is not the best choice for the mountains. In fact, everything about this journey seems to be impractical. He is more interested in the flowers and the exhilarating walk than in the possibly disastrous fall that may await. That's because he knows deep down that even if he makes the jump, the Universe will look after him.

I put the rest of the cards back and emailed Barbara to let her know that we needed an agency to help with a Russian adoption. She replied that she knew of one in Israel, which I promptly contacted.

HAVE WE DECIDED THEN? I AM NERVOUS! Rick texted at 10:00 pm.

YUP, THE ONE FROM ISRAEL, BARBARA'S RECOMMENDATION. X

I replied.

COOL, I KNEW YOU'D MAKE THE RIGHT CHOICE. SORRY CAN'T CALL, SPEAK TOMORROW, SLEEP WELL.X

Perhaps he did care. He was just being him, and I was being me. I was excited. Amidst all the bureaucracy, there now seemed to be the first inkling of humanity in the process.

♣

It was now Easter, a time of new beginnings, so we decided to go public with our decision to adopt. First we went to Rome, my home. Rick's parents lived in Italy as well, so we spent a joyous time there, sharing the good news. Despite a few minor misgivings, everyone was highly supportive, and many toasts were drunk to our happiness.

With the family and our best friends informed, it was time to let more people know. A very good friend, Alex, had invited me to her son's birthday party, so it seemed a good time to share. I didn't mind going to children's parties, even when I knew I would be the only non-mum attending. And I was buoyed by the reactions so far. As the sugar kicked in and the kids began to go feral in the garden, the conversation amongst the mums inevitably turned to children; toddler tantrums, babies in progress, stretch marks, breast-feeding and sore nipples, and how clever each child was. I sat there, just listening. Then Alex said:

"Did I tell you all that Francesca and Rick are going to adopt a baby soon? We are so excited for them!"

There was a long pause.

"Ah. I see you have decided to go for the ready-made family option," was Alex's mother-in-law's immediate reaction. I froze.

"Oh, I am so sorry you can't have children, I hadn't realised," said a mum. Others looked at me as if they'd just heard I was dying.

"Well, actually, Rick and I can have children. We are not infertile," I said softly.

"Are you some sort of celebrity wannabe then?" laughed another one. "I think it's terrible what Madonna does, going to countries to pick a kid and bring him home. Children should stay in their country."

"I agree with you, actually," I said. "People like her give us a bad name for the wrong reasons."

"I have to say I had thought about doing it myself," said someone else, "but I have heard it's really expensive. Is it true?"

"Yes, very expensive," I said.

"I think it's really brave, and you must have a good husband to come along with this," said someone else.

"Personally, I would never give up the best time in a woman's life. Being pregnant is just such a jolly good time! And there is no way your baby is going to bond with you after not having been in your tummy," said Katy, a quintessential yummy mummy who, only an hour earlier, had been moaning about her stretch marks and debating the possibility of a tummy tuck.

Her mate Felicity chipped in.

"Why are you adopting then, instead of having your own children?"

I thought I'd answer with a question to the group:

"So why did you have babies?"

The longest silence I had ever heard ensued.

"Well, you know, body clock and all that…" was all Katy could muster.

"I can't stand my job, but I was allowed a long paid maternity leave, so it felt right," said Felicity.

"I can imagine how wonderful it is to have a baby," I said. "I think it will also be magical to take our baby home, too, and give her a different life from what she would have had in a children's home."

"I think it's fantastic," said Alex.

But to the rest of them I was a freak, the 'fool', a woman who didn't want 'her own' children. So I just had to take it on the chin.

Sometimes I do wonder what is 'natural' about childbirth today in Western countries. Everything is planned to the nth degree. It doesn't seem to be a random act of nature left to instinct and *actual* body clock. There is a whole army of advice from obstetricians, GPs, friends, family and magazines who print articles like "Ten things you must know before you have a baby." You have to attend trainings where you are told how to breast feed, for how many months no matter whether you produce milk or not, how you are supposed to feel and how long your baby will need to sleep in the bed with you till it's ready to go to another room. Then there's the books, the 'baby bibles' that, as a friend put it, "hung over you like a black cloud of your own failures till you become fixated that you are not capable of ensuring your baby's survival" even in the safest, most equipped environment. What is natural about IVF, artificial insemination, surrogate mothers? And fundamentally does it matter how you bring a child into your life? Whether it's natural love, IVF or adoption, bringing a new soul into your family should be about one's ability to love and nurture another being. In my view, it's that simple.

"I better get going," I told Alex. "I don't like cycling in the dark."

"I'm so sorry..."

"It's not your fault. I need to get used to people's reactions."

I walked out, texting Michelle.

HELP, JUST BEEN AT KID'S PARTY, ALL POSSIBLE 'REAL MUM'S' REACTIONS CAME MY WAY!

IT'S JUST THE BEGINNING MY DEAR. STARTING THE HOME STUDY ON MONDAY. LOVE YOU, NOW GO HOME TO YOUR HUSBAND.

She was right. I just needed Rick. As he would point out much later, we were judged every step of the way. Always presumed guilty until innocent.

❦

It was a Saturday night when I heard the news from Russia. I had come in late and gone upstairs to read my emails, hoping for news about a baby. A stack of spam, and then I saw it: a message from the lady who ran the agency in Israel.

> Dear Francesca,
> Upon checking your documentation I would like to request your certificate of infertility. This is a compulsory requirement for adopting in Russia; please ensure you send it at your earliest convenience.

What? Nobody has told us this!
And then some helpful advice:

> If you can't find one you could pay a doctor to fake one for you or we can help you find someone in Russia who would do it for you, but this will cost a lot of money.

Yeah, great idea.

On Monday, back in my Geneva office, I found an empty room and called Rick. I didn't want anyone listening, as I hadn't made it public at work that we were adopting.

"Hey, Fra." He sounded busy.

I told him what the agency in Israel had said.

"That's interesting," he said.

"Interesting! Is that all you have to say? Rick, this is our life, not just mine!" I tried to stay composed. I didn't want people on the other side of the glass window to see how upset I was.

"Look, I haven't got time for this now. I'm driving. Why don't we speak when you are back in London?"

"Can you at least turn the music down? I can't even hear you. I don't want to wait for three days. I want to reply to the email. At least tell me, do you think we should try and get a fake certificate?"

"No idea. Listen, I'm off to a meeting and I don't want to be late. I'll call later, OK?"

That was it. He had no idea how hard it would be to decide on another country. That meant more visits from Barbara, and perhaps another rejection. He didn't even seem to care. I was doing the worrying for both of us.

But Rick has to think things through quietly, decide on a solution, and just get on with it. As it turned out, it would be he who made the moves that would prove to be decisive.

"Mexico," he said as we got in the car at the airport.

"Sorry?"

"We'll adopt from Mexico. Guatemala's closed to European adoption, the wait for China is long, and you're fluent in Spanish. It makes sense all round. I think a Mexican child would be a good match for us."

And just like that, the clouds cleared again. We knew already we wanted a baby girl, up to two years old. Plus we didn't feel we had enough experience with older children. As always, Barbara tried to temper our expectations.

"It's going to be very difficult to adopt from a country where nobody in the UK has adopted from before," she warned.

"We're prepared to be the first," said Rick.

Autumn came, and it was time for Barbara's initial report, together with our references, finance checks, police checks, and doctor's reports to be reviewed by a panel of twenty people. They asked us yet more intrusive questions, and we did our best to convince them that we would be great adoptive parents. One by one they gave us the 'yes' we needed.

"Don't get too excited," Barbara had whispered as we left the room. "Remember, you still have to get the piece of paper." True, we still needed the certificate of eligibility from the DCSF.

Save for that formality we were on our way. We had now settled on an American agency that helped place children from Mexico, and since the board had approved us, we could proceed. I wasn't sure whether to cry or throw up. Months of tension had finally given way to release. As soon as we left the room, Barbara, Rick, and I all hugged each other. We stepped out into the most glorious autumn sunshine, the red and yellow leaves on the trees clapping at our good news.

I called Michelle.

"We did it! They just had some doubts about us being able to adopt a newborn, but I put them right!"

"Yeah, with us it was more about IVF and whether I had mentally recovered, but it only lasted five minutes! See you guys for dinner soon."

It was 11:00 a.m. Champagne was called for, but we had chocolate cake and coffee instead.

"I can't believe it, Fra. In only a few weeks we should have a referral from the US agency, and our Mexican baby will be even closer. Are you even listening?"

"Sorry, my phone keeps on beeping," I said, rummaging for it in the depths of my handbag. "Look, it's mum, dad, Francesco, your mum, Paolo, Lilly from Australia! I'm so happy! We need to make sure we get a sibling soon too, a brother."

"You're already thinking about the next thing. So much for the woman who lives in the present!"

That night, Rick left for Leeds, and my brother Paolo arrived. To celebrate, we headed for a Greek restaurant, in memory of the single most inspirational woman in both our lives, our Greek grandmother. The next morning, despite the hangover, I felt on top of the world. I got up early, while Paolo was still snoring away, and opened my email, eager to broadcast the good news to my friends. And then, another shot through the heart, in the form of an email from the US agency:

Hello Francesca,

I have some sad news. I have been asked to suspend the placement of Mexican babies to European couples. Therefore, we cannot assist you in adopting from Mexico. Best of luck.

Best of luck? Is this about luck? How can they pull out now that panel have approved us to work with them?

I rang Rick, who was his usual quiet self. Unlike me, he had no need to articulate everything he felt. I reminded myself that he was probably just letting the thing ferment in his brain. It didn't mean he didn't care; he was just waiting for the right time to respond. It made sense. Nonetheless, at times like these, I would verbally prod and poke him and eventually there would be an argument, lame and useless.

And so there was.

"It's just like *Groundhog Day*," he said. "You're repeating yourself. Calm down, Fra. It'll work out. Remember, we're playing a long game."

"How long?"

"As long as it takes."

"Rick, we only have one week to find someone else to take us on, or we will have to go back to panel!"

"You'll find someone, I'm sure."

"Rick, can you please try and call them and convince them to keep us on? Perhaps if it comes from you it's better."

"Are you kidding? Like I haven't got enough to do. Anyway, you're much better than me at these things. Come on Fra, pull yourself together."

"You just can't be bothered!" I put the phone down.

I spent the next few days searching the web, and at first I found nothing. But things change suddenly in adoption land. When Rick came home that Friday night, we had a proposal for a match from a woman named Wendy at another agency. Happy? Yes, but also slightly confused by the text in the attachment:

Details of the birth mother:
Name: Maria Rodriguez
Height: 1:65
Skin Colour: Medium dark
Personality: happy and positive, non smoker

Education: Primary School
Other children: Two, ten and eight years old
Marital status: widow

Details of the birthfather
Name: Unknown
Height: Unknown
Skin colour: Medium dark
Personality: Unknown
Other children: Unknown
Marital status: Unknown

"I don't know about you, but I expected to be more excited," said Rick, as he poured us each a glass of red wine.

"I know what you mean. Something about these details feels very cold. Like, why is she giving up the child for adoption? Is it money?" I sat on the stool and watched him cook lamb chops.

"Yes, that's what we really want to know, and they are not telling us. Instead they give you all this stuff about how she has brown eyes and a nice personality. Why did she send us a picture of the mother, anyway?"

"To see her skin colour?"

"It could be. It just seems so superficial. I mean, is that all?"

"Maybe most people just want a baby and they don't care about the circumstance. I guess they assume that if they've followed the procedure from their end, then everyone else is doing what they're supposed to do."

"Still, it's a baby girl, which is good news," he continued.

"Yes, and they say the mother is healthy and a non-smoker," I added.

"On what basis are we supposed to decide, anyway?" asked Rick.

He had a point. We'd had our lives examined and documented in minute detail to ensure that we would get it 'right', but ultimately this thing was pretty random, a veritable turkey shoot. All the scrutiny of us by councils, social workers, and psychologists didn't matter a jot, because when the whole thing was laid bare, we were talking about timing and luck. We were cautious, especially Rick, who made it clear that he wanted to know why the baby was being relinquished.

I decided to call Wendy on the spot and see if I could get an answer to that one. She seemed unperturbed by the question.

"I suppose she's giving her up because it's out of wedlock. You know what Mexican culture is like. It's very Catholic, hardly emancipated. I am certain she can't keep the baby, though."

Rick didn't need any more information. He was happy. As we were eating our lamb chops and roast potatoes, he said:

"I think we should move to Mexico." He said it in the same tone you'd use to announce you were buying a kettle.

"What!"

"We should relocate to Mexico while we adopt. It makes sense to be on the ground."

"What about our jobs? We can't just throw them away!"

"You can use your maternity leave, and I will take holidays and sabbatical. Look, we have a daughter on the way. We need to be there at the birth and see the process through. That's important."

"You are mad! What happened to Mr Rational that I married? I'm supposed to be the crazy one."

But the thought of Mexico was appealing. It would help us expedite the process. Plus, I liked the idea of actually going to the place my baby was from.

Both of us instinctively knew this was the excuse we needed to put us in the same place. Our careers had meant large amounts of time apart for the past few years. We were ready to start the next phase in our lives, and like a lot of people, we needed a reason to change things. Now we had the best one of all. We were both world travellers, used to ambiguity and confident in our ability to deal with whatever the world could throw at us. Mexico was just another trip, albeit one with a serious mission.

Two weeks before leaving, we received an email from DCSF.

Dear prospective adoptive parents, apologies for my earlier emails, which I sent on the assumption you were adopting from the US. You are adopting from Mexico, a country that, like the UK, has ratified the Hague Convention on Protection of Children and Co-operation in respect of Intercountry Adoption. Accordingly, your case will be processed in order that it may be recognised under the Convention. This will mean that your application would be sent to the Mexican Central Authority, the Ministry of Foreign Relations and you will not be able to work with the US agency you had been approved to work with or accept a match via them.'

Do these people actually know anything about the adoption system? I wondered. They seemed dangerously slow on the uptake.

Rick and I had boxed up our lives and were ready to go. Mentally, we were in Mexico. We'd bought baby clothes, thought of names, and sat together at night staring at the birth mother, trying to figure out how our baby would look. I was incredulous that the panel had approved us to use a US agency when it wasn't legally possible. They didn't know their own rules. How could DCSF have printed off a certificate of eligibility for us to adopt from Mexico but then think we were adopting from the US? They were supposed to go through all the documentation with a fine-toothed comb. We tried to contact them, but it was impossible: the DCSF does not have a telephone number. Emails are met with an automated reply. Our only lifeline was Anne, the team leader at our local council.

"They are confused," she said to me. "They have never done this before, so they are trying to work out what is and isn't possible." And that was that. She tried to talk to them again, but it was as if they had disappeared from the face of the earth.

We were days from getting on a plane, and had no way of turning back the clock. The arrangements with work had all been made. To renege now would look bad, and we would never have this chance again. Wendy tried to do her best, sending us information from her agency's Mexican lawyer, Miguel, who stated that non-

Hague adoptions are possible in Hague countries. I didn't know what to believe. The chances of squeezing any sort of victory from defeat looked remote.

I even called the DIF, the Mexican equivalent of DCSF, in Guadalajara to ask for one more opinion. They, too, were against us pursuing this match. So we had to give it up.

But the next morning, Rick was unequivocal. Clearly this one had solved itself for him overnight.

"We're going anyway," he said as he spread butter on his toast. He was clearly in fighting mood.

It was at moments such as these that I was reminded just why I had married this man.

🖤

I really doubt anyone has got as excited as we did buying luggage for our trip. Despite being frequent travellers, we are both incredibly disorganised, so we didn't have a list. Mosquito nets, easy to dry towels, guide books, iPods, sun block, sandals, a diary for me, trekking shoes, folding speakers, one set of smart clothes, jeans. We were like students on their first big trip. When we couldn't find exactly the same backpacks, I traipsed all over London until I found the identical model and colour to Rick's.

It was a strange time. While everyone else was Christmas shopping and feathering their festive nests, we were de-cluttering, packing up our belongings and arguing over what to put in our bags. Rick was adamant we wouldn't need my Mac laptop, but I won. And very soon, we would be glad I did.

3

Is Mexico Really That Big?

"Rick, wake up."

"Mmmmm?"

"Wake up! I think someone's being killed!"

There was a high-pitched screech, followed by the sound of branches cracking under a heavy weight. Then came an almighty roar.

"It's probably a lion," said Rick nonchalantly.

We got out of bed and looked out of our treehouse into the dense rainforest. The deafening noise was coming from a group of howler monkeys, who were greeting the new day with their cacophonous dawn chorus. It was accompanied by a hailstorm of berries, leaves, and pods. The explosion of sound was incredible; I had read that howler monkeys can be heard up to three miles away. But for us, after the hubbub of London, this was peace. It was Mexico.

We had already spent a few days as tourists in Cancun, but the relentless noise and chaos of package tourism began to grate on our nerves, so we had moved to the Yucatan jungle. This was the real Mexico, the one most people don't see, and we wanted to experience as much as possible of the authentic side of the country our child came from—not the pre-packaged version.

There was another, deeper reason for leaving Cancun. We

needed to be calm and get in touch with ourselves. I believe that you need good energy to bring good things. So, we practised yoga and treated ourselves to healing Mayan clay massages. We ate nothing but raw vegetables, and we read books by candlelight, since there was no electricity. And in the mornings we'd wake up under our mosquito nets to the sight of misty jungle, blue skies, and a variety of creatures: jaguars, pumas, and armadillos, who were our breakfast companions after making their way into the sleepy sunlight to greet the new day.

It worked—for a bit. But we were not here for a vacation, and the desire to do something was bubbling up. Everything seemed like a distraction from the main event. I could not laze in a hammock all day and not think about the DCSF, or wonder when someone would contact us with next steps. I wanted something to happen. So, early each morning, I made the trek to the only internet café around. It was a tiny, airless place, so stuffy inside that the customers were nearly keeling over at their terminals. But bless them: they prided themselves on having the only 256KB connection for miles.

From here, I would speak to family and contacts in the U.K. Sometimes I'd call my Mexican colleague, Cetty, in Mexico City, or my great friend, Oscar, in Argentina. I'd talk to anyone who would listen. We'd chosen to come here, yet I felt lonely and abandoned, which soon led to guilt over not being able to appreciate my surroundings. I wasn't practicing the 'live in the moment' philosophy I so often preached. I was unhappy and stressed. I might as well have been sitting out winter in London.

February 6th was Rick's birthday, so we decided to go to Tulum, which boasts endless stretches of white sandy beach and turquoise water. In the distance, atop rugged cliffs, I could see Tulum's famous Mayan ruins.

"This must be paradise, surely," I said to Rick with watery eyes.

"If there is one, it must look pretty damn similar to this," he replied.

And for a few days, it was paradise. Tulum is home to the

world's second largest barrier reef, and we revelled in diving with turtles, eagle rays, and barracudas. But, as the Crowded House song goes, "You always take the weather with you," and soon the clouds came out again. We were not here on holiday. We had a mission to fulfill, and nothing was happening. The tension between us was increasing. Short words and irritation filled what should have been memorable moments.

My problem was primarily that I felt Rick didn't care, and it was all falling to me.

I was the one calling the central DIF, the employees of which appeared to have graduated from the same charm school as our own DCSF, the regional DIF's were a bit friendlier, but nobody was interested because we didn't have our documents of approval—the DCSF hadn't sent them, even though all they had to do was put them into the envelope we'd provided, and give them to the courier we'd already paid for.

Rick and I drifted almost silently through the week. I found Eyleen, a Chilean yoga teacher who gave classes by the sea every morning. She was beautiful, and she radiated a kind of centered calm. Her toned, perfect body was fully tattooed, and she would turn up barefoot, often with a huge, colourful butterfly poised on her arm. Her English was poor, but charming.

"Spread the fingers of your feet," she'd say. "We now look at the Eagle of the North to ask for peace."

Nobody really had a clue who the Eagle was, but we went with it because I think secretly we all wanted to be her. Rick would often join in, which made me feel at least that we were sharing something. But one morning he left the session halfway through, saying nothing. I was livid. Now he wouldn't even share this brief moment of calm with me. He'd brought us to Mexico, but now he expected me to do it all. The class finished, and I stormed back to our hut intending to pick a fight, but he was nowhere to be found. I ran outside. Nothing.

Has he left? Are we one of those couples who has become an adoption casualty? Is this all worth it?

"Fra!"

He was sitting on the roof of our *cabana*, the only place that had a tiny bit of internet reception, holding the laptop.

"What are you doing?"

"I've had enough."

Enough? Is he booking a flight without me? Is he leaving now? I broke into a cold sweat. The idea of being left alone in Mexico, of our marriage ending in this place, was just too horrible.

"I've found a guy who can help us. I think it's time we left this place and hit the road. We're going to do this on our own. Together."

🐖

Later that day we sat in a café in Tulum, a map of Mexico spread out on the table in front of us. Rick was shaking his head in the way that tradesmen do when they're about to tell you it's going to cost you big.

"I reckon we're looking at six hours driving at least. And that's if we don't end up in a crumpled heap somewhere."

He was referring to the number of car wrecks we'd seen in ditches already. I had to admit there did seem to be rather a lot. Nonetheless, I wanted to rent a car.

"Utter rubbish, Rick. Have you looked at the map properly? It's practically next to Tulum. I think we should drive. What's your problem?"

"Well, I *am* looking at the map, and I can see that Chetumal is next to Tulum. But we're hardly talking Rome to Florence here. Plus many of the roads between here and Chetumal are pretty ropey because of the last hurricane. You're talking hundreds of kilometres of jungle, and I'd rather look out the window than drive. Unless you do it all."

"Come on, how big is Mexico? It looks so small, in between the US and South America!" I said.

"Half the size of Europe, I think. Actually, the handbook says exactly two million square kilometers, and it's pretty empty, too. The population is the same as Britain. Still want to do it?"

I was amazed. American distances are always mind-boggling to us Europeans.

"Wooo. Shall we at least check how much a rental car costs?"

"Done that already. Fifty dollars per day, but it's not really an option when you don't know where you're going, or how long you're going for. Still want to do it?"

"Crikey. Hmm."

Our backpacking gene kicked in and decided for us: we'd do it by bus. The waiter came to take our orders. He turned out to be Australian, and he recommended that we travel to Chetumal by first-class bus, which was still dirt cheap but offered the luxury of a toilet. Surrounded by hippies, or perhaps eco-chic stockbrokers who had turned hippie for a couple of weeks, we bought tacos and fried bananas for the journey and waited for the bus at Tulum station.

"Who's a clever girl for photocopying our documents, then?" I was referring to the dossier that Barbara had prepared on us, as well as our police checks and everything else which made up our file. I had asked the translator to do it before she sent it all to DCSF. At least we could get started with these. We had already been waiting for a month.

Before we left, I'd checked out the guy Rick had contacted from the hut roof. It turned out he ran a private home in Chetumal. Lots of children, but it was no good for us. For a Hague adoption, we were required to work with children's homes run by DIF. However, the idea of contacting homes lit a spark, and we'd boarded the bus with the name of a DIF-run home for children in Chetumal which we could visit.

I'd phoned them and carefully explained who we were, emphasising that we were not American. Being Italian was an advantage in Mexico. Culturally, we have a lot in common, much more so than the English—although talking about football and Manchester United tended to improve dialogue immeasurably. I'd worked out my spiel in Spanish and practised it. It was my default introduction.

"We're a couple, a EUROPEAN couple. I am ITALIAN, and he is English." I mumbled the English bit.

The lady who'd answered the phone was delightful.

"You don't need to go to DIF first. Come and meet us. We have children available for adoption here, all girls. It will be lovely to help you, and we also need people to help us in every way they can here in Chetumal. You will understand when you come."

It was a four-hour journey, during which we saw nothing but jungle. Flat jungle.

Chetumal is the capital of the state of Quintana Roo, a stone's throw from Belize and Guatemala. The city, located on a huge bay in the jungle, has all the problems that come with being a border town, as well as a long history of being destroyed by hurricanes. Following each cleanup, Chetumal was reinforced by even more concrete, which did little for its appearance and not all that much for its ability to withstand the weather.

Weary from our journey, and also perhaps from wondering what lay ahead, we retired to a small, shabby hotel Rick had booked over the internet, and fell asleep on a bed with no springs.

The next day we got down to business. We'd each packed one good set of clothes for meetings: white trousers and black smart top for me, and cream trousers and polo shirt for Rick. We were full of anticipation. Already we had someone who was willing to speak to us, and there was also the possibility of meeting a child we could adopt. We were so nervous we even skipped breakfast, though we were pretty sure it would have been *huevos revueltos*, or scrambled eggs—a name we thought was hilarious. Who wants revolting eggs?

Outside it was unbearably hot and humid. The temperature was already over thirty Celsius, or nearly ninety degrees Fahrenheit. By the time our taxi reached the gates of the children's home, our clothes were damp and tacky.

We stood outside the high gates and pressed the buzzer, announcing ourselves and our appointment with La Directora. The rather large security people in their blue uniforms opened the gates and waved us in, then led us into a very clean, spacious waiting area with light green walls and children's drawings of animals and family scenes.

"Look at those seats," whispered Rick. There was nothing wrong with them, except that they were child-sized.

"Personally, I think it's a good sign."

"You and your signs, Fra. Still, I hope you're right."

I'd read horror stories about children brought up in homes. It didn't matter where in the world they were located—you never read a good news story about institutions. But this place was spotless, calm, and full of character. It reminded me of my primary school in Rome. The tiles of the floor were white and shining, and the small play area in the corner was piled with soft mats. The few toys were beautifully crafted of wood and all in good condition. Next to us were large boxes full of second-hand clothes, which had apparently been donated and needed sorting. Even this gave me a good feeling. It showed the home was connected to the community.

"Buenos dias, Francesca." The voice belonged to *la directora* of the *casa*, a rather minute lady in a flowery skirt and white top with short, straight, dark hair. We shook hands.

"Please follow me. I don't speak English. I hope you both understand."

"I can translate for Rick," I said as we followed her into her office.

"Please take a seat," she said, gesturing to two metal and plastic chairs.

She sat at her large desk, where framed pictures of children, and one of herself on what seemed to be a graduation day, were neatly placed.

I began our story. It was one I would retell countless times in the coming months.

"We're here to adopt a girl, up to two years old," I said. "We have been approved in the U.K., and we have moved here to get to know your country and find our daughter. We have been here around a month, making enquiries."

"Are you infertile?" she asked.

What a strange question.

"No, but this is the way we want to have children. It's what we believe in." I paused for breath. "We are still waiting for our papers to be sent from our government, but we have these." I showed her the photocopies. "Anyway," I continued quickly, "we are here to do the right thing the legal way, and we want to adopt under Hague."

"That's all very good, is Hague the city you come from?"

Oh, dear.

"Oh no, I meant the treaty…"

"No idea what it is. Anyway, you have come to the right place."

Rick and I exchanged hopeful glances.

"Here in this casa we only have girls, most of whom have been removed from their birthparents, either temporarily or permanently, for a number of reasons. The ones who are not being returned to their parents are available to adopt. We have a few of the age group you mentioned. However…"

Rick rolled his eyes, as if to say, *Here we go.*

"You cannot meet any of the children until we have the all clear from DIF. I will call them for you and make an appointment," she said, already dialling a number on a huge black rotary phone.

We were to go the DIF office straight away. Back in London, we couldn't even email the DCSF, here we could talk face to face with no formal appointment to a government official, even though we were foreigners. In less than forty-eight hours, we had shifted from hammocks to high gear.

"Let's get a cab," I said to Rick as we walked out into the blazing sunshine.

"Easier said than done. Look where we are."

We were nowhere, on a dusty road with only the children's home and a little shop a bit further on. The temperature was now around forty degrees—well over one hundred degrees Fahrenheit. As there were no cars in sight, flagging a taxi down was impossible. I went back and peered through the security gates. The guards were eating a breakfast of steak and chips. I yelled out to ask them if they could call us a cab.

"Senora! Un taxi? Noooo!" said one of them. Clearly they had never needed one, and neither had the children. No cabs, then. We walked to the little shop across the road. It was a *chagarro,* the equivalent of a corner shop in the U.K., but much smaller. It seemed to sell a bit of everything; groceries, cleaning products, drinks. We bought lots of sweets in anticipation of returning to the home later. When I came to pay, I asked the lady how we could get a taxi.

"Un taxi? Ha ha ha!"

More hilarity at our request.

"Where do you need to get to?" she asked.

"The DIF office."

"Oh, you must be important then. My son will take you. Pedro!" she shouted towards the back of the shop. "Pedrooo!"

Out came Pedro in his green shorts and yellow t-shirt, covered in sweat and dust.

"Mama! I was playing football! What do you want?"

"Take these people to the DIF, now, *cabron*!" she said, smacking him on the head.

"OK…" he said reluctantly, dragging his feet. He put his hands in his pockets and started walking.

"Sigame." He wanted us to follow him. We went through the back, via what seemed to be their home, and into a yard where chickens ran happily amongst some kids who must have been Pedro's football partners. Then we emerged into a small back street, where there sat a car directly from the 1950s. It was long and low, like the one I'd seen Gael García Bernal drive in the movie *Amores Perros.* Each door panel was a different colour, and there were no windows. Pedro, who looked no more than thirteen, motioned us inside and got in. He didn't have a car key. Instead, he connected two wires, and the car started.

I prayed to the Virgin of Guadalupe, spiritual protector of Mexico, to keep us safe as I held tightly to Rick, and he to me. And then, with a squeal, and leaving a cartoon-like cloud of dust behind us, we were off.

"Senores, todo bien?" Pedro seemed concerned at our silence. He wanted to know if everything was okay.

"Si… gracias." *Yes, thank you.*

"Le gusta Mexico?" *Do you like Mexico?*

"Si, si muchissimo…" *Yes, very much.*

The car screeched to a halt in front of the DIF building. We thanked Pedro profusely and went inside, grateful to have arrived alive.

"Ooh, look! We've gone back in time," said Rick. "I love this place."

From the large, noisy computers to the antique grey telephones and posters on the wall, we seemed to have left the 1950s and landed in the 1970s. The building was bursting with people. Each adult appeared to be struggling to control a bundle of at least four or five children, many of whom were crying. Older children sat by themselves on the floor. Presumably they had delivered themselves here, and were waiting to be seen. Meanwhile, men sporting huge cowboy hats swaggered up and down the hallways, smoking and looking like film extras.

"Are all these people in the right place? Are *we* in the right place?" I asked Rick.

"I'm trying to work out who's here to help and who is here to be helped," he said. "Do you think the ones in cowboy hats are officials?"

"Don't be silly."

We stood there taking the whole scene in for about ten minutes, until I figured that if I didn't ask, we might not get seen.

A woman came past carrying a bundle of papers that obscured most of her face. I decided she must be an official, or at least would be acquainted with one.

"Excuse me…" I said, gently touching her arm.

She stopped, causing the seething mass of bodies to hastily rearrange itself around her.

"We're here to see Lucia," I said.

"Yes, *la procuradora* is waiting for you. Follow me."

We walked up the stairs to the first floor. There were fewer people here, and lots of grey office doors. It looked more institutional. We were told to knock on the last door.

My first impression of Lucia was one of overwhelming femininity. She wore a floral dress and high heels. Her silky black hair was neatly tied back, and her skin was a lovely dark nut-brown. The way her hips undulated reminded me of a flamenco dancer more than a government official. In addition to pictures of children around the office, there was the obligatory image of the Virgin of Guadalupe. There were also ornaments, lots of them. My eye caught an improbable shelf of owls. Seeing me, she smiled.

"They are a symbol of the law," she said.

We all sat down and I got ready to tell our story for the second time, beginning with an apology for my Spanish I probably didn't need to give. It always felt polite to do so, even though I had no problem with the language.

"Don't worry, I do not speak English. At least you speak my language."

Once I finished, I looked at Rick and then we both looked at her. Her face was sympathetic, but there was a frown forming.

"There is a little mix-up. I am sorry to say you were somehow given the wrong impression at the casa, but we don't actually do international adoptions in the state of Quintana Roo."

What?

"But we were told that it was possible. The directora told us," I said. My voice shook as I grabbed for a reassuring hand from Rick.

"I'm really sorry, but we don't. We are not set up to do it."

Rick clearly understood the sense of what she was saying. He squeezed my hand for encouragement.

Lucia continued:

"The place you need to go to is Veracruz. It's the state that does the highest number of international adoptions in the whole of

Mexico. They are famous for it. In fact, the procuradora there is my friend. Here is her card."

She took it out of her purse and handed it to me.

"Tell her that I have sent you and she will do her best to help you, I am sure of that."

We were disappointed, but this was tempered by the fact we had somewhere to go on to. At least Lucia had been kind and honest. She'd given us a little hope, the lifeblood needed by any would-be adoptive parent. She also gave us her personal email, plus a mobile number in case we needed to speak to her.

Outside, the sun was searing. Though the day felt as if it had gone on forever, it was still only two o'clock.

"Well," I said, sitting on a bench outside, "at least it wasn't a complete 'no'."

"It wasn't." Rick sat next to me.

"And we have somewhere else to go," I said hopefully.

"We do." He was tired. We both were. Our adrenaline levels had suddenly dropped.

Veracruz would be our next destination, but first we were headed back to the home. Before we'd left, I'd asked if we could meet some of the children, and Lucia had agreed. After another night in our grungy hotel, we went back and were introduced to some of them.

First we met the toddlers who were too young for school. They all had thick, black, shiny hair, mostly worn in a bob. They each wore a white t-shirt and a skirt. They were adorable. Hearing visitors had arrived, they ran into the corridor to greet us. A carer took us to their bedrooms, which were all interconnected. On each bed, there was one teddy, no other toys. The white walls were festooned with flower stickers. The bathrooms each held a pink potty, and there were cups on the sink with tiny, different-coloured tooth brushes in them.

Rick and I sat on the floor and asked them for their names and ages. At least three of them struggled to speak. As I was repeating my questions, the carer whispered in my ear:

"They are a bit retarded. They are all from alcoholic parents. It does that to their brain." We had been told this during the training back in London, but nothing had really prepared me for this. These were real, little people on my lap. I hugged them even more.

"Chicas, jugamos a las escondidas?" *Shall we play hide and seek?*

Their eyes lit up, and they all jumped up and ran to hide so that Rick and I could find them. They giggled and ran around with us until the lady said it was time for a snack. Then they obediently sat around a table and ate some mango and sipped *agua de fruta*, a drink made with fresh fruit and ice.

"Now we must leave them to it."

The voice belonged to a middle-aged woman with short, badly-dyed blonde hair and a mouthful of golden teeth.

"Come, I will show you more."

She took my hand and led us through the rest of the rooms, which looked pretty much the same—apart from one. It was crammed with beds and clothes.

"Sorry this is a bit messy, but it's hosting twice as many children as it should."

"How come?" I asked

"The room of the teenagers is the only one we have not been able to rebuild after the hurricane of '97 destroyed most of the casa, so they're sleeping here with the seven-to-ten-year-olds."

"Oh, that explains why the rest looks so new. When will you build the missing part, then?"

"Tomorrow, so it's not so bad. A rich man gave us the material, and some people from town have volunteered to help. We can't wait."

"Ask her if they need one more person," said Rick.

"Well, we can always do with an extra pair of hands, señor!"

"Let's stay for a couple of days to help, shall we?" Rick had a sparkle in his eye.

"Yes! Though I am not sure I am the right build for carrying bricks!"

"You can play with the girls."

We asked the directora for permission to return the next day, and then we left, this time in a pre-arranged taxi. As we got in I hugged him.

"You are such a star. That was the best idea you've ever had."

"Well, not really. Remember, when we decided to adopt, one of the reasons was that we wanted to help children. Even if we can't adopt them, we should help them if we can. This is just another way."

"True, adoption is not the only game in town…Those girls were amazing, and so sweet."

"And the place is really well kept."

We were dropped off downtown where the afternoon siesta—which went from one to five p.m.—meant all the shops were closed.

"I really don't fancy going back to the hotel. Mayan museum, or walk along the bay?" I suggested.

"Bay. I need some fresh air, if it's even possible in this humidity."

After our walk, we had a delicious dinner of rice with bananas and beans fried in coconut oil.

"How do you feel now you've actually met children, real ones, in care, Rick?"

"There is something very affecting about them."

"Their eyes are so deep, like a path to their wounded soul. I thought about when I was a teenager and how much I detested my parents. What an idiot I was. These girls have nothing."

"It's good to see how lovely the carers are though, and amazing how happy everyone looked."

"Let's get the bill and walk home. We have a long day ahead of us tomorrow."

★

The next morning, Rick plunged into an ice cold shower at 6:00 a.m. We were supposed to be at the casa at 6:30 to avoid working when the heat was too bad. He put on his vest, shorts, and a cap. I wore a floral skirt, orange top, and sandals. The Mexico vibe was overtaking me. We went downstairs to the breakfast area, sat at a table draped with a red-and-yellow plastic tablecloth, and ate *chilaquiles verdes con pollo*, fried corn tortillas topped with chicken, green tomatillo sauce, and fresh cheese. It didn't look healthy or appealing to me, but Rick needed a big meal.

Arriving at the casa, we found a group of men already sawing, hammering, and carting stuff around.

"Hola, amigo!" It was Pedro, who'd driven us from the shop.

"What have I got myself in for? How am I going to get through this without speaking a word of Spanish?" Rick whispered, but before I could answer his amigo had claimed him.

I was taken to the toddler area. I was surprised at how natural it felt to take these little girls by the hand and explain the Italian version of "Ring-a-Ring-o-Roses", which involves double the amount of falling on the floor. It made them laugh, and in that place it was the most magical sound on earth.

At some point, I heard some shouting.

"Un, dos, tres!" I looked out the window. It was the men trying to lift a huge beam. I could see Rick's muscles bulging with effort, sweat pouring off him.

"Come on," I said to the children. "I know we can count, too. Let's help them." We ran over to the window.

"Un, dos, tres!"

Later, I ate quesadillas with the girls in the canteen. Outside, Rick was drinking beer and eating a burger with his new mates. They were talking in that special international men's language of football. Hearing the Mexicans shout, "Come on, City!" I knew Rick had made his point about his beloved Manchester City football team.

Hard reminders of why many of these kids were here was never far away. While I was trying to show one of them how to write numbers, I noticed some marks on her arm.

"Oh, what happened here?"

The girl looked down and carried on writing. I looked over to the lady who was sitting in the corner. My question was met with a gentle nod that suggested she would explain later.

There were similar marks on another girl. They were sisters.

"Cigarette burns," the lady told me. "Those girls were abused by their parents almost from the time they were born."

"Oh, God." I felt sick. "Why can't we adopt them then? Is there someone else on the waiting list?"

"Lucia told you why. No, there is nobody on the list, and there never will be. Mexicans only adopt newborns when they can't have babies, and then they pretend it's theirs. They don't even tell them that they are adopted, you see? Nobody is going to take two, especially at this age."

"This is awful, and so unfair."

I was fighting back tears. I didn't want the little ones to see me crying. Their lives were hard enough.

"Tell me, what's going to happen to them?"

"They will stay here until they are eighteen. Then they will leave."

"And go where?"

"Wherever, to work, to Mexico City."

Looking again at these two sweet little girls, I felt as if I was going to break down right there. It was really too dreadful to know that just because they had been dealt a raw hand in life, they would never know what it was like to grow up in the kind of home Rick and I had to give. These girls were a powerful reminder of what had been motivating me all along: the world is full of kids who need good homes. It was incredibly frustrating to know there was nothing I could do for them, beyond be with them in that moment.

I needed to be useful—and to stop my tears. I walked out past the men and saw that a new wall had appeared, and they were back on the beers. I headed for Pedro's mum's shop.

"Ah, la señora del DIF!" she said.

I bought flour, oil, canned tomatoes, cheese and yeast. Then I returned to the canteen, where I announced to the girls:

"Today we are making pizza!"

"*Andale*!" they said in chorus. Let's do it!

We started mixing and kneading. The girls joined in happily, and not once did they argue amongst themselves, despite the fact that there were not enough tasks to go round. You would have thought they were part of a harmonious family. And then I realised that they were. This place was their home, and the other children were their family. It might not have looked like the kind of family I knew, but it made me feel better to understand that they were not alone in the world at all. And things could have been much worse for them.

The two sisters stayed glued to each other throughout. I found myself drawn to them and took every opportunity to give them an extra cuddle.

"Please tell me I can shower in here!"

Rick walked in looking like he had just fought a long battle, dripping with sweat and dirt. The little girls laughed at him.

"Fra," he announced, "I am shattered, but this has been the best day of my life. The guys wanted me to go and drink with them, but I want to stay here. What's up with her arm?" He'd seen the marks on one of the sisters.

I explained. He just shook his head.

He came out of the shower just as the carers were putting the pizzas in the oven. He joined me in a chorus of "Old McDonald", which the girls thought was hysterical, as I did it in three languages: Italian, English, and Spanish. The same animals made different sounds in each language. Rick was incredibly animated. I'd never seen him like this. He held the sisters in his lap and exaggerated the animal sounds until the girls were in stitches. Gone was any of the resentment I might have felt for him. He looked like a natural father.

We ate our pizza, and then it was time to put the girls to bed. Rick helped me with the two girls. I suppose I shouldn't have been surprised at that point, but it was still impossible for me to hide my shock when I lifted the T-shirt over one girl's head and saw a vicious scar on her arm.

"Ohhh." I tried to say it silently, but the lady heard me and put a finger to her mouth as if to say: *Don't even acknowledge it.* Later, she told me the girl's father had broken her arm so badly that the bone had ripped through her skin.

It was both touching and sobering to be in the room where the girls slept, singing them to sleep as we held their hands. But in truth I felt powerless. How was it that I couldn't help?

"Those girls will remember this day with the gringos for the rest of their lives," said the directora affectionately as she caught up with us in the hallway.

"We are not gringos!" I said this laughingly, as I knew gringo was not exactly a term of endearment in Mexico.

"I know, just kidding. Truly you have been wonderful. I'll drive you to the hotel," she said, jangling a set of car keys.

When we got in, Rick threw himself on the bed.

"Muscles I never knew I had are hurting. Hey, are you OK?" He'd noticed my face was red from trying not to cry.

"No. I want to take those two girls home with me. Why can't we? Why?"

"Come on, come over here. I truly cannot move."

I lay next to him, staring at the ceiling fan.

"Sometimes, Fra, there is no good explanation."

"But it's crazy. They need a home. We want to give them one, and no one else ever will. Where is the problem? Stupid bloody system."

"You were great at playing with them. I watched you. You did a good thing."

"Yes, but I wish we could do more. I was proud of you, too."

"Will you be proud of me if I go to sleep in my sweaty clothes? I can't take them off, I'm so tired."

"Yes." I took my watch off and leaned over to put it in the side table.

"Today was special, wasn't it, Rick?"

No reply. I looked back.

He was already snoring.

Tequila and Teddy Bears

One doesn't usually celebrate St Valentine's Day by standing outside a toyshop swigging bottles of tequila, but that's what they do in Mexico. It might have been fun, except we were in Escarcega, which wasn't even a one-horse town; it was practically a one-house town. There was nothing more than a crossroads with a few houses, a few motels, and a hub for buses en route to somewhere else. There were also lots of people going wild, in love or not.

At midnight, every man, his dog, and his loony friends were out dancing, holding big teddies and red roses. They were necking vast amounts of tequila and singing at the top of their lungs to the songs of Vicente Fernandez, which were blaring from huge speakers outside the shop. We had just stepped off the bus from Chetumal, en route to Veracruz, and the scene was rather surreal.

The trip we were doing was long, over thirty hours, something we'd only figured out when we arrived at the Chetumal bus station. It made sense to do it in stages. We were both tired, the kind of fatigue that feels almost painful.

It hadn't been easy to leave the children behind. I couldn't stop thinking how the world was so messed up that governments couldn't even apply their collective brainpower to help kids like those sisters, so that they wouldn't have to spend their lives in a home. But then again, many governments hadn't even figured out how to move beyond war as a way of solving their differences, so what did I expect?

At that moment, however, our concerns were more immediate. We didn't want to dance with the mad people: we wanted to sleep. With few choices available, we checked into a motel. I knew it was going to be dire, but it was much worse than I had imagined. It stank of cigarettes and damp carpet. Everything in it was made of plastic: the bed covers, the small table and chairs, the linoleum in the bathroom, and the flowery shower curtains, which made me wince when they touched my skin. But I had no choice. I needed a wash. To top it all off, when I went to brush my teeth, I noticed that there were cockroaches in the sink. I decided against killing them, and carefully avoided them when spitting out the toothpaste.

When I went back into the bedroom, Rick was leaning out of the window. A small TV hanging in a corner of the room was playing *Casablanca* in Spanish. I joined him at the window and looked out.

People, high on drink and apparently with not much else to do, were still singing as if it was the world's biggest party. Get them lubricated and Mexicans can be the loudest and maddest people in the world.

"Do you think it's the bus drivers on a tequila break?" asked Rick.

"Possibly. Hey, for a hell hole this place is really expensive. We should try and get some sleep, at least."

We lay awake for a few hours on the cheap mattress, which was also covered in plastic; the room was hot and stifling, and outside we could hear the sound of people shuffling along, broken glass being kicked along the street, and some disjointed singing.

Rick suddenly jumped up as if someone had pressed 'play' on his remote control. He began pulling on his clothes.

"Come on, let's get out of here now."

I yawned.

"What sort of time is it?" Then I looked up at the big clock shaped like a Corona bottle. It said four o'clock.

"Hang on, don't you want to check out the guidebook and see where to go before we leave?" I said, sitting up on the bed.

"Anywhere's better than here. We'll work it out at the bus station."

I got up and was ready in seconds. I put my trainers and jeans on and crouched on the floor to get my rucksack on my shoulders. Rick was already outside, waiting. We'd had to pay in advance, so we didn't even have to stop at reception. We walked out, weaving through a group of teenagers doing shots and singing at each other. The speakers had been turned off and the teddy bears were nowhere to be seen.

It was a twenty-minute walk to the bus stop. It was still pitch black. We didn't see any taxis, but even if we had, we would have kept walking, since there was every chance the driver would have been one of the revellers, and therefore drunk out of his mind.

I went up to the counter to find out where the next bus was heading. We decided we didn't care, as we were getting on it no matter what. We'd get to Veracruz somehow, so long as we headed north.

"We're in luck. The next bus is for Palenque, in Chiapas. It's in fifteen minutes. And Chiapas is on the way."

Time is a fluid concept in Mexico. When you're somewhere naturally beautiful, like a lovely beach or a stunning city, it's wonderful to go with it and let it sweep you along. But when you just want to get out of where you are fast, it's depressing. We waited for fifteen minutes, which eventually stretched out to a Mexican hour and a half. We read our guidebooks and ate crackers. My phone beeped twice in my pocket. It was a text from my brother, Paolo:

ANY NEWS? HAVEN'T HEARD FROM YOU IN A FEW DAYS…

How do you summarise the events of the past few days in a text? You don't.

NOTHING MAJOR YET, WILL EMAIL WHEN I GET THE CHANCE. MISS YOU X

The bus arrived. I saw there were two drivers. One driver crawled out of a luggage compartment no bigger than a coffin, where he had apparently been sleeping, and took over the wheel, while the other took his place. A claustrophobic bus driver would not do well in Mexico, I decided. Even though we were exhausted, just knowing we were leaving that place made me perk up. Once on board, I pulled my hair up, crossed my legs, got my Mac out, and started on several emails that I would send later. Rick pulled his cap over his eyes and went to sleep against the window.

🐗

Once in Chiapas, we spent some time in the ancient Mayan city of Palenque, where we explored a stunning world of temples, pyramids, palaces, and ball courts, led by a guide who spoke only Mayan and Italian. We also visited the conflict zone of Chiapas, where, since 1994, a man known only as Commandante Marcos had led a popular uprising against the government because of its policy of stealing the land of the indigenous peoples and claiming it for itself. As a result of a US-backed military intervention, 25,000 natives had fled to the hills, where they remain to this day. I was deeply struck by the motto of the Zapatistas, the people who followed Marcos:

PARA TODOS TODO, PARA NOSOTROS NADA!
Everything for everybody, nothing for ourselves.

I was amazed by how patient the people of Chiapas were in their struggle for justice. And their slogan echoed feelings I carried in my own heart. It was not that they wanted to take away everyone's possessions, so that nobody owned anything. It was that they felt the best way to live was to make sure everyone had what they needed. After all, it was a similar feeling that had brought us to Mexico in the first place. We wanted to share what we had with a child who needed it. I took strength from meeting these brave people, and I took it as yet another sign that we were doing the right thing.

🐗

Perhaps that brief interlude into a world I had only read about on the internet gave me a taste for adventure. Maybe I wanted to relive our penniless backpacking days. Or maybe I just wasn't thinking when I bought two second-class tickets to Veracruz.

"Are you sure?" Rick wasn't.

"Look, we're only talking six hours or so, during the day. How bad can it be? Anyway, I won't miss air-conditioning. I can't stand it. Plus it's only two pounds." It was funny how a six-hour journey was now a 'short trip'.

We loaded up with grilled chicken and the customary fried bananas for the trip. The latter, in particular, are ridiculously addictive. We pushed and pardoned our way past men in cowboy hats and silky-haired women in traditional Mayan dresses onto the bus.

"This is fun," I said to Rick.

And that was pretty much the last coherent thing I said for the duration of the trip. The rest of the time I was holding my breath, gasping, breathing deeply, and praying in several languages. After starting up, the bus squeaked and rattled and then rapidly accelerated to a speed that I was sure was going to blow it apart in minutes. With the music box blaring, the bus skidded and swerved, while we hung on for dear life. I found myself digging my nails into my hands, convinced I was going to throw up at any moment. Everyone else was bouncing up and down in their seats, too, but the looks on their faces suggested that for them this was no more than a casual Sunday drive. Rick and I were petrified. When our food got tossed to the floor, we were too paralysed by fear to even attempt to pick it up.

"Never, ever again," said Rick, as he retrieved our bags from the bus.

With its splendid Spanish colonial architecture, Veracruz is one of those cities you immediately want to know. Everything is beautifully restored, and wandering the well-kept streets decorated with flowers and plants was a joy. Veracruz is also a port city with a long history as an international crossroads: Afro-Cubans, Spanish and the indigenous people have all contributed to making the city what it is today. The fact that it was a richer city than any of the others we'd previously been to made it no less crazy. There was still constant music and dancing in the streets, and some very peculiar local customs.

Sitting over what we'd agreed was our best ever coffee yet—and that's saying something, because it's all so good in Mexico—we were approached by a man carrying a big steaming blue pan.

"Would you like to try my *caldo de mariscos*?" he asked.

It's not every day a man in the street approaches you with a pot of fish soup, especially when you're already sitting in a restaurant.

"Oh no, no thanks," I said.

"Go on, por favor!"

"Well, we've already ordered our food here, you see. I don't think we can buy your food and then eat it here."

"Of course you can! You can have your food and this one too—for only a few pesos. Everything is possible in Veracruz, señora!"

It seemed that everything was indeed possible in Veracruz, especially getting your blood pressure checked in the middle of the street. The town appeared to have developed an obsession with blood pressure monitoring. The bizarre result of this was a steady stream of nurses in public places and cafès offering to take your reading.

"It's not really a good time," I would say, gesturing to our cups of coffee. They seemed to be oblivious to the fact that the reading would not be accurate, and it was incredibly hard to get rid of them. We let them do it anyway while we watched dancers and sipped espressos in the *zocalo*, the main square. At one point, a man sitting at a table near us leaned across conspiratorially.

"Do you know La Bamba?" he asked.

"Who doesn't!" I answered

"It's from here, from Veracruz!" he told us, proudly slapping his own leg.

The music that was being played was actually of similar style to La Bamba. The men all wore white with a red cotton belt (a *panuelo rojo*), while the women wore white dresses, black aprons, and accessorised with fans and jewellery.

"Do you see any difference in the women?" asked our new friend.

"Not really. They are all so beautiful!" I said.

He laughed.

"I am here to check out the ones with the flower on the right side on their hair!"

"What's so special about them?"

"They are the single ones!"

It would have been difficult not to feel positive in this city. Even the backpacker's hostel we stayed in was spotless, with very friendly staff. We kept bumping into people we'd seen in Tulum, so we ended up partying with a group that night. The next day we would have another meeting, for which our expectations were higher than ever.

When someone tells you a place is both used to doing international adoptions and does the highest number every year, it's hard not to get your hopes up. Especially if you have been sent directly to see the procuradora by one of her best friends. Buoyed by the possibility that we were getting closer to our goal, we got up the next day and put on our smart, albeit crumpled, 'parent' clothes. We hailed a cab in the street, and gave the driver the address of the DIF.

AVENIDA MARTIRES 28 DE AGOSTO 85

XALAPA, VERACRUZ

He looked at it and hesitated.

"Señores, are you sure you want to take a taxi? It's very expensive, because it's way out of the centre, you know?"

In a land where life is cheap, £2 an hour for a cab is a lot of money. However, we assured him that we did want to be taken there. We drove for about fifteen minutes, leaving the city behind us. I thought it was odd that a government department would be located out here. I could tell Rick was wondering the same thing, especially as we reached a shantytown where the roads were unpaved and barracks replaced normal buildings. Where there might have been pavement, filthy children were sleeping naked next to mangy dogs, while chickens ran around eating whatever crap (and I do mean crap) they found.

"Oh, my God. Where are we?"

"I am not sure this is right," said Rick, with typical British understatement.

The taxi driver was perplexed.

"Señores, I did ask you if you wanted to come here. This is no area for tourists!"

His tone was almost scolding, but I could tell he just wanted to protect us.

"This is the road that is written on your piece of paper, but I cannot find the number. There are no numbers on these shacks."

"Let's stop and call the DIF office," suggested Rick.

Children, many of them toddlers, approached the car, trying to sell us a stick of chewing gum from a packet of ten for one peso. It was desperate. I wound down the window to give them some money.

"Hey, gringo, don't do that! Put it up quick!"

The driver started the engine again.

"Ok, give me your phone. We don't stop here. We call as I drive, ok?"

"Sorry," I said, "I didn't know." I was well aware there was a Mexico we hadn't really seen; it was a poor, desperate Mexico, and this was one of its gateways.

I dialled the number of the Veracruz DIF and handed it to the driver so he could get the right directions.

"Yes, yes, I did take that road. I came off at that junction, yes. Yes, yes, I turned there."

And then: "No, there isn't a statue. Yes, I'm sure. No… there isn't a green gate… no… there are no traffic lights. I can't see any."

"We must have taken the wrong exit," I said to Rick.

The driver continued talking.

"Yes...yes... we are in Xalapa in Veracruz city. Ah, I see... no wonder! OK, I will tell them. Adios."

"Sounds like he's got it sorted," said Rick.

"Señores, you are in the wrong city! This address is correct, but it's for Xalapa the city, not Xalapa the area of Veracruz!"

We couldn't believe it. Right down to the road directions, this had been the right place. But it wasn't. In the state of Veracruz there is a city called Xalapa, its capital in fact, which is where we should have been. Instead we'd travelled to the city of Veracruz, also in the state of Veracruz, to an area called Xalapa.

We were stunned. And speechless. We rode back to the hostel in silence.

"You're back already?" said the manager. "That was quick."

"Not Xalapa the suburb," replied Rick.

The manager's eyes opened wide as he realised what had happened.

"Dios Mio! Xalapa the city? Oh, nooo!"

❧

You only have the moment. It's a cliché, perhaps, but nonetheless it's a philosophy I try to stick to: whatever the outcome of this whole journey, we had to make the most of our time in Mexico, rather than waving it by.

Wreathed in mist, Xalapa is a sedate town of Baroque and Neoclassical architecture and hilly, cobbled streets full of boutiques and cafés. We couldn't resist going for a walk. The park's terraced gardens featured views of Mexico's highest peak, the 5,600 metre Pico de Orizaba with its snow-covered tops, as well as the imposing Palacio del Gobierno.

I did my best to let this beautiful, laidback city overtake me, but I was feeling anxious now. I would find myself looking at a building or a statue trying to admire it, but my head was whirling with 'what if' scenarios, my brain locked in a battle with itself as positive and negative thoughts fought for supremacy.

Xalapa has a lot of hippie influence, so it's easy to find natural and alternative therapies. As we walked through a street market, Rick spotted a sign advertising reflexology massages.

"Do you mind if I have one? I really need to wind down," he said.

"Good idea. They do Tarot readings as well. That might be my way of getting a new perspective on things."

We walked up steep steps to a little shop displaying wooden animal figures, images of the Virgin of Guadalupe of every shape, size and material, woollen rugs, pottery, and amber jewellery.

"Please come in. Put your bags in this room. You look tired." The man who said this wore nothing but a pair of white cotton trousers. His bare chest was covered in tattoos.

"Can I help you?" he said with a lovely smile.

Rick announced he was there for a massage, while I went up a further flight of stairs to a tiny box of a room.

The woman shuffling the Tarot cards was nearing seventy, if she wasn't there already. She had long, white hair and a face lined from exposure to the sun and, I suspected, to life itself. She had the look of one who has not only seen it all, but who has jumped in without hesitation.

I will never forget her words to me.

"The adoption will happen, but it can only do so with one condition. *You* will have to make it happen. *Nobody* is going to do this for you. If it's going to take you sitting outside offices day and night, going on a hunger strike, writing to journalists, you *must* do it. You must do everything you can, as nobody will help you. This is your quest, it's yours alone to gain or lose. And you know what? If you feel you are bothering people, then think again. And don't give up. You are only asking them to do their jobs, and you are exercising your right to help a child. I know you really believe in this. Nothing in the world is impossible. Look at me: I decided to become a drummer in a rock band at the age of sixty-five, and I have done it. There is destiny in life, but nothing is as powerful as free will."

Sitting with her, I felt my purpose returning.

We know often the truth, and we are aware of what exactly must be done, but we just need the odd reminder to push us on. My Tarot teacher says the cards are a door to your intuition; they just allow you to step out of the circle of life and see what's in the circle. That's what they had done for me, again. I hugged the lady and headed out to meet a chilled-out Rick.

"Peace," he said jokingly.

"Yes, peace…" I replied, only half joking.

I wanted to contact Cetty, my colleague and friend in Mexico City whom I'd been speaking to since before leaving the UK, so we headed for an internet café.

"I have been worried," Cetty said. "I haven't heard from you since you left. So you are in Guadalajara with your baby?"

"Oh no, we are in Xalapa."

"You do remember Oscar lived in Xalapa when he studied journalism, right?"

"Oh, I thought it was Puebla."

"No, it wasn't. Now put the phone down and call him. He'll give you some pointers. You are such a silly girl. You never like to ask. I am here for you, OK?"

Next it was Oscar's turn.

"You went to the wrong Xalapa? Ha ha ha! Hey, you must go and see some people I know," he said, giving me a phone number. "Promise you will call them?"

"I will, Oscar. Thank you."

I called Oscar's friends, expecting that we might meet briefly and say hello. I hadn't factored in Mexican hospitality.

"Coffee?" said the man on the other end. "Absolutely not. You are a friend of Oscar's, and you are here for something very important and special, so you must stay with us."

A quiet man with a moustache opened the door. It was Carlos, the man we'd spoken with on the phone. He referred to Oriana, his wife as the *licenciada*, literally 'the qualified one". It's what everyone with a degree is called in Mexico.

Their flat was warm, decorated in hues of red and brown. There were two oak armoires in the kitchen, a wooden table and chairs, iron lampshades, and vases spilling over with flowers. We were shown a room with a beautiful iron bed and brown clay floor tiles.

"You will stay here with us." We tried to protest, but Carlos wouldn't hear of it.

Somewhere a door slammed, followed by children laughing. Teenagers.

"Hola, you must be friends of *la licenciada*," said fifteen-year-old Claudia. "Would you like a beer?"

"That's a lot of chillies!" said Rick, pointing at the kitchen bench where a number of them sat, ready for some wonderful Mexican concoction.

"Yes, in Mexico our chillies are very hot!" said the boy, and then he started laughing. Mexican men often make jokes equating chillies to their anatomical counterpart.

Claudia had the tall, lanky build of northern Mexicans, beautiful long, dark hair, and a grin to light up half of Mexico. She was absolutely gorgeous in her school uniform. *One day*, I thought, *I might have a daughter like that*. If only. She insisted that I should download some Mexican music to my iPod, but when we got to her room, she whispered that she had a boyfriend.

"Tengo un novio," she said, showing me pictures on her phone.

We went back to a room which housed only a TV and a hammock that could easily seat four people.

"That's where most of us have sex for the very first time," she said. "In a hammock like that."

Rick laughed when he heard the story, and said:

"Aren't you just so cool that teenagers want to tell you things. Still, I win. Marco confessed that he is gay, and his parents don't know!"

Oriana arrived at 7:00 pm. The *licenciada* was a journalist and, as was often the case in this matriarchal society, she wore the trousers. Oscar had told me stories of Mexican men coming to work with black eyes after being beaten up by their wives for coming home late, or something equally inoffensive.

Oriana insisted on hearing what we'd been up to. I tried to sound as nonchalant as possible. I didn't want sympathy, but she was wise and sensitive and tuned in straight away.

"Go and see my auntie," she said.

"Why?"

"You need to be at your best for the meeting tomorrow, no? You will go and see my auntie who is a hairdresser. She will make you look better. You can't go looking like that. You need to be smart to have the best chance!"

In England, the directness of this approach, even the idea, would have been an insult. Here it wasn't; it was genuine concern. We knew Oriana was doing it for the right reasons.

The auntie was a lovely little lady who spoke no English. She was waiting for us. Either that, or she simply had no customers. I had seen many hair salons like this in Mexico and wondered how they ever made a living, but maybe that was not the point. The décor was resolutely retro, with barber chairs and tools for steam and shave, so we shouldn't have been surprised when she produced a huge 'style' book with pictures for Rick to choose from. The men sported sideburns, quiffs, and of course mullets. She asked him to choose a style he'd like. Rick's hair was very short and it would have been impossible for him to have any style, even if he'd wanted one.

"Go on, you know you want to," I said, pointing to a classic footballer's mullet.

She just shaved his hair even shorter. Mine is curly and long, so she put some more colour into it and seemed very pleased with her handiwork. I chatted with her, and she confirmed that Xalapa was indeed famous for international adoptions; she'd done the hair of other foreigners who were there to adopt, she told me. Just hearing that made me feel better. I followed Rick, skipping out into the warm, night air to a snack of superlative Mexican coffee and sweet bread before returning to our hosts, who marvelled at our improved appearance.

We knew by now that there was no such thing in Mexico as an early night, no matter what you had to do the next day. Every day may as well have been Friday or Saturday. Our food was prepared by another auntie; it seemed to be the way of things here. We ate guacamole that transcended anything I have had before, and various stuffed tortillas and *puerco al carbon* (pork marinated in citrus). Rick and I decided this was absolutely the best food we'd had in Mexico. We drank a few beers and then went to bed.

The next day, following a hearty breakfast of revueltos with refried beans and coffee, and a final scrutiny of our appearance by Oriana, we set off for the DIF in Xalapa.

This office was a lot calmer than the one we'd been to in Chetumal. It even had a reception desk. The lady behind it took our names down with one of many sharp lead pencils. It looked like we were bottom of a long waiting list. We were told to wait on the chairs in the hallway.

Which we did. We waited, waited and then waited some more. Forty-five minutes passed. Nothing seemed to be happening.

"Would you really take two?" asked Rick.

"I am not sure about anything anymore. I certainly wouldn't split up two siblings, so I guess so."

"What are we going to do if she says OK? We don't even have our papers."

"Surely at that point, if we have a match or two, everyone will get their butts in gear." I didn't for one moment think anything would speed up. I just hoped it would.

I was getting impatient and thought I'd better make sure we hadn't been forgotten.

The receptionist was not happy to see me out of my seat.

"Is la procuradora here? Does she know we are waiting?"

"She is not here yet, but your name is down in the book. Don't worry, just sit down and wait." She said this while giving me a look that said, *What's your problem? Can't you just do what everyone else does?*

Chastised, I sat down again.

"She told you, didn't she?" said Rick. "Better not upset her. Sit up straight."

"Shut up, you!" He laughed as he ducked my hand.

"Oh, dear, you're getting to be one of those bossy Mexican women now."

Another forty minutes passed.

"I'm starving," said Rick.

"I'm so thirsty I can see cups of tea in the heat haze, but I don't want to move from here in case I get in trouble."

"If she has a match for us straight away, we would have to live here for a few weeks. I wouldn't mind. I really like the city."

"Yes, but we've been waiting for hours now. I'll try to go and sort this out."

I stood up again. As I did, the receptionist looked hard at me and made a gesture that told me I had to wait. Never mind my Italian impatience. This was too much even for a normal person. I got up again. The woman was fed up with me. She sighed.

"Yesssss, senora! She has arrived now, but she is in a meeting."

"Does she…"

Another sigh.

"Yes, she knows you are here. Her secretary will call you when she is ready."

By the time the secretary came out it had been three and a half hours. We were starving and thirsty, but we didn't care. We were where we wanted to be.

The office itself was surprisingly beautiful. There was a huge wooden desk, a sofa, and two elegant leather chairs. Lorena, la procuradora, fitted into this ambience beautifully. She was tall and aristocratic, and her long, dark hair was tied back into a ponytail, which served to make her bone structure even more prominent.

"I am ever so sorry that you had to wait, but I had an emergency. So I understand from Lucia that you would like to adopt a Mexican child?"

"Yes. We have been approved by the UK government," I said.

"Firstly, let me tell you Veracruz is the state that does the highest number of international adoptions. We are extremely proud of our work and of the families we find for our children. I myself have adopted three. Here are my angels," she said, indicating the pictures of children on her desk. "We mostly work with Italian and Spanish couples, as the language is not an issue for the children. Our processes are very rigorous, and we only do Hague adoptions."

This was music to our ears.

"That's fantastic. England is part of Hague, and that's exactly what we would like to do," I told her.

She nodded and continued: "Normally, the wait from the moment we receive the documents from the Ministry of Foreign Affairs is around two years. Right now we have eighty families on our waiting list. You should also know that our children are all at least three to five years old. They are institutionalised children who we have tried to keep with their birth families, but it hasn't worked."

God, no! So that was it. Our best chance had just gone. Rick knew it too.

Normally, I would have just thanked her and left. But this time I couldn't. I began to tell her our story: how we couldn't wait because we were on leave, and it would run out in a few months. There was no possibility of us going back to the UK to wait.

She looked concerned.

"Look, it's not all lost," she said, reaching for my hand. "You might be able to adopt younger children and have a shorter wait in Mexico City. Sadly, there are literally thousands in that state. Or perhaps you could try one of the poorer states where there are no Mexican couples able to adopt newborns."

As a rule, only Mexican couples are allowed to adopt newborns, so that the children would stay in their birth country. I thought it was an odd policy, as it was older children who would surely find it harder to be removed from their environment. Still, this wasn't the time to question it.

What happened next was an act of pure humanity. Clearly moved by our story, Lorena picked up her phone, opened her diary, and began the first of what turned out to be a dozen or more phone calls.

"Hi, I have a foreign couple here. Are you able to do adoptions of babies or young toddlers with non-Mexicans? What's the wait?"

Each time she put down the receiver she'd tell us the wait was going to be years, or that the children available for adoption were at least five or six years old.

"Hmm, this is not looking good, guys. But let's not give up."

Without pausing, she kept calling and explaining our situation. That alone was enough to make me cry; this woman was an angel. After a long afternoon, it appeared that our only hope was in Mexico City. However, nobody was answering the calls. Lorena had a final suggestion.

"If I were you I would just go, but stop in Puebla on the way and ask for Esmeralda, who is la procuradora there. She is on holiday this week so I can't call her. Cheer up now. Stay strong, and I am sure you will find the solution. I apologise, but there really isn't anything else I can do to help you. Do call me if you need any advice."

She had done more than enough, more than we had a right to expect. We thanked her profusely, and with as much dignity as we could muster, we bid her farewell.

At that point, emotional paralysis set in. The place we thought held the most hope had none. And while I was grateful for Lorena's intervention that afternoon, I felt somehow pathetic that I'd needed it. Rick was philosophical. Like a boxer, he reckoned we'd fight again. I was doing my best to bounce back with him, reminding myself of the Tarot reader's words: *You have to make it happen.*

As we prepared to leave Carlos and Oriana's place for the bus station, I wondered if this was a journey into insanity. I asked Rick:

"Is this how people go crazy? Obsessive? Following a goal they can't attain?"

"Perhaps we were crazy to start with, and now we are doing the right thing."

"Aren't you worried? I mean not just this, but our jobs as well. We only have a few months before we have to get back. Plus I know they are playing tricks back at my office. They were all waiting for me to leave to stab me in the back."

"I just know we are doing the right thing, and if we go back without a child, people who love us will understand. And no, I am not worried about the job; a job is just a job, as you always tell me. I can't wait to see Puebla. I have heard it's stunning." He kissed me passionately on the lips.

"Does that feel better?"

"Better do it again. You are my rock," I said.

☙

The Puebla DIF was in a colonial building with a huge courtyard and fountains. We only waited for ten minutes for Esmeralda. She was a round, chubby woman with a cream suit that didn't work well on her, and dyed blonde hair that worked even less well.

She sat at her desk in her messy office, chain-smoking. I began the ritual of telling our story, which by now was getting very long. I'd learned which bits to skim over.

"Oh, wow," she said. "You are definitely in the wrong place, guys." She was very no-nonsense. We hadn't raised our expectations for this one, so we didn't have far to fall. But it hurt.

"We have a wait of four years. From the moment we receive the documents, that is. And it's for older children. Have you tried Oaxaca or Chiapas?"

Oh great, another bloody place.

"Hang on, let me call my colleague. He might have better advice." She picked up the phone, and after a minute or so a man in a pinstriped suit and with huge amounts of gel in his hair appeared. He sat on the sofa and listened to us. He was, he told us, a lawyer.

"Hmm. I don't think you are going to be able to do this with Hague, not in your timeframe. And it will definitely be an older child. Why don't you do a private adoption?"

I had no idea what he was talking about. Private adoption?

"We have been told that we can only do Hague adoptions in Mexico…"

"That's rubbish."

"How do we do a private adoption anyway?" asked Rick through me.

"Well, say you meet a birth mother who wants to relinquish her baby. You adopt that baby privately here in Mexico, and then readopt the baby in the UK."

Oh, yeah, I thought. *What's the likelihood of us bumping into a woman in the street who wants to hand over her baby?* Instead I said: "But we don't know anyone here. What else can we do?"

"Have you heard of Vifac? They look after pregnant women who cannot keep their babies, and then they place them for adoption, but only privately, not via Hague."

Even though we could only do Hague adoptions from the UK, I wrote the name in my diary.

"Otherwise, try Chihuahua or Zacateca."

Another wild goose chase. Sure, we love it. Keep them coming.

Esmeralda was tough, but like the other people we'd met, she was also compassionate. She called a few more people, trying to help us.

Buoyed by the astonishing efforts of these incredible women, I began to contact people myself when we returned to the hotel. I called ten different DIF offices and got pretty much the same answer from all of them. Chiapas seemed most hopeful: the wait was a couple of months, and they did have babies. I also called Carla at the Guadalajara DIF, the woman I had spoken to from London when it looked like we were going to adopt from there. She suggested we come and see her.

We were getting worried. Our options were running out. Soon we would run out of viable states in Mexico, and that would be that. This time there was no dignity. In our lovely hotel with its gorgeous view, I sank to my knees and cried my heart out, sobbing from the depths of my soul until I was totally spent.

5

One Frappuccino and a Baby To Go

Calling my brother Paolo in Italy seemed like a good idea; I felt I needed some kind words from home, and he'd always been someone I could rely on. I'd been sending him our email updates so he knew how things were going, though we didn't delve too much into how we felt. I opened the computer and called him up on Skype.

"Hey, big sis."

"Paolo... So good to hear your voice."

"What's up, bella?"

I began to pour it out. How all we wanted was to meet our child and it was getting so hard, and everywhere we turned the doors opened slightly and then shut in our faces. How could the world be so unfair? What had we done to deserve this?

His reaction caught me by surprise.

"So what do you think you're doing?" Even through the crackling static I could tell he was annoyed.

"What do you mean? You know what we're doing."

"This is so typical of you. What made you think you could just fly off to Mexico and bring home a baby? *Here I come, Mexico, to save all your children. Oh, I don't know how to, and nobody else seems to, but I'm just that cool.* All you are doing is wrecking your lives with this mad quest. Come home now before you ruin everything."

"That's so unfair. You say it like we're taking something, and we're not. We're trying to give. Don't wind me up and belittle me. I feel small enough, I tell you."

"Well, I think you've gone too far. Couldn't you just wait? "

"How can you say that? You know it wouldn't change anything. We'd be waiting for years to come."

"Fra, you know more than anyone that you chose this. So you have to deal with it. Come back. It's all I can tell you."

I hung up. I wanted to cry, but I was so exhausted that nothing came. I was also shocked that my own brother should have taken such a brutal stand. Yet as I replayed his words in my head, I began to wonder if he was right. Perhaps we should have waited, and not rushed off to Mexico thinking we could wing it. He did have a point—especially since we'd taken leave from our jobs and told everyone we were coming back with a child. The consequences of coming back without one would be pretty major on all counts. And reminders of those consequences were not far away.

Before I'd left my job, I'd had my final appraisal with Thomas, my boss. Like the previous ones, it was good. In fact, it was more than good: every appraisal I'd had since joining the organisation had been close to excellent. I knew I'd made a difference, and so did they. In order to come to Mexico I'd taken maternity leave, to which I was entitled. My final chat with Thomas had been amicable but cryptic. He'd hinted at the fact that I would probably come back to a different role than the one I'd left behind. I didn't comment, partly because I was wondering if I would still want to commute to Geneva with a baby at home. Thomas was on my email distribution list, but we were not 'friends'. My female Southern European sensibility clashed too much with his male Northern European one. Nonetheless, I felt things were fine.

While in Tulum, I'd received an email from the human resources department. It was about some supposedly outstanding living expenses. I pointed out that they had been paying these for three years. But they insisted on proof, and bang in the middle of the jungle I had to somehow find evidence of the contractual agreement we'd made when I joined. Which I did. The matter was resolved, or so I thought.

While we were in Puebla, preparing to leave for Guadalajara, my loyal personal assistant sent me an email saying that Thomas did not want to pay the bill for moving my belongings from my flat in Geneva back to London. Just what I needed. I'm not one to leave things hanging, so I organised a Skype conference.

"You didn't tell me how much it would be," he said.

"You didn't ask," I countered. "It's my clothes and books that I used when I was there, exactly what you agreed. Surely you can't expect me to pay the cost of a work move?"

"Well, I will pay 50% of it out of my budget and you can pay 50% out of your budget."

I noticed he didn't even ask one question about the adoption.

Later, I told Rick that I suspected Thomas was trying to get rid of me. "He knows I'm emotionally low, and now he's playing all these dirty cards," I said.

"You're being paranoid," said Rick.

"I'm not. He wants me out. I can feel it."

"You're just being oversensitive."

"No. He's acting odd, even for him."

We had no appetite for another thirty-five-hour bus ride at that point, so we flew to Guadalajara.

It was a grim, ugly place. In the taxi from the airport we passed through a series of shantytowns, then found ourselves on a huge motorway. We could easily have been in one of the poorer parts of an industrial US city. There were huge advertising boards for Starbucks, KFC, and McDonald's everywhere. US fast food culture appeared to have been imported wholesale. Even the cars on the road were American-style gas-guzzlers.

Turning from the highways into the centre of town, we found enclaves of the old Mexico: taco stands, more men in cowboy hats, and of course the ubiquitous loud music. We felt no need to explore, though our hotel was in the centre of town. Things had definitely changed since Puebla. I felt a distinct sense of make-or-break now.

After the call with my brother and the tension with my boss, I was mentally worn out. Yet it also felt like some debris had been cleared from my brain. Guadalajara felt like our last stand. I was going to make a go of it.

"What about Miguel?" I said to Rick when we got to the hotel.

"Who?"

"Miguel? Remember, the lawyer from the American adoption agency who we dealt with back in London? He lives in Guadalajara. We should try and meet him while we are here. Remember, he said that private adoptions are possible. We might be able to adopt through him. Let's face it—as nice as the women at DIF are, we won't get anywhere with them, not in this lifetime."

Rick said nothing, so I searched through my emails and found Miguel's mobile number. Then I called him. Miguel spoke impeccable English. His voice was wonderfully mellifluous, with an American accent. I pictured him as tall and elegant.

"You may not remember us," I began, and told him briefly what had happened. "And so I was wondering if you could help us do a non-Hague adoption, so we could then readopt in the UK."

He seemed hesitant.

"Will you be doing this via Happy Parents?"

"I don't think we can," I said. "The DCSF doesn't approve of it."

"Well… then… maybe I can't meet you."

"Oh!"

"Well, you know, I am tied to them… but… look… because you have come such a long way, I will meet you."

"Oh, thank you! Thank you so much."

"Meet me at the Plaza del Sol, where there is a Starbucks. That's where the meetings between birth mothers and adoptive mothers usually happen."

Starbucks sounded kind of tacky, but this was no time to dwell on that.

"Sounds good. We will bring the photocopy of our documents with us."

I hung up.

"We have an hour to get ready and get there," I told Rick. "He sounds good and competent. I have a good feeling!"

Rick stood there, dripping from the shower.

"Well, let's not get too excited. He keeps talking about Happy Parents and wanting us to register. I don't like that."

I was making a supreme effort to keep on top of things, and Rick's comment riled me.

"Sorry for being too positive," I said.

"Well, maybe I'm just being realistic. I'm fed up with being led down the primrose path and pulled in all directions only to end up at the start again, Francesca."

"And you think it helps me if you are so pessimistic? Why can't you keep it to yourself? I don't need this right now."

"Well, not everyone is as naïve as you are, Miss Alice In Wonderland. For a smart lady, sometimes you amaze me."

I wanted to hit him. Or hit something. Instead I stopped talking and stomped around the room, making a big show of opening cupboards and shutting them again, pretending to look for things. On the verge of tears, I called the taxi. Rick said nothing. It may have been almost a hundred degrees outside, but between us there was a sheet of ice.

"Are you ready?" I was tight-lipped.

"Yep."

We sat in the cab. I stared straight ahead. Rick caressed my cheek. I didn't respond.

"It's getting to be too much," he said.

Another caress. This time I leaned into him. Words had become the most useless way of communicating.

I looked out of the taxi, watching Guadalajara's Old Town vanish again. In its place, the new, ugly, modern Guadalajara came into view.

The taxi pulled up in front of a tall concrete and glass shopping centre. It was the sort of place I wouldn't ever have gone into in the UK.

"I thought by plaza he meant a square, not a shopping mall," I said. We found the Starbucks. Rick, groaning, stood in the queue to order coffee he didn't want. As he was about to pay, a huge man with thick glasses walked up to him.

"You must be Rick. I will have an Americano. And that," he pointed to me, "must be Francesca."

Could this be Miguel of the well-modulated voice? He held a handkerchief in one hand that he kept coughing into, and in the other he held a briefcase. He was not at all what I'd expected. The skin on his face was pockmarked from acne. He wore a suit with a jacket that was too small for him, over a shirt with buttons that were dying to bust open. But it was his sweating that I found really revolting. Rivulets of it streamed from his forehead and stained his armpits. I decided if he tried to hug me I would smack him. Rick placed the coffees on the table as Miguel cleared his throat. He spoke in the manner of someone who believed he was supremely important, and that he was doing us a favour just by talking to us.

"You see, I wanted to meet here so you know what it's like to be in the place where the adoptive mothers meet the birth mothers. It's always so very moving. I never join those meetings; I think it's best for the mothers to be alone. It's a very special moment for both."

"You mentioned something to do with Happy Parents," Rick broke in abruptly.

"Well," he said, stroking his chin, sitting back in his chair, and eyeing us up, "you see, I cannot work with you unless you are registered with them. We have a deal that I can't break out of. It wouldn't be fair. I have been working with them for many years."

"But we can't work with US agencies, less so with Happy Parents. The UK authorities have been very clear about it," I said.

I expected him to take this comment with some gravity, but he seemed to brush it off.

"Hmm, OK, let's talk about that later. Anyway, the way I generally work is that I advertise my services in local newspapers. The cost for that is one thousand dollars."

Rick shot me a warning look. At the same time, Miguel reached over to rip a piece of paper from his files, and in doing so he spilled his entire cup of coffee on the photocopies of our precious documents. He seemed oblivious to what he'd done. He didn't even bother to apologise as I grabbed napkins and frantically tried to wipe the coffee from the only evidence of our eligibility to adopt.

"Then, two thousand dollars to pay for the accommodation of the birth mother before the birth. There will also be four thousand for the hospital, as we like to put our birth mothers in the best hospitals. And then two thousand for any follow up care or fostering of the baby while you are coming and going, to ensure the child is well looked after. In total it's about ten thousand dollars. Plus ten thousand for Happy Parents, of course."

He handed Rick the grubby scrap of paper with these huge amounts of money on it with all the reverence of a priest bestowing a brand new marriage certificate. Then he leaned back, folded his arms over his corpulent stomach, and asked me to get him another coffee. Like an obedient puppy, I jumped up to fetch him his Americano.

"Let's start all over again. What do you mean by advertising your services exactly?" asked Rick when I came back.

"Well, you know, there are many women who don't understand contraception here in Mexico, and they can't keep the babies. So I put an ad in the newspapers—carefully worded, which is why it is very expensive—and ask them to contact me."

"But it's illegal to pay birth mothers for their babies," I said.

"Aha. But it is legal to pay for pre-natal and post-natal care, living expenses, and time off work, which is what you would pay me for. Of course you can choose to offer extra help to the mother directly. That depends entirely on how much you like her, and the level of generosity you want to show a woman who has carried your healthy baby for nine months."

"And then what happens? What happens after the advert?" asked Rick.

"Well, the women get in touch, and we discuss how to proceed. You must know that I only work with reliable women, and I have a number of women that I've been working with for years."

"What do you mean by reliable?"

"Simple. My women never change their mind."

His women?

"Surely they are allowed to?" I was incredulous that he could think it was wrong for women to change their mind. Surely, if the situation changed, it was better that they kept the babies and changed their mind now rather than later?

"By law they are, right up until the day of the court hearing, where they represent their baby in court. But we try very hard to work with women that don't change their minds. You know it's devastating for the adoptive parents when that happens. We really care about our customers, you see; adoptive parents are very special people who have gone through a lot by the time we get to meet."

I looked at Rick, who seemed impassive.

"We are not here to take a baby at any cost," I told him. I felt I had to make that clear.

He dismissed my concerns.

"As an adoptive parent, you have rights, you know. And I can make this all happen within the timeframe you have left. It will be a newborn baby whose birth mother will have been counselled and checked by doctors, so the baby will be healthy. These are very brave women we work with. They don't take the easy option of abortion, but the one of making another family happy."

Ordinarily I would not have listened to this fool for a moment. I didn't like his mercenary attitude. But we were already feeling beaten by the difficulties we had encountered. And if there were women in Mexico who couldn't keep their babies, why shouldn't we be the recipient of one? At the end of the day, if their baby didn't go to us, it would go to another couple, so what would be the difference?

I needed to know what Rick was thinking. Did he see it as I did? Or was he disgusted by it all? I almost wanted him to save me the decision I was scared I might make.

"What would we have to do next?" I heard Rick ask. Jesus. He *had* got to that point.

"Well, it's quite simple. You sign a contract. I find you a birth mother, hopefully one who is already close to giving birth. Obviously it's very late. I normally contact women three or four months before they have the baby, because by the time it's born, it is all sorted with Happy Parents." He was stroking his chin again. "But we'll see, we'll see. If I put an ad, I should be able to find a pregnant woman. I know these places and I may be able to sort something for you."

"And then what?"

"And we move on the way I have explained to you. You can go and live in the same block of flats where all the American and Irish couples are either waiting for their baby or waiting to go back. It's in this area, and I am sure you will like it. It'll be just like being home!"

"What about Happy Parents? At what point do they get involved?" asked Rick.

"Ah, forget Happy Parents! I don't really like them. I just have to work with them, you see. We can do this amongst ourselves. I have done that before. Many, many couples who come back cut them out of the process. They are way too expensive, anyway."

"What do you mean the couples come back?" asked Rick.

"Well, they come back for another baby, of course! There is nothing like having a new bundle of joy, not like those bad kids who have been abandoned or have lived in homes and can be sad or violent. And the second time they contact me directly, without involving Happy Parents. Then I can make sure the birth mother sleeps with the same man, so that the siblings will look alike. Many, many couples come back with that request, and we make it happen. For you. And your children."

I was shocked. He was not talking about adoption; he was talking about women making babies to order and selling them. I looked at Rick, who wore an inscrutable expression.

"We would like to discuss this before we meet again for the formalities, if that's OK," said Rick calmly.

He really has crossed that line. I hoped he hadn't done it just for me.

"Well, of course, my dear. I can imagine you'll be excited and wanting to celebrate right now! Let me give you a lift to the restaurant of a friend of mine. You can eat all the steak and chips you like. And he speaks perfect English, so you'll feel at home."

"No, we'll walk. We don't eat steak and chips usually."

"No wonder your wife is so skinny." He laughed loudly. "Let me drive you. They will treat you like old friends."

Rick nodded and took my hand. We took the lift down to the car park, where Miguel's gas-guzzler was parked. We drove about two blocks to another soulless concrete and glass building. The owner was outside, writing on the blackboard:

2 steaks for the price of one!!!

Mexicans are obsessed with 2-for-1 offers. Drinks, food, massages, clothes, movies; I once even saw a strip bar ad stating you could have two women for the price of one. I wondered, in my worried and distracted state, whether Miguel would ever stoop to offering us two babies for the price of one. It seemed like just the sort of thing he was capable of.

"Hey, *amigo*!" shouted Miguel. "These are my friends. Treat them well, OK?"

Then he turned to us.

"I see you soon, I think. Don't forget to have a tequila to celebrate! OK. Bye."

It had come to this: a meeting in Starbucks in a modern, ugly shopping mall, discussing the transaction of babies. It seemed to sum up the whole business of adoption. I didn't know who to be more disgusted with: Miguel, or the adoptive families, who requested that these poor women sleep with the same man for... what was their cut, perhaps two hundred American? Surely the Miguels of this world exist only because there are people willing to pay. Did Happy Parents know? Was that what adoption was really about? About poor, needy, *reliable* women who procreate to order and put their babies on the market? I was used to discussing the downsides of globalisation, but this was something else altogether.

More to the point, were Rick and I one of those couples I was now judging? The thought made me sick. Miguel had been clever, very clever, and had sucked us in big time. What he was talking about was child trafficking, pure and simple.

We had just had our first encounter with the seamy underbelly of the adoption world. It would not be our last.

6

After the Devil, An Angel

We were shell-shocked. This is the only way I can explain how we came to be sitting in a crappy, touristy fast-food joint with red plastic chairs and laminated posters of model food. The owner insisted we order his steaks, even though we didn't want them. I looked down at the grey lump of meat and pushed it around my plate and back again until it had nowhere else to go. Meanwhile, we were drinking margaritas with the kind of urgency only the locals managed.

I was waiting for Rick to tell me what he thought about the whole Miguel meeting, but he seemed in no hurry to talk about it. I was relieved, since his silence saved me from formulating my own response and allowed me to push the whole thing to the back of my brain. Except I couldn't. Instead of obliterating the previous couple of hours, the tequila only had the effect of bringing it all back, until after about the third round, the drink wanted to talk.

"So, what did you make of it?"

"Of what?"

"You know, Miguel…"

"Oh, interesting… you know, what he said about definitely getting a baby."

So Rick was interested in what Miguel was offering. He didn't appear disturbed by it at all.

"Yes," I said. "And on time to return for work, ha ha."

Was he serious? Were we actually going to do this? Drop our convictions just so our trip to Mexico wouldn't be fruitless and we could go home with a baby?

"It wouldn't be *exactly* what we wanted to do," said Rick.

He was right. It wouldn't. It wouldn't be anything like it. It would be cold and empty, like the horrible steakhouse we were sitting in.

"But if you think about it, whether it's us or another couple, these babies won't stay with their birth mothers. They still need a family. So it may as well be us," he said. Was this the drink talking?

"And surely, we're better than those other parents," I joked.

"But... I guess the question is... could you live with your conscience?"

This man was my husband, a man I'd known for eight years, yet I had no idea what he meant. Had Miguel fried my brain with all his talk? Was Rick saying that he was ready to take the plunge, but wanted to know if I could do the same?

I had to stop this. It would be a betrayal of my convictions, and while they might not have mattered to anyone else, they mattered to me.

He sighed and leaned forward, taking my face in his hands.

"No matter how desperate we are right now Francesca, I can't. I really can't do it. But... I *would* do it for you if you wanted it."

Relief surged through me like a wave of pure oxygen. Despite an excess of tequila, I suddenly felt light again.

"I don't want this either," I blurted. "I thought you did. You seemed so unruffled about it all. I had no idea what you were thinking in there. Oh, Rick, I'm so glad."

I had tears in my eyes.

"How could you think I'd want anything to do with him? The guy is a fraudster. Worse, he's a criminal who knows how to roll the dice so it looks good for people like us."

"Ick. He made my skin crawl. So slimy and manipulative. When did it click for you?" I asked.

"Well, to be honest, I wasn't too disturbed until he mentioned the couples coming back to Mexico for another baby, and him making sure those poor birthmothers slept with the same men. He's scum."

"I just couldn't do it, Rick. I just couldn't live with myself if I knew a woman was doing it to order. Because you know that's what he was talking about. Babies on demand. God, I feel sick. Give me another drink."

I threw a shot of tequila down my throat.

"I don't care if this is our last chance. If we end up going through all of this and we go back to England empty-handed, then we do."

"Shall we celebrate?" said Rick.

"I'm drunk already." I was seeing double. I can't handle tequila at the best of times, let alone with my emotions running high. After a few more drinks, I was well and truly pickled. Rick decided we'd better go. We fell out of the restaurant into a taxi and a very heavy sleep.

The next day, we would be meeting Carla at the DIF in Guadalajara. While my hopes for this meeting were low, my mood had suddenly lifted again. I was happy to be in Mexico and to have this opportunity to meet lovely people, and to get to know their ancient culture. With it came a strong sense of spirituality and hope for the future. I knew the universe would deliver. It was just a matter of time.

The next morning, I felt rough. Heat and hangovers are not best friends. We usually bought bottled water for our hotel room, but being drunk we had forgotten. Someone in my head was beating drums very loudly.

"Rick, I can't look down. Please put my trousers on for me?"

"I don't know, I thought I'd married a woman who could hold her drink."

"Shut up and help me, please! I need my sunglasses, too."

"God, Francesca, you've turned into a South American dictator."

Several pints of fresh juice later, we were en route to see yet another DIF. This one was just a plain, grey government office that could have been anywhere in the world. There was, however, a stern-faced lady at reception. I decided not to tangle with her.

Carla was much younger than the other procuradoras we'd met, but no less knowledgeable. She reiterated what she'd already told us over the phone, and what we knew by now to be the standard line in Mexico: only older children, and a very long wait. Because of our mutual association with Cetty, and the fact that we'd spoken on the telephone a few times from London, I told her about meeting Miguel.

"Miguel Peron?"

"Yes, why? Do you know him?"

She sighed and raised her eyebrows.

"Everyone knows Miguel, everyone in the whole adoption system. Interpol is after him. It's common knowledge what he is doing with these birth mothers, but he is also very clever and cunning, so it's very hard to pin anything on him."

The fact that Miguel was being sought by Interpol didn't shock me. What did shock me was the fact that he worked for a well-known American adoption agency, meaning that he must have been known to the American government. Given their far-reaching powers, you had to wonder why he hadn't been caught and investigated.

"There are some institutes here that are partly run by the State, and partly by the Church or privately. They might be able to help you if they knew I sent you. Look, here are some addresses. Let me think of a good one… hmm." She scanned her diary. "I think you should try Isituto Cabañas. They have many children. Call Gabriela and say I have sent you. Here is her number."

"I would really rather you called her, please, Carla," I said.
She shook her head.

"She will be at lunch now, and I need to go now as well."

I don't know if she didn't want the responsibility for making the call. Something told me it would be better if she did. So I pushed my luck.

"That's OK," I said. "We will wait here while you go and have lunch, then you can call and introduce us."

She relented. "OK, we can try now, I guess, before I go."

Gabriela wasn't there. It was indeed lunchtime, which meant a two-hour break, something I envied Mexicans. It was amazing that anyone even came back to their desks. I was sure that there was a large proportion of people all over Mexico who disappeared at lunchtime and never came back until the next day.

Carla came back.

"OK, Gabriela is waiting for you. The place is walking distance. Good luck, guys. Let me know."

Guadalajara is not a place you would visit without reason. It is everything you don't want to see in a country like Mexico, a complete killer of any romantic fantasies you have about this part of the world. In fact, if you landed here first you'd probably leave the country. The institute wasn't around the corner, but a longish walk through uninspiring streets past dull buildings until we reached the correct address. The building sat behind a set of electric gates that gave it a prison-like feel. The security guard knew of us from the directora and let us in. Titles are very important in Mexico.

I instantly liked Gabriela. She had big, blonde hair—big as in Eighties-style American TV hair. In contrast to this, she was dressed very conservatively: a cream skirt reaching below her knees, a white shirt, black cardigan, and a gold cross around her neck. The overall impression was aristocratic, something that was emphasised by her extraordinary British accent, which she told us she had developed because her English teacher was from Eton. While her appearance— and that of her office—might have suggested an austere attitude, she had a warm twinkle in her eyes that endeared her to me. I wanted to know her.

And so we began our story *again*, which of course had several dramatic moments in it by this point, though clearly they were more dramatic for us than for her. When I mentioned the corrupt lawyer, she just said, "Ah, Miguel, a man of no conscience," even before I'd said his name. More importantly, our decision not to follow his route at any cost gave us her ear. She told us about her organisation.

"Here at the Istituto Cabañas, we have over five hundred children from various backgrounds, a lot of whom sadly are for adoption. We have quite a lot of young girls, and we do tend to do Hague adoptions, so for you it would be an older child."

It was Rick who interrupted.

"We don't mind it being an older child, but as we have the child's interest in mind, we would like to avoid bringing a child who is already at school age into the UK, where they wouldn't understand the language and would be more traumatised. Plus, I wouldn't be able to communicate with my own daughter." Rick was grasping the opportunity to speak English to someone with both hands.

"I can see your point, and I really like you guys. I don't meet people like you every day, and caring for these children is everything for me. I want them to go to the right family. I am happy to consider you to adopt a two-year-old girl. We have many. The only thing is that I need my board to clear the decision. It is only a formality, though, if I think you are suitable."

A formality!

"We meet on Tuesday. I need you to fill in the application form and bring it back with all your documents by Friday afternoon, so I can submit it for the meeting."

"We… don't have our documents I am afraid."

Rick again. "We only have the photocopies, but we are hoping the originals will be sent soon." For two and half months now, the DCSF had been ignoring every one of our desperate requests for our documents.

"That's fine. Copies will be sufficient for the submission. Then, of course, we will need the originals when you make a specific application for a child."

When you apply, not if. She was serious. Both Rick and I were getting excited.

"Clearly, I am the board chair, so my opinion matters more than anyone else's," she laughed. "So it should all be OK. You will have to find yourself somewhere to live, as the process takes about two months. But I think after you have dropped off all the documents you should go and relax and celebrate at the weekend. You won't get much rest once you have a child! Now, don't you want to visit the children and la casa?"

"We would love to!" I said, leaping up.

She smiled and led us out into a courtyard full of glorious sunshine. The place was delightful, laid out like a city in miniature. There were neat, double-storied buildings, and between each one there were gardens with little benches. The courtyard was full of children. As we walked, Gabriela stopped to talk to them. She seemed to know each one by name, and a great deal of their personal information as well.

"How is your tooth today?"

"Did you manage to sleep better last night?"

"Don't forget to call your grandma tomorrow, it's her birthday."

She had time for everyone. It was clear that this was a happy place where children were cared for, not the institution of my nightmares. As we walked past another building, an adorable group came out, all wearing bibs and walking in single file like ducklings.

"It's time for dinner for the five-to-eight-year-olds. Come with me. I will show you the canteen."

As well as being massive enough for five hundred little people, the canteen was so impeccably clean you could have eaten off the floor. There was fruit laid out everywhere, and the décor was colourful and happy.

We walked out again and headed towards the toddlers' room. Another queue of little people—boys—were following a lady with toothbrushes in their hands.

Another smaller group was playing football. Rick stopped to

play with them, and they were ever so proud they were playing with an English man!

We turned a corner and entered a room full of cots where little bundles of pyjama-clad baby girls were being put to bed for the night.

"It's time for a sleep," said Gabriela. "Would you two like to help?"

I looked at all those innocent arms reaching towards us. It was so beautiful and heartbreaking at the same time. They were gorgeous. One of them immediately diverted me. As I picked her up to say goodnight and kiss her, she clung on to me.

Gabriela was understandably stoic.

"This girl is available for adoption… and so is her brother. Would you be willing to take two? We don't like separating them. She is four… I mean two." I could tell she lied so that we would consider adopting the girl and her brother, but it didn't matter.

"We need to let them rest now. I will show you the baby room next door."

I put the little girl back in her cot, but she just wouldn't let go. She was holding onto my neck and crying so hard it was shattering to say goodbye.

Most of the very young babies we saw showed clear signs of being handicapped.

"They are abandoned on our steps when they are born, and the parents realise that they are disabled," explained Gabriela.

She walked through, introducing us to each of them in turn and telling us their stories.

"See Marco in that cot?" She pointed at a baby who was clearly larger than the others. "He is actually four years old, but his brain is that of a baby."

I went over and leaned down. Marco was lying on his back like a baby would, even though he was clearly not a baby any more. He was holding his feet in a position that in yoga is called 'happy baby', babbling. I tickled him, and he started laughing uncontrollably. He was just adorable, such a little angel. He gestured repeatedly for me to keep playing with him, which I couldn't stop doing. Rick was holding other babies.

Gabriela indicated a hammock. We looked inside at the tiniest little person I'd ever seen.

"She is only a couple of days old. We found her yesterday on the steps of the entrance. We named her Aurora."

I was touched by Aurora, and by everything we'd seen here. Angels did exist, and Gabriela was their leader. Scattered around in the room on armchairs or sofas, more angels were feeding the babies, changing their nappies, singing to them. The scene was one of perfect humanity, of love and care being given and received.

"They are all volunteers," said Gabriela. "I can't afford to pay many people, just the ten in the offices, but we are never short of staff. There are more good-hearted people than one thinks in the world. Let's go now."

We went back to her office and she gave us a form to fill in.

"Remember to include a picture of yourselves, and to bring everything back no later than Friday afternoon. Call me on Tuesday at 1:00 pm. God bless you."

I always wondered if people meant it when they said God bless you, or simply said it out of habit. But she meant it.

"And have a good break at the weekend. Go somewhere nice and fun and party!"

7

The Blonde in the White Mercedes

Puerto Vallarta is where young American college kids go to let it all hang out and take it all off. Unlike brash Cancun, it has its saving graces, one of them being that it is an old town with the surprisingly pristine prettiness one might find in Greece's smaller island resorts. There are cobbled streets and outdoor cafés, where you can sit and enjoy dinner to the sound of people dancing salsa with the gringos. Or you can enjoy grilled fresh fish on the beach, and this being Mexico, they will thoughtfully ask you if you want a side of cocaine with your king prawns. They don't whisper it, either.

"Gambas! Coca!"

Señor Frogs is where the recently arrived and freshly liberated young Americans head for a good time. It has the ubiquitous 2-for-1 offers in the most enormous drinking glasses I've ever seen, plus a bizarre game where young girls give you a tequila shot and then squeeze your breasts, even if, unlike a lot of the student girls, you don't have them hanging out. It was tacky and stupid, but it was fun. We found an amazingly cheap place to stay on a hill overlooking the bay, with gorgeous views and a jacuzzi.

We made friends with an American couple who were staying at the same place, and with them we drank and partied until late. But some things can't be left behind. So when the Americans asked us what we were doing in Mexico, they got the full story about our impending adoption and how we'd finally done it.

Before leaving we'd worked on the submission, filling in forms, getting Oscar to look at it and advise us, and having photos taken. When we dropped it off en route to catching the bus for Puerto Vallarta, there was a real sense we were now getting somewhere.

Now, as we boarded the return bus, clutching our snack of pork skin in tomato sauce, I felt quite emotional. As usual, the bus was late, so I would have to call Gabriela while we were travelling in order to catch her at the agreed time. Phone reception wasn't great anyway, and every time the bus swerved around a bend we lost it.

"Hi, it's Francesca. Is Gabriela there? I had a phone appointment."

"One second, I will—"

The signal went. Again. Fingers crossed. God, no, he's turning. I'll wait.

"Hi, I'm sorry, the signal keeps going."

"Oh, hi, is it you Francesca? She is busy right now. Can you call back in—"

I didn't catch the last bit, as we'd swerved and lost the connection again.

"Oh, shit. Can't this bus go straight just for a minute?"

"Keep your voice down," said Rick as we screeched round a corner.

We were driving straight again. I dialled quickly and was put straight through.

"Hi, Francesca, yes... yes, I have reviewed everything with the board. You are just the perfect couple—"

The connection disappeared. But this time I wasn't upset.

"Oh my God, Rick, she said we are perfect! The perfect couple! That's the best thing anyone has said."

Normally, on a Mexican bus, my heart would be racing because of the perilous journey. Now I was excited. I took a deep breath and dialled again. The secretary put me through straight away.

"Gabriela, that's great news," I began.

She interrupted me.

"Francesca, the lawyer on my board pointed out you that have only been married for two years."

I held the phone tightly to my ear as the bus bounced its way along an unmade road. Rocks flew up and hit the sides.

"Yes, Gabriela. What does it mean?"

"The law of our state, Jalisco, only allows couples who have been married for five years to adopt."

This is crazy!!

"What… but… surely there is something you can do to help…"

"Of course I can," she said.

Oh, thank God for that.

"In three years!" she laughed.

It wasn't funny. It wasn't fair. Frankly, I was struggling. It may have been the consequences of too much partying combined with tiredness. It may have been that and the bus ride. Or it may simply have been the last straw. Whatever it was, I had to throw up. Leaning across Rick, I put my head out of the window and let loose the entire contents of my stomach. Not surprisingly, I lost the connection. Nonetheless, I kept my mind on the job.

"Quick, redial," I said to Rick as I wiped my face. "Do it now!"

This time she answered herself.

"You said we were the perfect couple. Isn't that what you said?" I knew I sounded desperate, because that's what I was.

"Yes, I did say that, and you are…"

"So if we are, you can surely help us? I mean, there can't be that many perfect couples."

"There are not, I assure you. However, it's the law of Jalisco, and even I cannot change it for you. Sorry we can't help you. Your papers will be at reception for you to pick them up when you want."

"Can we not meet? Talk again?" I was clinging on to shredded hope, and I knew it.

"Sure, if you come tomorrow morning I will be here."

To get so close and be thwarted by a local rule was just unfair. If I was explaining this to someone in my position, I probably would have rationalised it. I might have told them that they hadn't really lost anything, because it's not as if they had it. I would have tried to explain that it was all part of a process where outcomes were never assured. It would be what is meant to be. The right child is waiting for you somewhere. I really would have done my best to make them feel like it was not them.

But right now, it was me. It was my heartbreak, and I was going to have it. I was sick of trusting the ways of the world, tired of believing and being battered by my own emotions. I didn't want them any more. I didn't want to feel a thing. I had no room. I put my head on Rick's knee and tried to cry, but I couldn't bring it out. I had nothing left this time.

We reached the bus station and took a taxi to the flat we'd rented thinking we would need a home for our daughter. Now it was just another place to crash. I was worried about Rick. He was losing faith, withdrawn, struggling to cope. Gone was the man of a week earlier. There wasn't much left to hope for. The DIF way was clearly out of the question. So was Miguel's option, and now the Church children's home. What was left for us to try?

But somehow, I found a crumb of faith that it would still happen. There must have been something in the spiritual power of Mexico that kept me going. I wasn't yet ready to abandon hope that we would be allowed to do some good eventually.

I also felt that motherhood was becoming more real to me, not by virtue of a growing stomach or social worker's questionnaires, but a true maternal instinct for the children I'd had the privilege of meeting in the homes. For them alone I had to keep going and not give up. I owed them something more than a promise of cash donations.

🐟

"Are you pregnant and don't know what to do? Call us, it's free.

VIFAC." These words were written on a huge billboard we drove past in the taxi on the way to our flat.

Vifac, Vifac... where had I heard it before? Ah, yes, from the lawyer in Puebla. I grabbed a pen out of my bag and wrote down the number.

While Rick sat quietly eating toast and drinking tea, his first 'English treat' in the rented flat, I fired up the computer and Googled Vifac. There was nearly one for every state.

My headset was broken, so my calls had to be made with me bending over the keyboard. I called about ten different Vifac offices. The answers were always the same.

"Yes, we have babies, but not for foreigners."

After several fruitless calls, Rick broke his silence.

"How do you do it, Fra?" he said, taking my hand. "How do you pick yourself off the floor and keep on going? You amaze me every single day."

"I do it the same way you do. I get low, too. But you pick me up. That's how it works."

And then I called the Vifac in Colima.

The line was so bad it was difficult to even work out what they other person was saying. I had to keep saying:

"Are you sure?" when the lady at the other end kept answering my questions in the affirmative.

"Yes, we have done international adoptions."

You are kidding me.

"Are you sure?"

"Yes, of course I am sure. Look, *el licenciado* Jose is away right now, but I'll ask him to email you when he is back. Or you can email him. Can you spell your name, please?"

With my head practically inside the keyboard, I spelt my name out, which took a full twenty minutes. Although I speak fluent Spanish, it is not so easy for me when it comes to spelling.

There was no time to lose. As soon as I finished the call, I got on the phone to Oscar.

"Oscar, you have to help me. I need to write a formal letter to this lawyer and impress him." We did it there and then, and I emailed it to Jose.

The flurry of activity didn't disguise the fact that the flat felt empty, as it wasn't being used for the purpose of accommodating our daughter. Every time I walked past the spare room I had to look away. There was no little person sleeping in there, no tiny socks, no teddy on the bed.

As it was the first time we'd had access to a decent internet connection, I was able to pick up my work emails, too. My loyal PA had again contacted me about my boss, Thomas. She'd forwarded correspondence that he'd asked his PA to send to her. Apparently Thomas now wanted to take the costs of moving my things from Geneva to London out of my salary! I now realised I hadn't been paranoid; he was trying to get rid of me, or at least make my life so miserable that I would leave.

I decided I had to take the advice of an employment lawyer, which meant contacting the UK. Over the phone, the lawyer helped me write a letter to Thomas and HR explaining that this was wrong and I wasn't going to let it pass. It was slowly beginning to dawn on me that whatever happened, I would not be going back to my job, and it didn't feel good. Right now I was nowhere; I had left everything behind, and so far had not replaced any of it. My life was speculation.

I wasn't the only one, as my friend Michelle's email reminded me. Their plan had been to adopt from China, but unfortunately their timing was bad, as China had decided to change its policies and was no longer easy to adopt from. Now, she told me, they were going to adopt domestically. Unlike me, she'd experienced that awful moment when the doctor says, "I am sorry it's not going to be possible," so her and her husband spent a fortune on IVF, but even that hadn't worked. But she was truly one of the most determined women I have met in terms of her desire to have children. It consumed her, occupying every waking moment.

Michelle really wanted a baby or toddler, and there are very few available domestically; most of the babies up for adoption are mixed race or black, and as we had found out ourselves, white families are generally dissuaded from adopting them. She could have just opted for older children, of which there are more, but she wanted a baby, and even though in adoption you are supposed to just feel grateful for whatever you get, she was sticking to her decision. During her gruelling domestic home study, she'd been told that in order to have a baby or toddler, she needed to be prepared to have its siblings. There was no other way.

The evening came with a plate of comforting tomato and basil pasta, the first in two and a half months.

And an email from Jose, the Vifac lawyer. He was very touched by our story and wanted to speak to us the next day. We had an office number to call, and something to look ahead to. That night we both slept heavily.

In Mexico, 'first thing in the morning' is not before 10:00 am. I was up at 6:00 in order to speak to the employment lawyer in Europe and to spend the next few hours stressing about, well, absolutely everything.

Rick and I walked to a shopping mall. The only place open was—you guessed it—Starbucks. Memories of the sublime coffee in Chiapas and Veracruz were fading fast as we took our caffeine-flavoured lactose solutions from the counter. We needed to warm up fast, as Guadalajara is about 2000 metres above sea level. The temperature in April was around 30 degrees Celsius during the day, or over 90 Fahrenheit. In the evening it plummeted to zero, so early mornings were, literally, freezing.

I started calling the Vifac offices at 9:00 am. Conception, the same woman who'd answered the phone the previous day, was there and put us through to Jose. He spoke no English.

"You have to be interviewed before being able to register with us. As you are in Guadalajara, I will ask the *presidenta* of the Vifac there to interview you, to avoid travelling to Colima for nothing. She is very nice, a little tough at first, perhaps, but don't worry."

I rang Vifac Guadalajara and asked for 'la presidenta'. While I waited, I could hear a voice in the background. At first I thought it was a man, as it was a very deep voice. Whoever it was wasn't too happy.

"No way. Like I am not busy enough. What does Pepe think he is playing at? Never trust lawyers, not even *licenciaditos*." She called him the 'small qualified one'. Why? I could hear the receptionist pleading with her, and eventually she came to the phone.

"Bueeeeenooooooo." It was the deepest tequila and cigarette voice I'd ever heard. She could have been a Mexican character in the Simpsons. However, she was serious.

"Hello, Aurora. My name is Francesca. I am Italian. I am so sorry to bother you, but Jose suggested..."

"Yes, yes, Jose suggested. Jose suggests always..."

"We are here to adopt from Europe... he said it might possible to meet you... we are at your full disposal."

"Hmm." That voice was intimidating.

I stumbled on.

"I am so grateful you are finding the time to even speak to me on the phone. You see, it's been so hard for us so far, we have now been here in Mexico, your wonderful country, for months..."

"OK, come today, in twenty minutes. I am telling you right now I don't have much longer than half an hour, and if you are late I won't see you."

🐗

The white Mercedes rolled nonchalantly down the hill and stopped in front of the office of Vifac, the Catholic Association for Life. We sat inside what was just another unprepossessing little house in a quiet, dusty road on the outskirts of Guadalajara.

The woman who stepped out of the car was about sixtyish, tall and blonde. She wore a cream suit and sandals that set her light tan off perfectly. There was something about her that immediately drew me in. She moved with the elegance and regal bearing of an aristocrat, but the way the cigarette never left her lips suggested someone who had seen it all and more besides. Even from this distance her charisma was palpable. I instantly felt drawn to her.

The clack-clack of high heels and an impossibly dirty, smoky laugh preceded her imperious entry into the office. Flourishing her cigarette and pushing her sunglasses back onto her head, she gestured out of the window towards the car.

"It's my new baby. Isn't she super, Chita?" she said to the receptionist.

A very large Chita, who was also puffing away on a cigarette as if her life depended on it, emerged from behind a huge, old-fashioned computer monitor to look out the window.

"Oooh, Aurora. *Que linda*! Talking of babies," she added, gesturing towards us, "you have a couple of foreigners waiting to see you. They've been waiting over an hour. Apparently they have a meeting with you."

"Well, I'd better get a move on then." She motioned to us to follow her.

"I expect a lift home tonight," yelled Chita after her as we disappeared into her office.

There was another woman in the room who was already reading our file. She was tall and elegant, though much younger and less imposing than Aurora. Nonetheless, the presence of these two evidently strong Mexican women was intimidating, reason enough for both Rick and I to locate ourselves at the far end of a large table.

"Do you mind me smoking?" asked Aurora.

"No, not at all."

"Then come closer! I don't normally bite at this time in the morning." She laughed.

She placed her two mobile phones and shiny car keys on the table, and then nodded to the other woman, whose name was Anna, as if giving her royal assent. Anna leaned back in her chair, placed the folder in front of her on the table, and crossed her arms.

Oh God, here it comes, I thought. *The Mexican Inquisition.*

This looks like it's going to be tough. These two are going to make it hard.

"So why do you want to adopt a baby? Can you not have one?"

No, please, don't ask me this question again.

"We feel very profoundly that we want to give a child who has no chance of a home an opportunity they might not otherwise have."

"Is that it?" Anna asked cynically.

"You should talk about your work in children's homes, and your adopted brother, your general commitment to this," Rick whispered, tapping my knee.

"I have worked in children's homes for many years, and I have an adopted brother, so this is not a whim, although you might think it sounds like one. We have discussed this and spent a lot of time making the decision. I think the fact that we have made this journey should tell you that we are serious."

The questions were exactly what I'd expected. I'd worked on model answers, but as with any interview situation, it's the luck of the draw whether you actually pull it out of the bag at that moment. Thankfully, Rick was on good form and provided the prompts.

As the interview wore on, there were hints of what looked like approval appearing in the faces of both women. When they began smiling and nodding at each other during my answers, I began to think I was making some headway. Still, I wasn't going to relax.

"What if the baby was of a different colour, say black? What would you do, ha?" This was Anna asking, leaning forward in her chair and staring me in the eye. She had her own special way of asking questions that was somewhere between playful and deeply inquisitive. It was hard to tell if she was joking.

Rick was tapping me again.

"Tell her about our godson, Daniel, who is black, and all of our friends from different countries. Come on, Fra, don't give up now," he whispered.

"Of course we wouldn't mind. We would love any child unconditionally, whatever their sex, age, size, and colour."

"As you know, Francesca, we do this work for the sake of God and His will. We host women who decide against the brutality of abortion and help them decide whether to keep their babies or not. We just want the best for our babies, for these new lives," said Anna. She sounded like she truly meant it. "This is primarily about caring for life, not about giving unwanted children away. Do you see what I mean?"

"We do know, and we completely admire and respect what you stand for and the work you do," I said. I started feeling bolder and more confident. Rick was holding my hand. Aurora sat with her arms crossed without saying a word, just puffing away and giving the occasional look to Anna, who seemed to be relaxing.

"If the women decide not to keep their babies, we will place them for adoption just a few days after their birth, once they have been legally relinquished. With the right waiting family, of which we have many, of course. It happens very quickly, as we want the baby to be with its family straight away, and we are not equipped to look after babies. This is a place of women for women, you see. Do you feel capable of dealing with a young baby who has just been taken from its mother?"

Anna moved forward and stared right into my eyes, this time in a definitely confrontational fashion. But for me it wasn't threatening. It was an indication that I needed to understand how serious this was.

"We would do everything we could to make that child feel loved and wish for nothing else but to be given that honour," I said.

Aurora nodded again. Did she approve of what I'd said? She smiled. They were both silent as were we. Just as it got uncomfortable, Anna spoke.

"Welcome to the Vifac family. We will be sure to help you once all your documents have been checked. The world needs more parents like you!"

I jumped up and hugged Rick. Had we finally made it?

"I hope you don't mind waiting for a couple of years," added

Anna. "We will make sure we keep you posted at all times, of course, while you are back in London."

No, no, no no! I was shaking.

"Wh...What do you mean?"

"Well, our waiting list is between two and four years at present, but the good news is that we are pretty confident we can make things happen for you rather quickly—maximum two years," replied Anna. The words tumbled out of me, seemingly of their own accord.

"But... we don't have two years to wait. We don't even have one year! We packed it in at our jobs nearly three months ago to come and find a child. And we are supposed to be back already. We have travelled this country top to bottom and back and front, working with children, helping schools, going from one promise to the next. We are running out of time. If we go back now without a child, we will both lose our jobs..."

"Look, Francesca—" Anna tried to speak.

"This was our last hope to be able to fulfil our dream and the hopes of another human being. Perhaps it's just not meant to be."

Anna managed to interrupt my melodrama.

"I am sorry. We can try and speed things up, but even then we are talking a few months minimum. As hard as we try, we can't make miracles. That's something only God can do."

"Thank you for being so lovely. We appreciate it. Maybe we have come to the end of our road and our journey has finished. Thank you for being so lovely with us and best of luck for your wonderful work." I turned around to translate, but when I looked at Rick I knew he didn't need me to.

I got up, took his hand, and pulled him up too.

"Let's go, amore, I am sorry." I don't even know why I apologised. I had started to feel responsible for having been the one who wanted to adopt. I felt like I had coerced him into this mad plan without even knowing what I was doing. I'd gotten him so excited he moved to Mexico for it. And we were about to go home empty-handed, and possibly unemployed. These two ladies were adorable, but it had become clear that there was no way forward, either here or anywhere. Paolo was right. I had been stupid. The trainers were right when they said the obstacles can become insurmountable. And Barbara was right, too; we shouldn't have tried a country that no one else in the UK had yet adopted from.

"Wait." It was Aurora's deep, raspy voice. She got up and came towards us.

"I didn't know all this, and I want to help you. I think you are a wonderful couple and I will do my best to help you in the time you have available. I promise, I *will* help you. I will do all I can to help you before you go. Just give me time."

By now I was feeling sorry for myself, and ashamed and embarrassed by my outburst. I just wanted to run away. I didn't want reassuring words; in fact, I didn't want anyone to be kind to me.

"Thanks, Aurora, you are wonderful, but we have no time, we truly don't," I said. She put her cigarette out and took my hand.

"Go home and relax a little now. It looks like you need to. Just take some time," she said.

"We know how hard this is," added Anna.

We hugged them both and walked out to the reception area, where Chita was eating a burrito with refried beans. She waved at us, smiling, her mouth full.

"Francesca?"

That voice again.

"Yes, Aurora?" I turned around, but I couldn't look up at her. I felt like an ashamed school kid.

"Look at me," ordered Aurora, lifting my chin with her finger.

I looked up into Aurora's firm, unflinching face. She took my hand, squeezed it, and whispered: "When I say I will help you, I will help you. I will send you back with your baby girl. You have my word. God bless you girl, you have a heart of gold. Now go home and get some sleep. Ask Rick to look after you."

There was something about Aurora that made me believe her. She was not a woman who made promises airily, I could tell.

8

Between Life and Death

I once read a book called *Emergency Sex,* about how people in war zones felt the need to be physically close and let off steam. Back at our hotel that's what we did, wordlessly and endlessly. And then we fell asleep.

We were definitely re-energised and closer than ever. This trip could have taken our relationship either way. Luckily, it had made us bond even more. We had even found things to like about Guadalajara. The place had its graces. The 'Pearl of the West', as they call it, is the city of mariachi. In their wide-brimmed hats, you'll find mariachi singers in every corner, singing songs about the city. Sometimes they're sitting on horses, looking like they're in a film. Guadalajara is also conveniently located next to Tequila, the town where the drink originated.

I liked Aurora, and most importantly I had a really good feeling about her. I sincerely felt she would be true to her word. But while we hadn't lost hope, the ability to get excited appeared to have left us. It wasn't something we discussed, but I think we'd come to a tacit agreement that we'd leave excitement for the day we held our daughter.

Very early the next morning, I turned over to see Rick out of bed, already dressed.

"What's up?"

"I need to focus on something else. I saw on the net that there is an English bookstore near here, so I'm going to walk there, OK?"

"Sure. Do what you have to."

But you're going without me, I thought.

He was doing the right thing. No pun intended, but we really had been on top of each other for the past few months. It was the most time we'd spent together since we'd met. Time out was necessary for both of us, so I kissed him goodbye and sat in bed reading. I had stopped to get a drink of water when the phone rang.

"Francescaaaa!" rasped the smoky voice on the other end.

"Aurora?" I pulled the white sheet over me, as if she could see that I wasn't wearing anything.

"Si, *claro!* You haven't forgotten about me already, have you?" she laughed.

As if I could. As if anyone would dare.

"You have to meet with the psychologist today. She is off for the US tomorrow, and we cannot waste any time."

"But… where… what psychologist?"

"Call her. This is her number." She rattled it off quickly.

"But… Rick is out!"

"Well, go and get him. Hey, listen, stop mumbling and hurry up. Let me know how it goes. And Francesca, one thing, OK?"

"What?"

"Lie if you have to. You know what psychologists are like. Anyhow, you are a smart girl; you know what I mean, make sure she is impressed. My other phone is ringing now. Bye!"

🐖

Gabriela, the psychologist, had sounded amiable enough on the phone, but she needed to see us quickly. As in now.

I went straight into panic mode.

"Where are you?" I asked Rick over the phone.

"In the bookstore, about half an hour's walk."

"Get in a cab immediately. We are going to see a psychologist. I'll wait for you downstairs. Hurry up!"

I ran to the bathroom and confronted the mirror. My hair was all over the place, and I just didn't feel 'right'. I felt hot and clammy, so I took a cold shower and quickly dried myself. My all-important black top was clean and didn't need ironing. I pulled on jeans, hoping they wouldn't be a deal-breaker. That is what endless scrutiny of your life does to you, I guess. Now the good luck 'amulets'. I couldn't leave home without a clutch of objects: my mum's ring, my dear friend Lilly's necklace, and the little red handbag Paolo had given me. I grabbed Rick's watch and his polo shirt so he could get changed in the cab.

I got into the lift, closed my eyes and breathed deeply. When I stepped outside, Rick was already there, waiting in the taxi.

"That was quick of Aurora," he said as I got in.

"Here, wear this," I said, handing him the polo. He got changed.

"This is exciting!" he said.

"Hard not to be excited, isn't it?" We sat in the cab, hugging and grinning.

"Fra, are you sure this is the right place? I mean, look!"

He had a point. We'd stopped outside a full-fledged Buddhist temple, complete with miniature paths, statues, and courtyards fragrant with flowers and incense.

"Hmm, well, yes, it is rather incongruous. Oh, look, she's waving at us. That must be Gabriela."

"Pretty cool," whispered Rick.

Gabriela was barefoot, wearing yoga pants and a loose top. She had a butterfly tattooed on her left foot. I smiled. My grandmother used to say, "When you see a butterfly, just know that I am thinking of you."

We went into a room. It was empty, save for three yoga mats.

Gabriela spoke calmly and straight from her heart. No textbook questions, no mundane bureaucracy. No backtracking to "Why can't you have children?" Telling her that Aurora had invited us to attend an *entrega* elicited a very positive response.

"The fact that she has invited you to attend must be a good sign. She would never want you to witness an entrega unless she felt that yours was coming up soon. It's a very emotional moment. I can understand why Aurora likes you guys, and I think she is really determined to make sure you do realise your dream of adopting."

The *entrega* was the Vifac ceremony where relinquished babies were handed over by a priest to their adoptive parents. It takes place in a church, and is considered a spiritual birth, where God blesses you with this new life whom the adoptive parents won't have seen until that moment.

After what was more of a friendly chat than an interrogation session, Gabriela gave us both a warm hug and waved us off.

"Good luck with it all."

While not quite walking on air, I felt unusually peaceful. Rick seemed to have picked up on this, and there was definitely a pervading sense of calm. And hunger. We headed for Karne Garibaldi. It's a restaurant where they only serve one main dish: *carne en su jugo* (meat in tomato sauce). And they do it fast, very, very fast. They hold the Guinness World Record for fastest service—13.5 seconds. A hearty meal, copious beers, and not a bad day at all. We went to bed contented.

I was cocooned in deep sleep when the mobile phone rang, or at least I thought it did. I was obviously dreaming, so I let it go. Who would ring at this time? It rang again, more insistently. Now I was awake. It was 4:00 am, or so the old-fashioned clock on the bedside table told me. At first I thought it was wrong.

"Rick, wake up. The phone is ringing…" I got out of bed to look for it.

It had stopped ringing, which made it even more difficult to find in the half-light. Something was wrong. I just knew it. Something lit up at my feet. I put my hands on it, picking it up from my jeans pockets, and saw the little envelope symbol on the screen. It was a text message from my sister-in-law, Fiona.

FRA CALL AS SOON AS YOU ARE UP X

There was another one as well, from Lilly.

CALL FIONA URGENTLY. SHE RANG ME TO CHECK IF THE NUMBER SHE HAD FOR YOU WAS CORRECT. XX

Fiona from the UK was asking Lilly in Australia for our phone number? That's when I knew it was Rick's dad. Something serious was wrong with him. I had no logical reason to think this, but the voicemail from Rick's mum confirmed it. She didn't say why we needed to call, but her voice gave it all away.

I lost it and screamed at Rick.

"Wake up! Something has happened to your dad, and we need to ring them!"

I dialled Rick's mum with Skype on our battered computer. Rick sat next to me and had to lean close to the tiny speaker. *Why hadn't we bought some new headsets?*

"Mum, it's Rick, what's up?"

"Hello, son." Her voice was strained. "Your dad is poorly. He collapsed in the middle of the night. We're in hospital with him now. The ambulance brought us, and thank God they were very quick."

"What's wrong with him, mum?"

A sigh.

"They think it was a heart attack, but they're looking into it now… I think that's what they said… you know my Italian isn't great, especially with medical language."

"Mum, are you sure? How is he now? What did the doctors say?"

Rick's grandfather had died of a heart attack at a very young age. His dad was in his mid-fifties, same age.

"I am waiting, Rick, I need to go, they're calling me. Call me back in half an hour." She hung up.

🐦

Rick was crumpled in the chair, sobbing. When you see your macho husband turn from a rock into little grains of sand so quickly, it's truly heartbreaking.

"Oh my God, my dad, my dad."

I couldn't waste any time. I had to get my own family out to the hospital to help. They were about two hours away. At least they would understand the doctors. The only problem was they didn't speak English, so they still wouldn't have been able to translate for Sue. But my brother, Paolo, could. I quickly dialled his number.

"Paolo...Jack is very ill."

"I know. I am in the car, heading out there with mamma."

"Text me as soon as you get there."

I looked up the name of the hospital on the internet, then called and asked to speak to the doctor in charge.

"Hello, I am Jack's daughter-in-law. Can you put me through to the doctor? The family do not speak good Italian, so it's imperative I speak to him."

"You can't speak to the doctor on the phone," said the woman on the other end.

"But I have to. I am with his son now, and we need to know what is happening. We are in Mexico. We need to understand what's happening so I can tell his wife."

A different person had taken the phone.

"It's fine. We can make an exception."

I looked at Rick, who was shaking. The doctor came on the line.

"Hello. I am afraid to say the situation is very serious. Jack has had a major heart attack, truly a very big one, and is in between life and death as we speak. He is in intensive care and we will not be able to tell whether he will survive for another 48 hours. I'm sorry, but that's all I can give you right now."

I always wondered how doctors can give people such bad news in a factual manner.

I looked at Rick as this was being said. I didn't want him to hear this. OK, maybe the heart attack, but not the other bit. But I had the loudspeaker on, so it was too late, and he understood enough Italian to know things were pretty bad.

"Ask them if I should be going home," he said quietly. "I will leave straight away."

From what the doctor had said, Rick was damned if he did go home and damned if he didn't. If Jack did survive those 48 hours, he would need an operation anyway, but then he would improve, so Rick didn't need to rush. All that would mean was that he'd get there while his dad was having a major operation. If Jack didn't pull through, Rick would not be on time to see him, as the travel from Guadalajara to Mexico City, Milan, then Rome, and three hours' drive would have taken more than two days.

I relayed this to him as he paced the room.

"Maybe you should call my mother and explain all this properly to her. I doubt if she has understood the nuances involved," he said. Then he burst into tears again.

"Don't worry, Rick, everything is being done. I'll call Sue now."

She sounded surprisingly calm.

"Look, I'm OK. Everyone will be here soon. Matt is flying here and Paolo is picking him up. I'll have a lot of support. My friends here are being wonderful, too. They have been with me all night."

Rick shouted into the computer.

"Are you OK, Mum?"

"Yes, I am, but I'm worried about you two, and Matt."

"Geez, Mum, don't worry about us. It's Dad we have to think about. And you."

"Look, just don't do anything silly. Don't move from where you are. Just wait for the news, OK? I have to go now."

We were used to waiting. We'd spent the past few months in Mexico doing nothing but. But this was different. We were waiting for someone we loved to live. Or die. I didn't want to even contemplate the latter.

"I'm going to have a shower," said Rick, his face sticky with tears.

I sat on the bed and began to meditate, sending Reiki healing to Jack's heart. I was trying to connect to Jack's mother, Ruby, who had passed away just prior to us leaving for Mexico. We all adored her. I asked her not to take Jack away from us so soon. He was only 56, and we needed him; we needed his love and joy for life.

Bad news is stifling. The room was oppressive. Outside it was still cold with the early morning chill. We put our red thick knitted Chiapas jumpers on and headed for the local Starbucks, where we sat and talked about what to do. We knew we couldn't really do anything, but somehow just being away seemed wrong when everyone we knew was no doubt pulling out all the stops.

Even if something is not about you, it's human nature to bring it all back to that intensely personal place. In this instance, Rick and I began to wonder if we were selfish, with all the attendant questions—rational and otherwise—that brings with it.

By the time we'd had what passes for a strong coffee in Starbucks, we'd reached that "What the hell are we doing here" stage. Now, in the face of the possible death of one of our parents, our desire to adopt when we didn't need to seemed completely superfluous.

"I want to go back and be near the laptop in case they ring us on Skype," said Rick. "They'll be all together soon."

"Look, Rick, a church. I think we should go in." I didn't need to suggest it, for he was already making his way through the doorway. We were welcomed not like the casual interlopers we were, but with warmth by a very sweet man. We sat at the back of the church and prayed silently. When we got up to go, the same man came over and asked us if we'd like to become Mormons. We'd had no idea where we were. But who cares? There is only one God for everyone, as far as I am concerned, and that day we spoke to Him. I felt better; it was as if I could feel that Jack's heart was healing, too.

We got back to the flat just as Rick's mum called.

"Your dad is awake. He has a black eye and is chatting up the nurses, so he must be feeling OK."

Rick didn't hear any of it. Somewhere along the way he'd become convinced he had to go home.

"Mum, I'm looking at flights," he said, while browsing the net. "I am coming back. Francesca will stay here."

"No, you are not coming." Her reply was delivered unequivocally and firmly. One of those times you know you should not disagree with your parents.

"Mum, I have to."

"Rick, I said no and I mean it. We mean it. I asked your father if he wanted you back, and he was clear as day: he doesn't want to see you until you come back with his granddaughter. These are his very own words. Please do it for him."

Rick tried to argue, but his mother was adamant.

Soon I would come to think that it would have been much easier if she'd given in, because Rick became lost in a way I'd never seen him before, and it seemed nothing but going home would work for him. We'd go for a walk, and suddenly he'd turn around and say we should get back near the laptop in case someone tried to call us on Skype. Then we'd go back and look at the computer as if waiting for a miracle, and he'd decide that he needed some fresh air and demand to go out for a walk again.

Rick was used to solving problems—in work, in our own lives— and this was something he was powerless to do anything about. And so was I. Both of us are the eldest siblings in the family. That, coupled with our personalities, has always meant that we were the ones to provide. Now we were thousands of miles away, and it would fall to Matt, Rick's little brother, who was treated as if he was six, even though he was thirty. He had no choice but to step up to the challenge to look after his dad and mum, in a foreign country, and to be the 'man of the house', not the baby of the family.

And he did so brilliantly. Paolo, my brother, was driving my mum back and forth and acting as a translator, and my dad, who isn't always someone to act quickly, was on the motorway driving at a hundred miles an hour in his tiny Fiat 500, only a few hours after the call from Paolo. Everyone was racing around doing the best they could. And the two families were bonding in a way they probably they wouldn't have otherwise.

The most amazing revelation of all was Sue, Rick's mum. I don't know where she got her strength from, but I remember being amazed at how every time we spoke on the phone she sounded so calm and strong, even when she was telling us that she wasn't sure Jack would pull through. I marvelled at how she gave strength and hope to Rick. It made me reflect on the role of mothers and whether I was ready to become one. Could I ever be an amazing woman? Like Sue? Like my mum? Like my grandmothers had been?

Until this point, we'd fallen so madly in love with Mexico that we had even thought about selling everything and setting up a few huts in Tulum, child or not. But right now we wanted to be home. Yet Jack's heart attack and his request for us not to go back without his granddaughter was a responsibility. We couldn't fail. Now we were more determined than ever.

🐟

Somehow we slept and woke to another day suspended in the ether of uncertainty. I'd suggested going to a lake, called Ajijic, near Guadalajara. Rick was agreeable, so we went and bought the tickets. He then changed his mind, so we walked back home. Then he reneged. Eventually we set off in the afternoon, the middle of the night in Italy, hoping against hope that we wouldn't get a phone call then, since it would certainly be bad news.

Chapala, the main town near Ajijic, had a lazy, Sunday-morning feel, with mariachi playing for the passers-by, kids messing around on the sidewalks outside the houses, families promenading in the *zocalo*, and people asleep under trees. We took it all in and had lunch near the lake, during which I tried to distract Rick with my family's stories of mafia and the Italian way of adultery, which usually drew a smile from him.

After lunch, we wandered aimlessly in a delightful older area with cobbled streets and saw a classical concert in an old convent. I knew Rick was on edge, but I figured there was no point feeding that part of him any further. I had to hold on to my beliefs to help him get through this.

He received calls: from his friend Ian, who'd been through similar things with his father, and from his best friend Dave, our other referee, who was busy chanting mantras for Jack. This encouraged him to talk a bit more, which I felt was a good thing, and we discussed our families and how much we loved them. I knew, however, that Rick was waiting to hear how Jack was; forty-eight hours had nearly passed.

By the time we got back it was time. We dialled the hospital. I felt sick listening to my thumping heart competing with the ring tone.

"He is through. He will need an operation, but he will be fine." I made the doctor say it twice. And then I turned to Rick, and we hugged and cried our eyes out. I closed my eyes and smiled. *Thank you, Ruby.*

Dolores, A Soap Opera

OK, God, I think we have a misunderstanding. You see, when I asked you to help Rick's dad, I wasn't doing a swap. I wasn't saying, "If you help Jack get better I'll go without a child." See, because Jack doesn't want us to do that. He wants a granddaughter. And we want a daughter. And what we want is not just good for us but also for the child we adopt. It's about love and care for one of your creatures. I hope there hasn't been a misunderstanding or you don't think I can't have both. Thank you.

My confusion was the result of a phone call with Aurora straight after we'd found out that Jack was going to recover. For about half an hour, we were able to feel that everything was on track again. We had planned on meeting her in a few hours to finalise things. Until I heard the now familiar:

"Buenooo," on the other end.

"Aurora?"

"Si, Francesca. Listen, we have a problem"

No, no we don't need any more problems.

"Look, I called the Mexico City Vifac to see if they had any babies, as we don't have any right away, and I wanted to speed things up for you, and…"

This was not going to be good.

"Apparently I am not supposed to be giving newborns for adoption to foreigners. I didn't know."

Go on, just shove that arrow through my heart now. End it here.

"Oh, no. Aurora, please don't do this, not you. You said… Jose said… even Conception said…"

"I know, I know, I am sorry, I really didn't know… but look, we will find a solution."

"But we need one now. Rick's dad has just had a heart attack. And we have promised him to go back with his granddaughter. What are we going to do now?"

"Oh, dear. Listen. Wait. Wait. When I promise something I mean it. Let me think. Perhaps you can ask your friend in Mexico City, what's her name…?"

"Cetty?"

"Yes, her. She can write a letter saying that you work in Mexico for her right now, so you'd be resident here… that would make you as good as a Mexican, right? Or… hmm, what else can we do, I know there must be a solution, just give me a few hours, OK? And tell Rick's dad I will be praying for him and he will get his granddaughter. But let's not meet 'til we know how we are going to do this. I will see you at the entrega anyway. *Un abrazo*."

"OK," I whispered.

And then something really odd happened. The phone rang immediately.

"Hola, it's Jose. I have some good news for you. A two-year-old girl is available for adoption. Now."

"Really??"

"Yes. Her mother is mad. She has tried to commit suicide, so the girl is not safe with her. Do you want to come and meet her?"

I was taken aback. On the one hand, this was great news. On the other, I couldn't believe that a suicide could be viewed in such an opportunistic fashion.

"Meet her? Where? How? When? Why did she try and commit suicide??"

"Here in Colima. I'd be at the meeting, of course. Don't worry, you'll be fine." *Fine?* We were going from madness to madness.

Jose had told us all we had to do was get to the bus station in Colima, and he would meet us there. All very easy to say, but buses to Colima were not easy to find. They all left from the Central Station, which was very far from Zapopan, where we were staying. Eventually we found out that if we stood by the motorway outside Guadalajara, a bus might come by.

"It's not actually a bus stop," said Jose, "but buses do stop there. You have to stand by the food stalls and hope that one stops. It should say Colima on the front."

And so it was that at 5:00 the next morning, we stood hopefully in the cold, next to the fried banana vendors and cowboy hat-wearing, guitar-toting men. I was so cold I wore my orange pashmina over my head, though it would be hot within a few hours. Rick wore his blue vintage Adidas zipped top. We looked and felt exhausted and clumsy, but underneath the odd, mismatched pieces of clothing were two human beings who were not giving up hope.

The decrepit vehicle that picked us up had certainly once been a bus, but today it looked like a risk you didn't want to take unless you had to. I tried to distract myself by listening to the blaring music, but while the tune was a happy sounding one, the lyrics always seemed to be about death and love intertwined. In Mexican songs a lover could, and often does, kill for love.

🌶

With my iPod playing ABBA to cheer me up, I tried to focus instead on the winding cliff roads and not think about death for the moment. Maybe it was the heightened emotion of the past few days, but I was terrified of losing everything now. I spent the whole journey staring ahead without saying a word, while Rick held my hand and tried to be reassuring. Crossing bridge after paper-thin bridge over a two-thousand metre drop wasn't helpful. Neither was the fact that far below I could see the wrecks of buses that clearly hadn't made it to their destination. The combination of height, speed, and a barely roadworthy vehicle meant that by the time we arrived, the colour had all but bled out of me.

"You look like a ghost," said Rick.

It was now midday, the sun was high in the sky, and in contrast to the chilly morning, the temperature was around 35 degrees Celsius. As we stepped gratefully off the bus, a car came screeching into the dusty car park. A tall young man emerged from a blue Volkswagen Polo, his dark hair gelled, sunglasses atop his head, and a big smile on his face.

Oh, dear.

I remembered that Aurora had referred to Jose as el licenciadito. Adding '-ito' to the end of a word could indicate a small version of something. It could also be a term of endearment or a means of belittlement. At first I had thought Aurora simply meant that Jose was short, but upon meeting him I realised she had meant the third option. Jose was the 'little qualified one' because he was so young. In fact, he looked about twelve.

"Hola! Mucho gusto! Jose, your saviour!" he said, vigorously shaking our hands. "You can call me Pepe. Andale, andale!"

He literally pushed us into his car and got in. The music came on.

"I love The *Chemical Brothers*!" he shouted, nodding his head to the music and throwing a few shapes for good measure. He pronounced the 'ch' like 'che' , as in Che Guevara, which made us smile. I knew he didn't speak any English so I turned to Rick, who was boxed into the back seat, and said, "Do you think he should even be allowed to drive? Look at him. He's a baby."

"I'm just praying for my life right now!" replied Rick, gripping the seat tightly.

"We are going to my office first, then we can go and pick up Dolores and her daughter," said Pepe. We turned through a gate and came shuddering to a halt. An immaculately dressed lady in her forties came out to meet us in the sunny courtyard as we got out of the car.

"Hello, I am Conception, the office secretary. We spoke on the phone a few times. It's lovely to meet you in person at last. Please come in, take a seat. I will get you some water."

We sat on two chairs facing one of the two desks in the office. As she left, Pepe ambled towards the stereo, blasting us with 'the Chemicals', as he called them, once more. Both desks had big leather chairs. There was a bookshelf with a picture of a short man hugging a very tall woman, a large stereo, and a red leather sofa behind us. Pepe opened a drawer underneath the shelves, and after scrabbling around for a few moments, pulled out a dusty folder.

"Ah, here it is! As you can see, we have worked on international adoptions before," he shouted, handing it to me.

"Do you think you can turn the volume down?"

"You don't like the Chemicals, Francesca?"

"Oh, I love them, and Rick actually knew them in his university years. It's just that I can't hear what you're saying."

Pepe reluctantly turned the stereo down.

"Noooo!" he said to Rick." You know them? ¡Híjole! You are cool, man! What are they like?"

Rick ignored his question and blew the dust off the folder.

"Fra, this is dated 2001!"

I looked over his shoulder at the contents.

"And the adoptive father was Mexican anyway!" Then I said to Pepe, who was looking rather pleased with himself:

"Is this the only international adoption you've worked on?"

"Yes, but no problem, no problem! You are in good hands!"

"It would seem so," said Rick sarcastically. I decided to move on.

"Did you have time to read our papers? I sent them three days ago. Have you got them? Are they OK? Will we be able to adopt this girl?" I said.

"Your papers…? Ah, yes, they arrived! I haven't read them yet, but don't worry, don't worry."

But I worried. Pepe was no more than a teenager. He probably knew nothing of the law, and he could only produce one file, which wasn't even an international adoption.

"What is the story with Dolores, then?" I asked him.

"I don't like her or trust her. She sleeps with gringos, you know. I hate gringos!"

"Oh, fantastic, even more promising," said Rick, who'd understood.

"OK, but what's her situation? What should we be expecting from this meeting?"

"Well, she is mad, basically. She has tried to commit suicide, and her daughter is not safe with her. She now wants to give her up for adoption. Bah!" He said this as casually as if he was telling us about someone changing cars.

I briefly explained to Rick, who nodded. His Spanish had improved to the point where he was capable of understanding most of what was being said.

"God, that sounds awful," he said.

"Pepe, it's so tragic. Do you think she will want to talk about it? And will the girl be there?" I asked.

"Of course the baby will be there. You need to meet her. She will be your daughter! I don't really know if she will want to talk about that stuff, though... hmm, let's just go and see."

"What, just like that?" I was a bit taken aback at the rapid and somewhat casual nature of it all.

"Well, yes. What else do you want to talk about?"

"Well, err, nothing, really." I replied. We obediently followed him outside to the car.

"Bye!" Conception waved from the window. "Good luck!"

We arrived at a small house painted bright pink. This was the Colima Vifac residence. Normally a woman wouldn't still live there after having had a baby, but Dolores had nowhere to go, and as she was going to have her baby adopted they allowed her to stay.

Pepe got out of the car and went into the house. A few minutes later he emerged with a petite woman. It was difficult to tell what she looked like, since she was wearing a long blonde wig that was curled in movie star style. She was dressed in a suit that was far too big for her and wearing sunglasses. In her arms was a toddler, her hair in pigtails. She was wearing a floral vest and nappy. As Dolores approached the car, she glanced around suspiciously. Then she got in, passing the baby to Rick and I, who were in the back.

Pepe started the engine, and with it the inevitable Chemical Brothers, and off we went.

"Pepe, turn it off," Dolores said. Then turned around to shake our hands.

"I hope you don't mind Beatriz in the back with you. It's best that she gets used to you both as soon as possible."

I could understand the sentiment, but something about this felt incredibly sudden and strange. Beatriz looked well cared for and seemed happy. She had straight dark hair, deep, black velvet eyes, and chubby legs and cheeks. She seemed at ease in our company, giggling with Rick, who was playing with her. Meanwhile Dolores talked non-stop.

"She feels very comfortable with English speaking men. Her dad… well, not her dad, my ex-partner… well, it's too complicated now. Anyway, she is used to hearing English being spoken to her."

Her constant patter ensured there was no time for awkward silences, which was good, since the situation was highly uncomfortable. She talked about the food Beatriz ate, her sleep patterns, and the fairy tales she liked, while Pepe drove us almost all the way back to Guadalajara, ostensibly searching for somewhere to have lunch.

The restaurant he'd chosen was an isolated rancho surrounded by a lake. Once out of the car, Dolores's moves were deliberate; she walked ahead with Beatriz cloistered in her arms, looking furtively around. Eventually, after some deliberation, she chose a table by the window, some distance from the other customers.

Again, Dolores issued orders on proceedings.

"Pepe, you sit next to me. Francesca in front of me, and Rick next to Francesca. I want to be able to see you both as I speak. Beatriz can run around."

Slowly she removed her sunglasses and placed them on the table. Apropos of nothing in particular, she began to tell us her life story.

"I was adopted myself by a horrible family. This is why I have asked to meet you. I want to make sure Beatriz goes to good people. I ran away from home at twenty, when I found out that that wasn't my family, that's why they always treated me differently than the other kids, and I never went back. Six months later, I got married just so that I could have my family. But my husband was horrible, too. He divorced me when he found out I couldn't have children."

"But…"

"Let me finish. Of course, I was then to find out that I could have children. I got pregnant by a man who used me and ran away when he knew I was expecting."

A classic tale of a damaged child looking for a way out. Or was it? Neither Rick nor I thought to question her story. After all, what reason did we have to? She was a poor woman in Mexico with a baby she couldn't keep. There were many more just like her.

I looked closely at her face. She looked as if she were on the verge of crying. But nothing came. Nonetheless, she reached for the tissues and delicately patted her non-existent tears.

"It sounds very sad. I am so sorry. What did you do after that?" I asked.

"Don't ask questions. Let me finish."

Her retort was aggressive, but I figured that was the mark of a woman who'd had a hard life.

"I lost my job, but for the first time in my life I found love. He was an American man. We dated for six moths, and he promised to marry me. Our wedding day was supposed to be on San Valentine, last month. He had moved me and Beatriz to Barra de Navidad, to his beach house, while he sorted his documents out in Florida."

She was briefly interrupted by the arrival of grilled steaks, chicken, and cerveza. Pepe, who up until then had been busy playing with his phone, distributed the food. I watched as Dolores took a tiny nibble of chicken.

"I have lost my appetite, you see," she said, as she took a larger portion and gobbled it up. "But everything was spoiled when a man in the village got obsessed with me and started telling everyone that we had an affair. The news got to my fiancé, and he called off the wedding. I was devastated."

Now she was crying while she ate.

"Oh, but couldn't you—"

"I don't want you to ask questions. I need you to listen," she snapped. Rick looked at me and raised his eyebrows as if to say, *She's loopy.*

Dolores's eyes filled with tears. Real ones this time.

"That's why I tried to commit suicide. I took lots of tablets, grabbed Beatriz, and we both jumped into the dark freezing sea at night."

That effectively killed the conversation. Not that we had been allowed to speak.

"Anyway, we finish now, Pepe. Take me back." Dolores was done. For now. In fact, she'd stopped crying and was now intently hoovering up the food on everyone else's plates.

"She didn't ask us one thing about ourselves," pointed out Rick as we settled the bill. Pepe and Dolores had gone ahead.

"I know, and did you see how she wouldn't let anyone else speak?"

"What did you think of her story? You know, the suicide stuff and all that?"

"I don't know what to think. Listening to Dolores has blown my head apart."

Somehow, six hours had gone by. By the time Pepe dropped us back at our hotel, we were mystified and exhausted. I had never felt so drained in my life. Colima in the late afternoon is dusty and airless. So was our hotel room. Rick fiddled with the grimy air conditioning unit attached to the wall.

"This thing doesn't work, and if we open the windows we will be eaten alive by mosquitoes," he said.

We were staying in the Reina Margarita. Ostensibly it was a four-star hotel, which in most places would at least guarantee a bed that wasn't lumpy. Despite the website's description ("high standards… swimming pool with waterfall…maximum comfort") it was actually just a dumpy motel situated on a busy road, and was inhabited largely by boisterous teenagers on their way to more exciting places. We showered and sat on the bed in our towels.

"Part of me just wants to leave. I didn't get a good vibe from Dolores, but Beatriz was just so lovely," I said, wrapping my hair in another towel.

"She's absolutely adorable. She doesn't deserve that mother."

"And yet I think Dolores loves her daughter. I really do."

"The question is, did you believe her? I had no idea what was true and what was made up."

"What about Pepe? What do we make of him?" I asked Rick.

"Hmm. I am not sure if he is a young man trying hard to fill his boss's boots while he's away, or if he is just playing."

The hotel phone rang. I reached over to answer.

"Hola. It's Dolores."

"Dolores!" I made a face at Rick. *How did she know we were in that hotel?*

"I need to speak to you, I am coming around. My friend can give me a lift."

"But… what… what do we need to talk about? Is Pepe coming with you?"

"No way! And don't tell him that I have called. I will bring Beatriz with me so you can practise with her. I will be there in fifteen minutes." Click.

We looked at each other .

"She's coming in fifteen minutes. How on earth did she know that we were staying here?"

"More importantly, what did she want?" said Rick.

"She is coming around for us to *practise* with Beatriz and talk. What do we need to practise? Plus, she doesn't want Pepe to know."

"What? I bet you she will ask us for money." Rick quickly pulled his jeans on.

"Do you think I should call Pepe? After all, he is our lawyer. What if she is dangerous? The woman tried to kill herself!"

Rick sat down, head in hands. Suddenly he pointed to the phone.

"Call him."

"Do you think we should?"

"Yes."

My hands were shaking as I dialled Pepe's number.

I would have expected Pepe, as the Vifac lawyer, our lawyer, the person who introduced us to Dolores, to be even a little protective of us, or to be at least slightly knowledgeable. He wasn't.

"Ha! Bloody typical!" he said.

"What do you mean by *that?*"

"Well, I think she will try and manipulate you and cut me out of the deal. I told you I don't like her."

"What *deal?*"

"Don't worry, relax! But call me when you are finished. I am curious now!' Click.

"Useless as usual," I said to Rick.

The hotel phone rang. It was reception.

"A lady called Dolores is waiting for you down here."

"Oh, my God, she's already here! Rick, can you go and pick her up please? Please? Look at me!" I was still wearing nothing but a towel.

"What will people at reception think? A gringo who doesn't speak a word of Spanish, escorting a young Mexican woman with big sunglasses, fake blond hair and a toddler in tow to a motel room? In the UK it's enough to get arrested!"

"Well, we are not in the UK, we are in the middle of Mexico. Please go! Please go, go!"

Rick reluctantly shuffled out of the room, hands in his pockets. I quickly got into my jeans and t-shirt and sat on a chair next to the window, watching for Rick. Poor thing. He came back holding the little girl's hand in a way that looked anxious and overly attentive. He looked like a policeman who has had to take charge of a child after some sort of catastrophe.

What were we to make of Dolores? Was she unstable? Or was she cunning? The one thing I was absolutely sure of was that she loved her daughter desperately. It was obvious from the way she was with her. I was sure then, and I am sure now, that Dolores was lying about a lot of things, but she couldn't have been faking that. The rest—what she actually wanted, for her daughter and for herself— was anyone's guess.

Guided by Rick, Beatriz tottered along. Dolores, now wearing a floral dress that was far too small for her, was striding ahead, this time without a wig. Her hair was straight and had highlights. Clearly she wanted to be blonde, a 'gringa'.

As soon as I opened the door, she threw her arms around my neck like a long lost friend.

"*Querida* Francesca, it's so good to see you!" I stood motionless. Rick was still holding the baby's hand.

"I'm sorry there isn't much furniture here. Would you like to sit on the bed?" I pointed at the garish covers of our lumpy beds.

"To tell you the truth, Francesca, I am here because there are some things you need to know." She plonked herself next to me on one of the beds and took my hand conspiratorially. "I think it's best that your husband goes and plays with Beatriz in the pool. She loves water and will only whine if she stays here."

"Please take notes, Fra. I want to know everything. I've got the mobile with me," said Rick, grabbing two towels and ushering Beatriz out of the room.

"What did you think of Pepe?" asked Dolores.

"Well, he is… young."

"Exactly! Un *jovencito*. I see that we agree already. Too young.

And he is inexperienced, Francesca. We cannot put the life of our daughter in his hands."

Our daughter?

"Francesca, I want you to adopt Beatriz, but I am not comfortable signing the relinquishment papers until Alfonso is back from his holiday."

"Who is Alfonso?"

"What do you mean? El licenciado! Pepe's boss."

"Where is he?" I got up and got some water out of the fridge.

"In Europe."

"For how long?" I poured myself a glass.

"Eight weeks."

"What? We can't wait that long! Dolores, we have limited time. Do you want some water?"

"No, thank you. I though we could use the time for you to practise with Beatriz..." She took a tissue out of her bag, wiped her forehead, and fanned herself with her hand.

"What do you mean by practice? Do you want to go outside? It's boiling here. The air conditioning doesn't work."

"No, *que loca*, nobody can hear us or see us in here. Anyway, you can get used to her, know what she likes and doesn't like. For example, if you ever need a couple of hours to clean the house or something, you can put *The Jungle Book* on. She loves it. Anyway, Alfonso is a true friend, and has our best interests at heart. I would trust him with my life, Francesca. He is such a good lawyer, and he speaks perfect English, so Rick will be able to speak to him, too. Think about it, Francesca, we could move in together until he comes..."

Whoa, hang on there.

Dolores was looking at my ring. Why?

"I can't decide anything unless I speak to Rick, but I am pretty sure he wouldn't agree."

Dolores tried another tack.

"Pepe is superficial, Francesca. He is only interested in money.

He doesn't care about people. To tell you the truth, he's not even a qualified lawyer."

By now I was getting irritated. When someone prefaces their sentences with 'to tell you the truth' and uses your name at every opportunity, it implies a bond that doesn't exist. Plus I was finding the noise of the people in the pool and the smells of fried food annoying. I shut the window, which made it even hotter .

"Alfonso is such a wonderful man, Francesca, he has given me a home when I didn't have one and has looked after me and Beatriz without ever asking for anything in return. Everyone loves him and respects him in Colima, Francesca."

"I understand, but we can't wait. Rick and I have already been here for three months. We need to go back in a few weeks or we will both lose our jobs."

"But… but…"

"And I really don't think it's a good idea for Beatriz that we move in together for so long. It's only going to hurt her more when you leave. You will need to let go of her, Dolores, and accept you will never see her again. This is what giving her up for adoption means." I sat next to her and held her hand.

"I… guess… I had not thought about that, Francesca…"

Dolores's bottom lip was trembling and she had tears in her eyes. Surely she wasn't faking those. I took her other hand.

"Are you sure about this, Dolores? It's a big decision to take. You clearly love Beatriz. Perhaps there are other ways to help you."

"I still want to wait for Alfonso."

"I will discuss it with Rick, but I know already that we can't wait."

"Hmmm… I will email Alfonso and tell him about our conversation. Perhaps he can come back sooner. I know this is so important to—"

As Dolores was about to finish her sentence, Rick came in, smiling, with Beatriz, who also looked delighted.

"We had such a great time. She loves the water! She was

splashing everyone and giggling! Oh, and she loved the slide! And…
oh, sorry, are you not finished?"

"You didn't take her nappy off!" Dolores laughed, pointing at
Beatriz' soaking wet nappy dripping on the old carpet.

"I am so sorry. How embarrassing…"

Dolores's phone started ringing.

"Hola, Pepe… yes… yes…"

Pepe?

Just like that, Dolores grabbed Beatriz's hand and walked out
of the room with the little girl running after her, wet nappy dangling.

10

One Madwoman and a Baby

If you have ever thought the story of the birth of Jesus didn't make sense, the Mexicans have it sorted. There, St Joseph is the protector of adoptive parents—because he wasn't the biological father of Jesus. You have to love the logic. We knew this because we'd been invited to attend the *entrega* on St Joseph's Day, March 12th. Parents who had adopted would have their baby handed to them by the priest, with God's blessing.

Given that it was a special day, other families who had already adopted were also invited to join with their children. We were concerned that we'd feel out of place, as we didn't have a baby to collect. But we didn't. We had met our daughter, and she was waiting for us in Colima. The Vifac family of women welcomed us with open arms. This was about as matriarchal as it got. I found it very comforting.

Anna, Gabriela, Chita, and the wonderful Aurora were all there, congratulating us for having found our daughter at last. But before the ceremony began, Aurora took the opportunity to take Rick and I aside for a little chat.

"I am not sure, Francesca," she began.

"Not sure about what?"

"You know, I don't know if I trust this woman Dolores. She is taking a long time to decide, and in my long experience this is not a good thing: the women who give up their babies generally do so without this type of carrying on and constant negotiation. Once they have made up their mind, which is a hard thing to do, they just want to move on and allow their babies to do so. As for young Pepito... well, he is both very young and a lawyer, a dreadful combination in my book. You know we are always here for you if things don't go the right way, and I have your best interests at heart."

"We already love that girl," I told her, "especially Rick. He seems to have bonded very quickly. We are returning to see her in Colima after this."

"Oh, then you will want to take my car. I don't like the idea of you catching a bus on those crazy roads," she said, handing over the keys of her brand new Mercedes.

"Aurora, I wouldn't dream of taking your new shiny baby anywhere. Honestly, we have travelled in buses up until now, and if it's good enough for the locals it's good enough for us, really."

It was now sunset, and everyone was gathering in the small courtyard outside the church. A lot of the parents seemed to know each other, and so did the kids who were running around chasing each other. People had brought gifts for the expectant parents, who were themselves holding a Moses basket and a blue balloon. I looked at the various groups of families and friends, hugging and taking pictures of one another. It was all so gentle, humble, and heart warming.

The church itself was a modern white building. At some point, Anna gestured that people should start coming inside. The parents-to-be walked in first, holding hands. Standing at the back of the church with Rick, I looked around at the paintings. Instead of the usual depictions of key Biblical moments, there were paintings of a man on the moon, of kids playing with sand castles, and of a woman cooking. God's creatures, just those of the modern world.

The entrega was beginning. There they were, the two indigenous parents in their best clothes, which looked like they had never ever been worn before—the man's shirt still had creases in it. It was all so utterly sweet and innocent, just like the baby they were about to receive. Surrounding them were an expectant group of family and friends, all eager to see this delightful bundle of joy that would soon join them. He was the tiniest baby I had ever seen, but what he lacked in size he made up for with a lush coating of thick, dark hair. His tiny eyes were firmly shut.

Today Anna was in charge of proceedings. She said a few words, and then the priest came out cradling the baby, blessing him and handing him to Anna, who in turn passed him to the overjoyed parents.

The whole thing was so simple and charming that I wondered why we didn't do this for all babies. We have christenings, but that is a different ceremony altogether: this is far simpler, incredibly meaningful and special.

Holding their tiny baby, the parents were asked to swear that they would look after him and watch over him, asking God and the Virgin of Guadalupe for support. Such tenderness. Such love. Though I didn't cry, I can't deny I felt more emotion in that church, and a greater sense of what we were about to undertake, than I'd felt in a while.

Buoyed up by the entrega, I even found the bus journey less daunting this time round. There was also much to discuss about the impending adoption of our daughter, Beatriz.

"My dad would love her," Rick kept on saying.

"So would everyone else," I said.

"Isn't she so cute when she smiles?"

"And what is all this about the terrible twos? Beatriz is so cheerful and well behaved!"

But I also had my doubts. Beatriz was not a baby but a toddler, and unsurprisingly she was very attached to Dolores. I knew that taking her away was not going to be easy for anybody. I wondered if she could grow to love me, let alone see me as her mother. While Beatriz had developed an attachment for Rick, whenever I got close to her, she'd cry.

Children feel it all. Of that I have no doubt. And I think that Beatriz was feeling both my tension and my reticence when we were together. She knew I wasn't relaxed, so how was she going to be relaxed around me? We were about to adopt a child with attachments to people, places, and things. She was going to have to make sense of her new reality with two people whose language she didn't even understand, and who couldn't understand her.

Beatriz's strong attachment to her mother was creating a dilemma for me. Were we doing the right thing in taking her away from a woman who loved her and who, it must be said, did not seem that anxious to give her up? However, every time I asked Dolores, she was adamant: "I have decided, Francesca. Beatriz cannot stay with me. Nothing will make me change my mind. I cannot raise her. She is making my life impossible, as no man in Mexico wants a woman with a kid. Nobody even talks to me. It's all about appearances. And this mere fact is making me lose the plot. I am on medication, and when I stop God knows what I'll be capable of. Trying to kill myself and her again might seem like a good plan. She is not safe with me."

Somewhere along the line, Dolores had designated herself my new best friend. I'd given her my mobile number, and now she was on the phone every couple of hours. Because she had very little money, she would let the phone ring once and then I would have to call her back. She wanted to talk. And talk and talk. Much of it would centre around her views on Pepe.

"Francesca, I don't trust Pepe." Fair enough, but I knew that immediately after she'd said that to me, she'd be on the phone to him. Or Conception, the secretary in Colima, would say that Dolores had been around to chat with Pepe. One day, out of the blue, she said: "I have been thinking that I would like to go to Egypt, where apparently my birthmother was from. Then I will be able to trace my roots. I have no future in Mexico."

Where is this coming from?

It was always difficult to know if Dolores had an agenda or not.

I didn't want to judge or suspect her, but some of the things she came out with made me wonder. I decided to try and keep the discussion as light as possible.

"In my experience, Egypt would be very hard for a woman alone, Dolores. It's a very different culture. Women don't go around travelling on their own in the Middle East."

"Hmm. Do you think I should buy a car and drive to the US instead? I know men there wouldn't mind a woman being single at thirty-five." *Another bolt from the blue.*

"I guess that might be better. But you haven't got any money. How do you plan to do this?"

"Well, I was hoping you would help me. After all, I am enticing you with my daughter."

Enticing! It was as if her daughter was some sort of trinket for trading. I was emphatic in my reply.

"We won't, Dolores. I could never live with the thought that we bought Beatriz from you. When we set out to adopt, we tried to make rules about what we would and would not do, and exchanging money for a child is something we would never do."

"Oh. So you will not help me?"

"Look, if you need help and want to keep Beatriz, I can see what we can do. But it's important that you decide. If you think there is one chance you two could be together, you should make that happen. If not, then we can maybe buy a flight ticket for you AFTER the adoption is completed. But right now, this sort of talk is complicating things, Dolores."

"But adoption is a long way away."

"No, it's not. We are coming to finalise things with you."

"I don't want to sign the relinquishment papers until Alfonso is here. I don't trust Pepe. I am not sure he is doing it all properly, or even knows what to do."

Oh, here we go again. Back to square one. It was maddening. We had gone again to Colima to meet her, in order to decide on next steps and to make a date for the relinquishment papers to be signed.

And here I was wondering if she even wanted to give up her baby. If not, what else was she playing at? While I was growing to like Dolores, I always felt on shaky ground with her.

When we arrived back in Colima, she insisted on seeing us alone first.

"Francesca! It's so good to see you!"

The funny thing was that she barely acknowledged Rick. When I would interrupt her to say I needed to translate for Rick, she'd look at me as if to say, *Why on earth do you need to do that?* It was very odd. I wondered if it was because she had trust issues with men. It certainly seemed she'd been let down by them before, and her lack of trust in Pepe was further evidence of this. Maybe she didn't trust Rick. But then she'd tell him to take Beatriz for a walk or an ice-cream, so she certainly trusted him enough to loan him Beatriz.

While Rick and Beatriz were becoming great buddies, I was trying to figure out whether Dolores was seriously unstable, incredibly cunning and manipulative, or just another lost soul whose feelings were all over the place. Given what Aurora had said, the biggest question was, of course, whether she was seriously interested in giving up her daughter.

Dolores went to great lengths to tell me how she adored children.

"This is very hard for me, you know, Francesca. I love children. I worked in Istituto Cabañas for years and have glowing references from them."

Istituto Cabañas? How could it be that everyone we knew was connected? There are six million people in Guadalajara alone. Who else was going to come out of the woodwork?

Despite all this talk, nothing was any clearer than it was on the day we'd first heard about Dolores. We were increasingly spending more time with them—well, me with Dolores, and Rick with Beatriz. We weren't getting anywhere, though. She didn't seem to want to sign the relinquishment papers. While Pepe was trying to convince her to do so, he kept telling us he didn't like her, and we should stay away and wait for Aurora to come up with another option for us.

We decided to give Dolores an ultimatum, via Pepe.

"We don't have four weeks to wait," I told him. "And this is proving very painful for us. We are bonding with this little girl without the security of knowing that she will be our daughter. So in order to end this crazy cycle we're in now, we've decided to go to Manzanillo by the sea. Once we know that there is a date for the document signing, we'll be back to do it."

"Good idea!" said a semi-attentive Pepe. "I bet you she will sign now."

"Yes, but we are going to have to do this both swiftly and via Hague. We need some legal help from DIF."

"I have never done that before, but I can work it out for you."

Hmm, that was reassuring.

"Well, we would need someone from DIF to send the details of Beatriz to the UK government, who would then need to approve them before we can take custody."

"Ah, I have excellent contacts at DIF and Vifac is connected to them. My friend from college works there. I tell you what. I will come and see you in Manzanillo and you can explain everything about Hague to me. My brother is having a birthday party there, so I'll come on the way."

Manzanillo is a beach town by the Pacific Ocean. Rick had booked us a lovely hotel room right on the beach. But we didn't want to do any of the typical tourist things. We just wanted to talk the issue through, as many times as it took.

We sat at the restaurant of our hotel on the beachfront, eating delicious seafood and drinking white wine, watching the ocean calm down for the evening. I smoked cigarettes and got drunk, two things I only do if I am very stressed, which is rarely. And then I began to cry. It all came out.

"I don't know if I can do this. I still don't understand what Dolores is all about and whether we should be taking this little girl.

She loves her mum so much. How could I ever replace her?"

"We are doing the right thing, Fra. However nice Dolores might seem, there is no doubt that she is an unstable woman. And the girl isn't safe with her. She tried to kill her. And if she didn't, she is evil for making such a story up. This is all we came here for, to help a child in need, and Beatriz is definitely one of those." He was right.

"A whale!"

"Who is a whale?"

"No, Rick, look, look! A whale! A real whale!"

It certainly was. The majestic creature was passing by in the distance. It was the first time in my life I had ever seen one, and it made me even more emotional, but at least I stopped crying about Dolores.

Manzanillo was peaceful. We took long walks on the beach, and on Saturday evening ate oysters and champagne by candlelight to celebrate, as Rick put it. I could tell he was over the moon, but I was still feeling cautious. There is something special about being by the sea for both of us, but neither of us felt that it was an actual celebration.

Saturday went and Sunday arrived in a blaze of sunshine, but still no sign of Pepe. I rang his mobile repeatedly, but it was always switched off. Eventually, I found he'd left a message for us at reception: *I am sorry I was late. I will see you tomorrow morning.*

"Where is he?" asked Rick? "He's bloody useless."

I decided to meditate on the terrace with the waves breaking on the beach as the only sound for my ears and my soul, until my phone rang. A single ring. It was Dolores. I really didn't feel like calling her back, but I did. With my legs still crossed, I reached over for the phone.

"Hi, Dolores, what's up?"

The uncertainty of our situation was such that I never knew if I should ask after Beatriz. I wondered if it would make her happy because I cared, or alternatively she might think I was being intrusive. We were walking an emotional tightrope.

"Francesca, how did it go with Pepe?"

"He didn't turn up."

"See? I told you! U-n-r-el-i-a-b-le."

"Yes, you are right…"

"Francesca, we cannot let him mess this up. We cannot put the life of our daughter in his hands."

Our daughter. Why does she say that? It's too weird.

"I have had an idea."

Yep, just what we need right now. Another crazy idea from a woman who isn't sure of her own mind.

"I have Alfonso's private email address, which Conception gave to me. Though he's in Europe, I have been emailing him all the time. I think you should write to him and explain the situation. That way he can draft the papers, and then I will trust that it has all been done properly. And you don't have to wait till he is back."

I sighed wearily.

"OK, let's try that. We cannot wait much longer, Dolores, and we are still not coming back until you have signed. Please give Beatriz a kiss and hug for us."

I woke up at 4:30 am to review the Hague convention, one of the most absurd and convoluted of documents. It was supposedly issued in order to smooth international adoption amongst ratifying countries. And in reading it, I discovered we had already screwed up. Apparently we shouldn't have even met Beatriz without consent from both DCSF and our local council. The fact that we were next to her and they were on the other side of the world didn't matter. That was the rule.

OK, that could be solved: we could explain it to our social worker. Then we needed someone at DIF to send her details to DCSF, who would in turn send them to our council, who would then send them to us. We would then discuss her before we could meet her again.

Then—and only then—could we visit her regularly, but we could not take custody until DIF, DCSF, and the Home Office had ratified article 17C of the Hague Convention by writing to each other a few times and agreeing that it was the right thing to do. Naturally, there would be a few translations in the middle.

Making this happen meant putting ourselves in the hands of the unreliable Pepe, who finally turned up in our room at around 12:30, stinking of alcohol. I began to explain the Hague procedure to him, but soon realised all I was getting was blank looks. Meanwhile, Rick was sitting at one corner of the table, scribbling.

"Rick, help me here, please."

"Ah, but I am." I looked at the paper in front of him. He'd produced a neat flowchart of all the steps that needed to be taken. That left brain of his had taken over. I translated it for Pepe, who looked at me with all the interest of a bloke who clearly had imbibed enough alcohol for a small Mexican town. Suddenly he sprang up. *Oh, good, he's got it,* I thought.

"Francesca. *Una pregunta.*"

Even better. He has a question.

"Can you adopt from Mexico?"

"What the hell?" Rick jumped up.

He's going to strangle Pepe, I thought.

Frankly, it might not have been such a bad thing.

11

I'm Just a Teenaged Lawyer

I rarely raise my voice. So even I was surprised by the strange, high-pitched shriek that came out of my mouth.

"For God's sake, Pepe, what sort of question is that?! CAN WE ADOPT FROM MEXICO? What do you think we're doing here? Have you been listening to our story at all? You have two sets of our precious photocopies, with everything you need to know. And WE HAVE A CERTIFICATE OF ELIGIBILITY TO ADOPT A 0-2 YEAR OLD GIRL FROM MEXICO. It's the first thing I told you ever since we spoke on the phone, and I've repeated it about one hundred times!"

Pepe didn't look perturbed in the least.

"Just checking," he said casually. And then, as if nothing had happened:

"I have an idea."

"Best not to," I replied under my breath. I sat down next to Rick.

"Why don't you come back with me in the car? I am picking up Aurora on the way—she has a house near here—and we are going to Colima, so that will work out nicely."

"That's OK. We'll go by bus." The thought of Pepe's crazy driving, along with the fact he reeked of alcohol, was not appealing. "OK, see you soon." And he headed out.

Rick was still fuming. He stomped around the room, picking up clothes from the floor and chucking them in his rucksack without even bothering to fold them. Then he sat on the balcony to smoke. I thought I'd better leave him. I decided to contact Alfonso and ask for his help.

I had been thinking about what Aurora had said at the *entrega* about Dolores not really wanting to give up her baby. She had said repeatedly that she wanted to help us, but also she let us know that she could not give us any certain timeline, as it was complicated at Vifac. It certainly was. Though the women ostensibly came to the Vifac casas because they were thinking of adopting their babies out, often they changed their minds. Their pregnancies are often the result of incest or rape, so their initial reaction is of wanting to give up the baby. But frequently, with the benefit of psychotherapy, these women overcome the trauma and just want to keep the baby. For others, it's the worry that they have no visible means of supporting a child, so Vifac does their best to teach them simple but useful skills—using a computer for instance, or administrative skills—and this empowers them.

Aurora had emphasised that Vifac was not an adoption agency: its mission was to make sure babies did not get aborted, and had the lives they deserved. So, even if they knew when the next babies were due in the casa, they could not guarantee that any of them would be available for adoption. Vifac respected the birthmothers' wishes, so long as the mothers were respectful of the babies' lives, too.

My mind went back to our meeting with the oily lawyer, Miguel, at the Starbucks in that awful mall. It seemed like another era. I imagined his description of these women would be '*unreliable*', a word which even now made me shiver. It was quite right that Vifac should give them every hope and chance of keeping their baby. The compassion shown by these women was wonderful, all the more so because it was staffed by volunteers. People often decried Mexico as a third world country, a country of poverty and primitive attitudes, but this type of care was way ahead of that shown to women in so-called affluent nations.

These women were not unreliable: they were poor, alone, confused, ashamed, and incredibly fortunate they could go somewhere like Vifac. Aurora had told me that as many as 80% of women who turn up at the Vifac casa will change their mind about giving their baby away. Some will register because they simply have nowhere else to go, and they know they will be cared for and have a place to stay during their pregnancy, right up until and including birth. Aurora acknowledged that though this was not ideal and did use up Vifac's financial resources (all obtained via donation), there was simply no other course for these women. And she wasn't going to let them down.

Everything Aurora said made absolute sense. I couldn't hurry the process along. What we needed now was luck and timing. We'd discussed this at the entrega. She knew how anxious we were, and she did her best to reassure me that she was doing everything she could. Yet she couldn't guarantee a specific time frame.

Right now, therefore, our only option was to pursue the adoption of Beatriz. We had started bonding with her, and she was beginning to occupy much of our thoughts and conversations. And her mother was adamant that she was going to give her to us for adoption. If not us, it would have been someone else. But still I was cautious about Dolores, as much as I had come to like her. She was unstable, and it seemed she could pull the rug from us at any time.

Dear Alfonso, I wrote:
So sorry to bother you during your holiday. As you will know through Pepe, we are a European couple approved to adopt a 0-2 year old girl from Mexico. We have been introduced to Dolores and are in the process of starting the adoption procedures with her for Beatriz. Dolores will be signing the relinquishment papers tomorrow. Given the circumstances, we would very

much appreciate your support and advice in this matter to prepare our case for the court hearing. Dolores has been so kind as to provide us with this email address.

We hope not to have troubled you too much.

Kind Regards,

Francesca and Rick

We were having a reasonably uneventful return bus journey to Colima. Pepe would be meeting Dolores at 4:00 pm to sign the relinquishment papers. He phoned to let us know that we should not call him at all. He would call us at the hotel room as soon as the meeting finished. And then he threw a spanner in the works.

"Why aren't you guys considering a Vifac adoption with Aurora? It's so much more straightforward, and it would be a newborn."

Talk about planting seeds of doubt. I wasn't sure if he was simply stating what he thought would be best for us —to wait for Aurora to come through—or whether there was a subtext that he wasn't telling us but wanted us to know. Or was he just messing with our heads because he was inexperienced? Again and again he'd let us know he didn't trust Dolores—and she felt the same way about him. Yet we knew they called each other constantly.

While we were on the bus, Conception phoned. It seems they had found Dolores in Alfonso's study, 'reviewing' our papers.

My initial response was, *At least someone has read them*, but then I became suspicious. Why had she done that? Was she interested in knowing how much we earned? It was very odd for a woman who had not asked us a single question about how we lived or how we proposed to bring up her daughter. It seemed this had set off an argument between Dolores and Aurora, who'd had a screaming match. Dolores had stormed out and left Beatriz in the office.

I called Dolores.

"What happened?"

"Aurora is an evil bitch! She shouted at me and called me a liar. I will never give Beatriz for custody to her!" She was sobbing.

"Custody to her? What happened? Where are you now?"

"Ask her. I don't want to speak to anyone now." Click.

"Aurora?"

"Bueno, Francescaaaa."

"I just spoke to Dolores..."

"Yes, Dolores, well, I have had the pleasure of meeting her... let me tell you something, Francesca. Do not trust that woman."

"I have heard this before, Aurora, but why now?"

"Well, first of all I found her 'reviewing your documents' in Pepe's office, i.e. checking how much you guys have in your bank account. And your London address. That woman is going to be after you. If you ever manage to adopt the girl, that is. If a woman is seriously thinking of relinquishing her daughter, the last thing she should be worrying about is how much money you have. Unless she is doing it for money, of course! Secondly, I saw the way she was playing with Beatriz. Francesca, I have counselled women who give up their children daily for twenty years now, and I can tell you I can spot one who isn't going to do it. Dolores is one of them. She loves the girl. There is something dodgy here, I am telling you. And I told her. To her face, of course. You do what you want, girl, but I don't want you to be deceived by this woman."

Who to believe? I believed Aurora had our interests are heart, but she was also fiercely protective, and a hard woman. Was her judgement clouded by her Catholic beliefs? I believed Dolores was unstable, but I wasn't sure if she was really a con artist. I believed Pepe was fundamentally useless, but I felt he somehow had our best interests at heart. I believed Conception, but it was clear she was caught in the middle. Whose side was she on?

But, as Rick reminded me, we were here now. Waiting for Pepe to call with news. We sat on the bed in our tiny room watching television. The choices were limited. There were soap operas based on the global cookie-cutter template of glamorous/slutty women, sleazy men, and everyone sleeping with everyone else. Or there was the news: the kind that makes our own look like feel-good stories.

The Mexico Rick and I experienced had, for the most part, been friendly, warm, quirky, fun, and naturally beautiful. But there is another Mexico, the Mexico of the border, where drug cartels battle each other and where, despite the Mexican government's deployment of 45,000 army troops and 5,000 national police, the land is lawless. You can argue that army deployment wasn't the cleverest of methods. But that's the situation. The prize for the drug lords is a big one: the biggest market, the US, and they'll stop at nothing to make their claim. Guns bought legally in the US flow south via El Paso, Texas, while drugs, women, organs and babies are shipped back to the US. The new generation of drug cartels isn't just interested in gang warfare; desperate and drugged up, they kill for the sake of it, just to prove they can. It's a status symbol, like the latest T-shirt or jeans. It's better to join a gang than to be an innocent teen at a party where people are gunned down just for the thrill of it. One report detailed how a victim's face was found cut from their head and stitched to a soccer ball. While all around the world there are tribes, religions, and countries fighting for their beliefs, these people aren't fighting for anything. Just for the fun of it. This is just the way it is.

In Mexico, 40% of the population lives below the poverty line, 78% of legal activities are infiltrated by crime, and in just one city—Juarez, the most violent city in the world—an average of seven people are killed each day. That's alongside the abductions and kidnappings that can't really be counted. The news reports had the flavour of war bulletins. And as we sat there watching it for hours, we felt rather pathetic about our own worries.

We waited, not wanting to leave the room in case the call came through. We thought of leaving the room in turns, but neither of us wanted to in case we missed out on the call. We ordered guacamole and little cans of beer to be sent to our room.

Against Pepe's advice, I tried to ring the office a few times, but Conception would answer and say, "They are still meeting." Mexicans start working late, but they do finish late too. Or was Conception lying? Or was she in the meeting too? Thank God for the internet. I looked up the time zones: Australia was awake, so I would call my friend Lilly. It was so good to hear her voice.

"Hey, darling, any news?"

"Not really. Oh, Lilly, I don't think I have a good feeling about this. We still haven't worked out what game Dolores is playing."

"I have a surprise to cheer you up!"

"Go on, then, please, I need it. New man on the horizon?"

"Not a man, but me!"

"What?"

"I've booked my plane ticket! I am coming to see youuuuuu!"

"Are you serious? You said you would come when we met our daughter, and we haven't got her for you, I'm afraid."

"You know what, Fra? I don't care. I want to. Look, you need me, and I need to celebrate my 35th birthday, and youuuu are the person I want to celebrate it with."

"Lilly, that is the best news ever. When? Where?"

"I am arriving in Cancun on the 10th of April, in two weeks!"

"Fab! We can go to Tulum then. You will love it! I am going to try and convince Shannon to come too. It's such a short flight from the US."

"Already done, sweetie."

"Oh, Lilly, you've made my day. We just need one more bit of good news from Pepe now."

"Hopefully I've been your lucky charm. See you soon darling. In Me-hi-co!!!"

By 11:30 pm we had switched from TV to books when the phone rang. Weighed down with guacamole, beer and boredom, I answered it.

"Andale." Pepe sounded tired.

"So?" I asked.

"I am on my way to see you. Meet you by the pool."

We left that room like hesitant teenagers on our first date. Although after seven hours of waiting, we had even less to say than two fifteen-year-olds out together for the first time.

"Here he comes," said Rick. Pepe wore a denim jacket and white trainers, and was toting his seemingly indispensable six-pack of Modelo.

"Virgin of Guadalupe, that woman can talk! I am shattered," he said, opening a can of beer for each of us. I hadn't drunk beer before I came to Mexico. But then, I hadn't done a lot of things.

"So?" I asked.

"Let's have a drink. She has decided. She is going to sign."

Rick managed a half-baked "Oh" while I thanked Pepe. I think we were all out of positive reactions. The stress was palpable amongst our little group. We had a drink and smoked cigarettes in the chilly evening.

"She is going to sign at the end of the week. She likes you and is happy to do it, even though Alfonso is not here."

"What about Beatriz?" asked Rick. "Under Hague, we can't take custody of her."

"Vifac."

"Vifac?" *That's what Dolores meant with the custody thing.*

"Yes, I suggested that Beatriz be left with Aurora. That would get us around the problem of custody. Plus, as you've repeatedly pointed out, she shouldn't keep the girl with her once she has signed the papers. DIF will be more likely to help Vifac than Dolores anyway, so it should ensure a smoother path."

Smoother path, after the row they just had?

"Will DIF send the details of Beatriz to DCSF?" My eyes were heavy. I almost felt jet lagged, but I needed to know everything.

"I think Zoila, my university friend, will do it. We'll see."

"What do you mean, we'll see? We have to tie these things down, Pepe!"

"Don't worry. It's going to be fine."

"Yeah, of course…" Rick was worn out.

"Right, OK, so what happens now?" I don't even know why I thought he would know.

"I am going to have a small but necessary operation at the end of this week, just before Easter. It's such a shame, as I had a trip booked to go to Cuba. I will leave Dolores in the capable hands of Conception, who will help with the relinquishment papers and move Beatriz to Vifac." *Conception? But she is a secretary!* "They are going to go to the notary and sign, together with two witnesses."

"And what do we do?"

"Leave."

"What?"

"You shouldn't be around. You are not supposed to have even met the girl, according to your Hague thing." *Oh, like you're a Hague thing expert now.* "Plus, it's all going to get too messy. But if you go away, by the time you return Alfonso will be here, and he can help you."

"What's your gut feel, Pepe?" The question just came out of me. I think I was starting to warm up to Pepe. I didn't *trust* him—he was, after all, a lawyer—but he seemed like a well-intentioned kid, even if those intentions were haphazard.

"You want the truth from me?"

"Of course."

"If you ask me, I am still not convinced. I like you guys and I think you should wait for a Vifac baby. Aurora is a tough woman, but she is cool. She does things straight from the heart. She doesn't take kindly to strangers, but I know she really likes you…"

I didn't need to hear this. I didn't want to. I knew he was trying to help, but after a long hot day followed by the chilly night air of Colima, it was messing with my head. I couldn't afford to consider it.

"Beatriz needs us, and we want to help her. This is not just about having a shiny new baby," said Rick.

"You asked," said Pepe. "Let's meet at my office tomorrow." He looked at his watch, probably the first time he'd done so in a long while. "Well, I mean today! We can finalise everything."

We slept for a few hours, taking turns to wake each other up and announce that it was really happening, before dropping off to half-sleep again. At five Rick got up to phone his mother.

"Mum, it's best if you tell dad gently, but it seems like we will soon be coming back with his granddaughter. I am so excited. She is adorable."

"He will be delighted, but are you sure things will be OK? Are you doing things correctly? Is the lawyer a good one?"

"Mum, I promise you, all is good. We'll see the lawyer in a few hours. He's young, but his boss is coming back."

"Do you know the boss? Is the baby healthy? Can we see some pictures?"

But weirdly, we had not taken any pictures of Beatriz. We felt it would have been intrusive. We didn't want to upset Dolores—either that, or we simply didn't believe it would happen.

I rang my brother, too.

"Nooooo wayyyyy!! Mamma is here right now. Mum, hurry up! They have got their baby! I think."

"Well, nearly! We are a few papers and days away."

"Oh, it will be your Easter present!" *Easter? This time last year we were announcing our intention to adopt.*

We felt we needed to do something to mark the end of our 'searching' phase and the start of our lives as parents.

"We should go to Tulum. I don't have it in me to travel and visit new places. It's not what our trip is about any longer. I just want to unwind and get prepared spiritually."

Rick had a point.

Unwinding was what we needed, not a holiday, but a preparation. We would leave early the next morning. At about 1:00 pm, we went to see Pepe as planned. Conception was there with big hugs for us.

"I am so pleased for you both. You are the nicest couple I have met in this job, and I tell you I have seen a few. Pepito is waiting for you."

"Hola!" It was Pepe. "Andale, sit down my friends. Actually, you know what, don't bother. I am taking you out for lunch."

"Shouldn't we talk first?" I asked.

"No, let's go, let's go. I'll take you to a really cool place!" We'd forgotten lunch *is* work in Mexico. It's when things happen.

The restaurant was the loudest place we had ever been to, and that's saying a lot in Mexico. There was a stage with mariachis. People got up randomly to sing at the top of their voices. Other lunchers would join them, standing on tables and singing songs that had nothing to do with the tune the band were playing.

There were a fair number of big groups celebrating their birthdays, with balloons and, of course, huge teddy bears. The place was fiercely cheap, and guaranteed to get you drunk. For about £3 you received assorted tacos, which came with "free" buckets of beer. It was utterly mad, and the least likely place to discuss our daughter's adoption.

Rick seemed reluctant to join in, but after a few beers he got into the spirit of it all. I don't drink more than one beer, so I just sat there taking it in. Pepe got drunk and then drove us back to his office. We'd taken our lives into our hands almost daily on this trip, so what was one more drunk drive?

Once there, he sat at his desk and tried to look serious.

"I have some bad news," he started.

"What the hell, Pepe? Tell me it's the alcohol talking, you idiot," Rick exploded.

"Well, Dolores called this morning."

We waited, Rick looking almost bloodthirsty.

"Well... she said that she will sign the papers, but only on one condition."

"What is it?"

"She said that she wants to be able to say goodbye to Beatriz properly, and would like for you to pay for a rented flat for them for two weeks in Barra de Navidad. Beatriz loves the sea, and that way Dolores would keep the memory of their last days together as a happy time."

I looked at Rick, as I had done so often when decisions had to be made.

"How much would it be?"

"About $500."

As a woman, I could empathise with what might have been

going through her mind. Either that, or I had entirely lost the plot. Fortunately, Rick hadn't.

"Well, it's not that much to ask," I began.

"Yes, it is." Rick's tone was firm. "Not only that, if Dolores is making such a tough decision, she shouldn't be worrying about money and holidays. I am not paying a penny. Not to Dolores."

He had a good point.

"Can you ring her and tell her?" Pepe didn't want the responsibility. That's what you get for having a teenage lawyer.

"Are you crazy?" I said. "You are the lawyer, and you are the one she said it to. No. You ring her."

Part of me was wondering if she had even asked for this money. What if the money was for Pepe instead? Or Pepe *and* Dolores?

"I want you to call her on the speakerphone." Rick wasn't taking any chances now.

Pepe dialled the Vifac casa.

A lady answered and put him through to Dolores.

"Pepito." Dolores's voice sounded sweet and relaxed.

"Hi. I have told them about your request."

"Yes?"

"They don't agree. They don't want to be paying for their child, or for a holiday for you."

"OK... I guess... that's fine." She sounded resigned. She didn't even try to argue.

"What does this mean in terms of you signing? "

"I will sign anyway. I better go, Beatriz is crying."

The other lady came to the phone. She sounded desperate.

"Pepe, help this girl, please, and get her out of here. She is so demanding and always asks for things. The other women here don't get or expect anything. She is always trying to strike a deal. Plus Beatriz is always crying."

Crying? That wasn't the Beatriz we had come to know. Was Dolores different with us then? Did she mistreat Beatriz behind the scenes? Nobody was telling us anything.

Our flight was really early the next morning from Guadalajara, so after getting our usual bus, we checked in an airport hotel. It was grim and dark, but there was an email from Alfonso. Finally!

Dear Francesca,
 Nice to meet you!!! Unfortunatelly I checking this mail too late, I writing tomorrow better. Just I want to let you know I supporting you, Dolores know. Keep you inform. Take care and I'll do as muchas thingas I can to make this to do possible.
Best regards,
Alfonso

This was the man whose fluency in English was supposed to be integral to getting this whole business sorted.

12

It Could Have Been Me

"I writing tomorrow."

In his 'fluent' English, Alfonso had promised us he would write to me. But mañana came and went with no communication. I began to send him daily reminders. I wondered if the delay was because his English wasn't good enough to discuss things like the Hague Convention in detail. And then, as much as I tried not to feel suspicious, my mind would inevitably throw out suggestions of a conspiracy: was Alfonso plotting something with Dolores? Who was to say he wasn't orchestrating some sort of deal where everyone would benefit?

Meanwhile, the unpredictable Pepe was about to go into hospital for his operation and was unreachable. I emailed the Hague procedures to our translators in London and sent the Spanish version to both Pepe and Alfonso, thinking that with the signing imminent they might feel it necessary to respond. Nothing.

Dolores was her usual needy, edgy self, and while I understood this, I was sick of being told not to trust Pepe. Whenever she'd say this, I'd point out that Alfonso had not replied to any of my emails, despite being made aware of the urgency of the situation. In fairness, his PA, Conception, who had been left holding the baby and everything else, had been wonderful. She was encouraging and caring, and amidst the craziness that was Pepe and Dolores, she was an oasis of calm. She told us that Alfonso had not been emailing her either lately, and that she was worried, as it was unlike him. I honestly started wondering if he was dead.

So with chaos reigning supreme—the normal state of affairs, it seemed—we decamped to Tulum with the aim of completely detoxing both body and mind. In our hut by the Caribbean sea, we ate fruit, meditated, and asked the Universe to grant our wishes and help us do the right thing, whatever that may be. The moon was full and it was all rather magical. Mexico can be like that. It wasn't a complete retreat, since we had to keep our mobile on. Unfortunately the only people calling us were Conception and Dolores, who now seemed to have bonded with one another. I wasn't sure if I should be worried or relieved, but right then it didn't really matter.

One day Dolores called, sounding more frantic than usual.

"Francesca, your daughter is sick."

Suddenly she was *my* daughter. I didn't mind her being called that. I just didn't like feeling like I was being manipulated.

"She has the flu and I have to take her to the doctor. Can you hear her coughing in the background? I was thinking it would be a good idea for her to also get her missing inoculations."

"Guess so…"

"As you know Francesca, I don't have any money. Perhaps you could be so kind as to send me one hundred dollars?"

What do you say to that? I accepted the girl I was going to adopt wasn't well, and yes, she probably needed the jabs. Still, I wasn't going to be taken for a ride. A hundred dollars in Mexico is enough to cure the flu for a hundred children. I called Conception.

"Is Beatriz really sick, Conception? Tell me the truth."

"Yes, she is, Francesca, but it won't cost that much. And you will need a doctor's report for the UK authorities to allow Beatriz into the country, so we could do it all at once." At that point

Conception's knowledge of Hague was superior to both Pepe's and Alfonso's. Plus she was the only one making any effort to move things forward.

"Dolores doesn't have a bank account," continued Conception. "But if I give you my details you can transfer the money that way."

Were they going to share the money? I was not accustomed to having to think about things this way, but it seemed to be business as usual in Mexico. I agreed to send twenty dollars on the grounds that it would be plenty to cover everything we'd discussed.

I heard Dolores saying, "But Beatriz needs nappies, too."

This was becoming ridiculous.

"The twenty dollars will cover that too," I said.

Tulum has a village, consisting of a few shops, a bank, and a church. We hitchhiked there but found the bank was unable to transfer the money. The account number Conception had given us was two digits short. I called her.

"Oh, sorry, I can't read it out to you because I don't have the card."

"Have you lost it?"

"No. That was my auntie's number. I don't have a bank account either."

Her auntie. This was turning into complete farce.

"This is madness, Conception. Shall I send it via Western Union? That way Dolores can pick it up directly."

"Oh, that's a good idea!"

The Western Union office was nearby. It was also still closed. It didn't make sense to go back, so for three hours we sat on the pavement in the dust and waited for the office to re-open.

"Remind me how we ended up in this situation," said Rick. "That poor little girl is not even well and she's being dragged around by her mad mother."

Another phone call. It was Zoila from the Colima DIF.

"Francesca, Pepe left the photocopies of your documents for me to review. You see, DIF always has to review the documentation, whether it's a Hague or private adoption. At first glance they seem absolutely fine."

Yes!!

"However…"

Uh oh—here comes the dreaded 'however'. Time to adopt the emotional brace position.

"He suggested that we send Beatriz' details to DCSF for them to approve the match, and I don't think we can do that."

"Why not?"

"Well, we can only really send details of children residing in a DIF institute. I am only an intern though, so I might be wrong. I will check with my boss when she is back in two days and let you know. She knows Alfonso well, so she might be able to help him make things work for you anyway."

OK, so a bit of a setback, but not a major one. A couple of months ago it might have been a big deal. However, we had become quite philosophical about it all. Meanwhile we managed to send the money, having called Dolores to alert her in advance.

I called her to check immediately after we'd made the transfer.

"No, I am standing here, but it hasn't arrived."

"What do mean? We sent it to the Western Union in Colima, in your name!"

"Oh, no, there isn't a Western Union in Colima. The one listed as Colima is in a nearby town. You must send it to Telegrafo, not Western Union. Didn't Conception tell you? I want to go to the doctor today. As you know we are going to go to the notary tomorrow, and I don't want her to be unwell then."

We returned to town to send the money. The day after was going to be momentous: it would be the day Dolores would sign the papers that deprived her of any legal maternal rights to Beatriz. Needless to say, we didn't sleep all night. We tossed and turned, prayed, chanted, danced, cried and laughed. If that sounds insane, then it was only a reflection of the madness of the situation, and perhaps a rare release of tension.

It was both rare and brief. The next morning was fraught. We woke up stressed. I rang Dolores's mobile. Unusually for her, it was turned off. Then, as I did most days, I checked my email inbox. No, it couldn't be. Surely not. But there it was. A note from the DCSF.

Dear Ms Polini and Mr Bowden,
  The Department for Children, Schools and Families (DCSF) is now in a position to dispatch your application. The collection address is the loading bay, DCSF, Staindrop Road, Darlington, DL3 9BG, Tel: 01325 392434. Please get the courier to ask them to ring the Intercountry Adoption Team so that we can bring the package down.
    The delivery address is:
Ministry of Foreign Relations
Legal Department
Ricardo Flores Magon No 1
Ala "A", 2o piso
Colonia Nonoalco Tlatelolco
Delegacion Cuauhtemoc
06995 MEXICO , Distrito Federal

Ninety-two days after they had received our pre-paid envelope, DCSF were actually ready to send our papers. Exactly three months to the day. It had only finally happened because Rick had emailed our MP, begging him to support us, which he'd promised to do. There was only one problem. The documents were being despatched to the wrong address.

It seemed that the files at the DCSF were not up to date. The building to which they were sending our documents had actually been knocked down a few years ago. I found this out only because the address that DCSF had provided didn't look anything like the one to which I'd posted our photocopies, and which I knew to be correct. Luckily I had a contact at the Ministry of Foreign Affairs. My continuous begging and pestering has yielded some very useful contacts, and now I was able to call on one of them, Maria.

"Maria, we are in a bit of a mess."

"The right address is the one you mailed your parcel to, Francesca. Get them to send it to my attention. I'll be looking out for it!"

Not surprisingly, they didn't believe me. Their file said that the address they had, the non-existent building, was the right one, and that's where they would send our papers. Nothing I said convinced them otherwise. I even sent a link to the website showing the new address. My efforts to persuade them produced this email in reply.

Dear Ms Polini,

I understand that this will be very frustrating for you but I do need to make further enquiries as we are required to send the documents to the address in our file. I will try to make contact with Mexico today but given the time difference I may not receive a response before Fed Ex are scheduled to collect the papers. I will be in contact with you again as soon as I receive clarification.

Thankfully, clarification did come from Maria herself, and our documents, those papers containing our whole lives, were sent at last. Their first stop: The Mexican Ministry of Foreign Affairs.

We had no sooner dealt with one crisis than another popped up.

"Hola, Francesca."

"Dolores. At last."

"Speak to Conception. I am too upset."

She was crying. I imagined she would have been. How hard must it be to give up your daughter forever? Despite the chaotic, unstable package that was Dolores, we'd become friends. She wasn't a young student who had got pregnant by mistake, or a drug addict, or a woman off the streets. We were about the same age; we even had a similar slim build. More importantly, we had similar interests; we liked the same music and films. Like me, she loved children and had volunteered for children homes. She was politically aware, concerned about the world, and had a sense of humour. We had all of that in common. But for the grace of God, I could have been her, and that very thought was distressing. How would I be feeling? What would I have done in her position? It would be facile to say I would have acted much differently. I might have, but I wasn't in her place. There are situations where it is very easy to state what you might do. But we never really know until we are there. How much could I really feel?

For all intents and purposes, Dolores's action had been prompted by her concerns about being able to look after her child properly. When she allegedly threw herself and the child into the freezing sea, she realised that it was her blue-lipped, shaking daughter who would die first, and she couldn't live with that. She would be killing her own daughter whom she loved so much, when in fact it was she who wanted to die, so she changed her mind and dragged her out in time.

I knew if I allowed myself to succumb to these feelings I would feel guilty. I think it was part empathy, and part female solidarity. Call it whatever you like, but at this moment I was alongside that woman, rather than opposite her. Rick didn't comprehend any of this. For him the girl was better off with us, where she'd have a future, our unconditional love and that of our families and friends. For him, we were doing the right thing.

Conception took the phone. Apparently they had gone to see the notary, and the documents left by Pepe were not complete. The end result was there had been no signing.

"Dolores is really upset. I am going to take her home with me and look after her and Beatriz. Have you been able to speak to Pepe at all?"

Logically, if he wasn't speaking with the office PA, why would he speak with me?

"No news from either him or Alfonso, I'm afraid. Total, complete silence."

"I am starting to get really worried about Alfonso. It's not like him at all to disappear like this," she said.

You have to hang on by your fingernails sometimes. You don't acknowledge that's what you're doing, just in case it weakens you. But there were many, many times when that was all we were doing, holding on with tenacity and faith. We were also both lucky to have parents who were behind us the whole way. They were our rocks, even though we didn't speak to them all the time. We just knew they were there. And if they thought we were on a mad quest, they never let on. They just gave unconditional love and support, though at times, like many parents, they would have loved to stop our emotional pain and just say: "Kids, just come home. You gave it your best shot." But they never did. Other than the phone call I'd had with Paolo, who was only looking out for me, nobody had told us to give it up.

Dolores and Beatriz went to the doctor the following day, which meant I had the official description of Beatriz that Zoila at the DIF in Colima required. This included a passport picture of Beatriz, and details about her age, size, weight, eyes and hair colour, which DCSF and our Council were supposed to be agreeing on before we could meet and eventually take custody of our little girl.

I also sent the photographs to Lilly. After so much talk, I wanted to share something visual, and showing my dear friend that tiny picture on the doctor's form felt therapeutic. But I felt too unsure and superstitious to show the picture to anyone else, even our parents.

Conception had finally managed to speak to Alfonso and to get the right documents for Dolores to sign. So things seemed to be on track again, although the track was never a straight one.

Rick's good friend, Ian, and his girlfriend, Lisa, had turned up to meet us. It was great to see some familiar faces. We were invited to a wedding of a mutual American friend in Tulum, and it was great to be with some people where the only thing on the agenda was talk, laughter, drink and food. And a few tears. As the margaritas flowed on the wooden platform by the sea, with 'From This Moment On' by Shania Twain in the background, we tried to tell them what had happened in the past few months.

But where to begin? How did you tell them about the corrupt lawyer Miguel, who sold babies to order? How did you explain the many different versions of adoption that we had discovered? How did we begin to describe Pepe, Conception, and Aurora? How did we tell them about Vifac and DIF?

How did we explain the anger and frustration of having to beg, coerce, and plead to be considered adoptive parents, using our frankly illegal photocopies, while DCSF struggled for three months to put the same papers in an envelope? And now they wanted to send them to the wrong address, insisting it was the right one.

"You guys are stars, and you're doing the right thing. It will work out for the best. You are so close now." Ian and Lisa were wonderfully supportive as we gave them edited highlights of our journey thus far.

The day of the wedding was the day Dolores was finally heading to the notary to sign the relinquishment papers. It was uncomfortable trying to be joyful for friends while thinking about her. We were in an exquisite Caribbean setting, the sunset was over the water, the champagne glasses tinkled, and all round us were the sounds of laughter, love, and people having a good time. I wanted to enjoy it, but all I could think about was the signing, about Dolores in that office.

And then came the phone call. I saw my phone light up. Without thinking, I dropped my glass and ran inside with no shoes on, tripping over my long cotton black dress. I called back.

"Francesca, it's Conception. Dolores is too upset to speak. She has signed the papers. It's all done. Beatriz is legally not her daughter any longer. We are heading home. She said she wants a camomile tea and to go to sleep. It's been a big day."

It was done. Was I happy? Not at all. It was as if there was a firewall between my actual emotions and those I was supposed to be feeling. Was this all the past few months had amounted to? A kind of semi-guilty emptiness?

All I could think of was Dolores. It could have been me.

13

There Might Even Be a God

Dolores had *one* more request, relayed to us by Pepe: she wanted to move in with us. She wanted to help Beatriz settle in. Any adoption agency would have said this was madness, and likely to create trauma rather than ensure harmony. Generally, the principle behind handing over a child is to do it swiftly and cleanly. On the other hand, what did I know about children? I wasn't a mother, and deferring to Dolores's sense of what was better for Beatriz didn't seem to be the worst idea.

"Oh, whatever," said Rick, who saw it as part of the fine print of the deal. Knowing his objections to Dolores's previous demands, I asked if he was absolutely sure. He was. However, we both agreed that actually living with Dolores simply would not work. So we put a limit on both space and time. We decided we'd do ten days maximum, and we'd live in separate flats: Beatriz with us, and Dolores in another one near enough to be able to come and go. I still felt uneasy wondering how Dolores would finally leave. However, Rick was confident that we could manage it.

Fortunately, our eco-shack in Tulum had WiFi. We looked on the internet and located two serviced apartments in a modern building in Colima that Pepe told us about. It was normally used by Americans who were retiring in Manzanillo and who stopped by on their way for a few days.

It seemed like a good idea to phone Dolores to let her know that we'd agreed to the request, and also to tell her where the flat was so that she could check it out if she wished. The phone rang, but she didn't answer, which was unlike her. It occurred to me that she could be avoiding us. However, given her form, it wasn't a thought I wanted to contemplate. Instead I proceeded to book our 4000 mile journey, which would comprise of a bus to Cancun, a flight to Guadalajara, and finally a bus to Colima.

I was totally absorbed in making our reservations when Aurora called and offered her congratulations. I assumed she'd been informed that Dolores had finally signed the papers.

"So you know then?"

"Know what, Francescaaa?" I loved the way she dragged out vowels.

"That Beatriz is finally going to be ours, and we are soon moving in with Dolores."

"No, I did not know. I have a baby for you."

"A baby? For us?" I broke into a sweat that had nothing to do with the heat. "But… you said it would take time. Where did it come from?"

"Where do you think babies come from, Francescaa? *It* is a she. And she is the baby girl I had in mind for you all along, but of course I wasn't going to tell you until the relinquishment papers were signed, and now the birth mother has done so. And she has left. Which means you can have this most beautiful baby girl to call your own."

Aurora didn't want to give us the faintest glimmer of hope until she was absolutely sure she could help us. And now she'd delivered.

"I'm sorry, Aurora, but we have already decided to take Beatriz. We have come a long way to get to this point, and both Rick and I feel it's the right decision."

Did we?

As always, Aurora was very calm.

"OK, Francesca. But I know you and I want you to think about it. This is the most important decision of your life. Talk about it with Rick and your family and see what they think. It's a major decision."

Really, this was quite remarkable of her. Considering we'd turned up on Vifac's doorstep begging for an audience with her and were now turning down her newborn baby, she was being incredibly kind and understanding.

"You are an angel, Aurora, but there isn't much to think about. We have a moral obligation to Beatriz, and Dolores has relinquished her daughter so that she could go to us. She will end up in an institute if we pull out now. She couldn't stay with Dolores any longer. By the way, have you heard from her or Pepe about taking custody of the girl in the short term?"

"What do you think? Hey, listen, I know everything you say, but I want to give you and Rick another twenty-four hours, no more and no less. We speak tomorrow at 1:00 pm."

I was well aware that to turn down this baby would mean her being given to the next waiting family, probably by tomorrow. As for another baby becoming available, well, the chances of that were slim. If we said no to Aurora and something went wrong with Beatriz' adoption, would Aurora still be there for us? I doubted it.

"OK, Aurora, speak at 1:00."

Rick had fallen asleep on the hammock outside and hadn't heard anything. I put my scarf on my head, as it was hot and this wasn't going to be a quick conversation. I sat in our hammock and kissed him on the forehead.

"Amore."

"Gosh, I was dreaming of being back in London, at the airport with Beatriz and everyone was waiting for us with balloons, like in an American movie."

"Aurora called." I told him what she said.

"A newborn would represent the Holy Grail for most adoptive parents, but we are not those parents, Fra. We have a bond and obligation with this little girl."

"Oh, I know. We came to help a child who needed a family. Right now both of these little girls do, but Aurora's baby is likely to find another family relatively soon. The same can't be said about Beatriz, so why am I so unsure about things still?"

"Beatriz doesn't have a hope in hell of finding a family. She will end up in a place like Istituto Cabañas, as nice as it is, but for the rest of her life, like the sisters of Chetumal. Is this what we want for her? Nobody in Mexico will adopt a two-year-old."

Knowing all this did not diminish the numerous niggling doubts we had about Dolores, and indeed about the bizarre nature of this whole saga. Rick jumped off the hammock.

"Put some shorts on. We are going to town."

"What for?"

"We are going to call our parents. They must know what's right."

I got off and obediently found my shorts and vest. Skype wasn't working too well in our eco-chic shack, possibly due to the structure literally being in the sea. We grabbed a cab and headed for an internet café in Tulum. Squeezed into the same cubicle together, we phoned my mother, then my father and brothers, to tell them of our decision to take Beatriz and our rationale for not opting for the newborn instead. As always, they offered no objection. I guess they figured we knew what we were doing. Feeling slightly more confident but still looking for reinforcement, we phoned Rick's parents and told them.

"Yes, you're doing exactly the right thing. You must follow your hearts." Sue had no doubts.

Then, after a walk outside into the bright sunlight, we wondered if putting our lives in Dolores's hands was really the right thing to do. She could still disappear. And even after signing the papers, a birthmother can change her mind right up until the day of the court hearing. How did we know Dolores wasn't going to make further demands or change her mind altogether? So we decided we'd better do the whole thing again. We called our parents, who agreed again, even though it was the opposite of what they'd just heard from us.

And so the calling cycle continued for hours.

I decided to call Dolores again. I wanted her to understand exactly what was going on: if we said a final no to Aurora and Dolores changed her mind, then we were well and truly stuffed.

"I am on a truck heading to Barra de Navidad," Dolores shouted down the phone. I could hardly hear her.

"What for? Hasn't Pepe told you that we are moving in together tomorrow?" I shouted down the phone.

"Yes, but I need some papers..."

The line was cut off. I tried to ring over and over again but there was no reply. Not wanting to think the worst, I assumed there was no reception, or that her battery had gone flat. Still, it was disconcerting. I also worried about Beatriz, the poor little soul now being dragged to Barra on a truck. In Mexico it's pretty normal practice for a working truck driver to pick up passengers along with whatever else he is carrying. I had images of Dolores holding little Beatriz in a truck full of corn or tomatoes.

It was the end of a highly charged day. Europe had gone to bed, and we were exhausted but happy. We were going to stick to our guns. Not even the prospect of a shiny new baby was going to change our minds. We had a moral obligation to Beatriz, who was about to lose the only person in the world who'd showed her any affection. And we had an obligation to Dolores, who had entrusted us with her daughter.

"Ok, well I think we've sorted it," said Rick.

"Yep, we have."

"No need to think anymore about it."

"No, definitely not. I'll phone Aurora back now. No sense prolonging this."

Aurora was somewhat nonplussed. "I said twenty-four hours, OK. Keep thinking. You must be exhausted now. It doesn't make any sense speaking. I speak to you at lunchtime tomorrow."

I told Rick, who shrugged.

"Well, what did you expect? She's a tough lady. We have one more day in Tulum and then we become parents. Let's enjoy it. I'll go and get a cab while you check your email."

There was one from Alfonso. It was terse and distant.

Francesca,
Please do not bother me while am in Europe. Pepe take care of things while I am away. I do not need involved.

"Goodness, what's his problem?" I said to Rick. "How very odd."

We let it go and headed back to our shack. It was going to be real. We were going to be parents. Neither of us was normally given to big pronouncements. But this was big. And so I can clearly remember that we spoke about Beatriz on our balcony that night, under a clear sky full of stars, in tones a little louder than usual. Perhaps it was us just wanting to make it real.

The next morning, after an early meal of fruit, we said goodbye to our hut, and to our nomadic life. We had little to say to one another, but standing there watching the waves crashing on the shore that morning, there was a sense we were beginning a new phase of our lives.

We were loading our rucksacks into the cab for the journey to the bus station when my mobile rang. I had one leg inside the car and one on the pavement when the call came. It was Conception, though at first I could barely make her out, as she was sobbing profoundly. Conception is a deeply religious woman, so when she told me she'd been up for the past few nights asking God for a sign, I knew something was up.

"Conception, please don't be upset. Tell me what is bothering you."

"Francesca," she wept, "I have to tell you something. After not sleeping all night I went to the notary in the morning and there was a woman with a baby, a baby girl she was giving up. I looked at this girl's eyes and they were the most beautiful I had ever seen. I knew this was the sign I had been waiting for from God."

Now I had tears in my eyes. That was Aurora's baby, the one she'd told us about. There is only one notary in Colima. The taxi driver looked at Rick, who just shrugged. He turned the volume of the radio down so that he could hear.

"But what sign, Conception?"

"Look, Alfonso is not a bad man, and he is a good boss to me. You must not ever tell that I am talking to you about this, but he had a plan with Dolores, and that is why they delay you. Alfonso told Dolores a story about an American couple who bought a house for the birthmother so that they could go and visit her regularly with the child. Dolores wanted you to do the same. When you said no to Dolores's pleas for money and holidays, they knew you wouldn't do it, so they fell out. Alfonso told her there was nothing else he could do and to be reasonable, but she is after the money at any cost. So the licenciado didn't want to be part of it."

That explained Alfonso's nasty email. But it's what Conception said next that would change our lives forever.

"When I went with Dolores to the notary she did sign, but there was only one witness. It was me. You know you need two witnesses for the relinquishment papers to be valid. She did it on purpose, so that if you did not buy her a place to live she would take her daughter and run."

Which is probably what she was doing now.

Conception was sobbing loudly again.

"Oh, my God, what have I done? Please forgive me for this, I am so sorry. And you, Francesca, you are too wonderful to deserve this. Stay away now."

How was I going to explain this little fork in the road to Rick? Meanwhile the taxi driver sat there listening to loud music and looking in the rear view mirror as if to say: *These gringos are all about the drama, always drama.*

"Conception, please be assured I will not betray your confidence to a soul." I said this as I got out of the car at the station. "Neither Alfonso nor Pepe will ever know this conversation happened. It is gone. Meanwhile, Rick and I will do what we must do. You are a star, my darling Conception, and I am sure God will understand why you did this, because I do."

I said all this calmly as the cab drew up to the bus station. Now I had to explain it all to Rick. There was absolutely no time to lose. It wasn't lost on me that the day was in fact April 1st. Were we being taken for a ride? Maybe by a whole lot of other people, but I was convinced Conception's heart was pure and her words true. And now I had to explain that all to Rick.

So it was there, amidst the excitable backpackers and the bus drivers shouting at each other through their windows, that I relayed the story to him that would change our lives. He stood wordlessly, just listening, while I gave him Conception's news as impassively as if I were giving directions. It wasn't that I didn't feel anything. On the contrary, I felt an extraordinary lightness, as if the storm had passed and now there was pure clarity. It was as if everything was suddenly illuminated. And Rick saw it too.

It was one hour until lunchtime.

14

Internet Date

Destiny or free will? Do any of us ever really know the difference? I have always believed that the path to wisdom consists of surrendering to the will of "the Universe", a belief my husband always teases me about but which I know he understands. Yet I also know that it is impossible to achieve a goal without pursuing it wholeheartedly. It is not enough to simply want something. You have to be willing to fight for it, sometimes against seemingly insurmountable odds. And yet I always wonder if the outcome of these struggles is pre-ordained, or if it is purely my own creation. I had been sure Beatriz would be ours, but the rug had been yanked from under our feet in an instant. We were confused, heartbroken, worried and afraid. The only thing we were completely sure of at that moment was that merely a single exhausted, desperate yes to just one of Dolores's demands would have had us well and truly conned.

But we didn't wallow in self-pity. It wasn't us who'd been dealt the dud hand; it was poor, wretched Beatriz. We were not going to be the ones allowed to help her in this life. It was not meant to be. We might have fought for her, maybe even have contacted the authorities to report Dolores, but we knew we couldn't have Beatriz taken from her mother; after all, we had no proof of anything. And this was not our country. They did things differently here, and if we had decided to report Dolores, we would have probably just sounded like pathetic gringos who hadn't got what they wanted.

It was less than forty minutes to lunchtime, a watershed moment that would mark the end of the twenty-four-hour waiting period imposed by Aurora. The whole thing had a providential air about it: her phone call, Dolores's absconding with Beatriz, and the fact that there was a baby waiting for us. In that moment, even though I was exhausted and emotionally drained, the whole situation appeared to be part of some larger plan.

"Aurora," said Rick softly, as we plonked our bags down on a red metal bench.

I nodded and got up. It was a conversation that deserved dignity and privacy, both of which were in short supply at the bus station. I walked over to the bus parking lot, where their engines were spewing out filthy smoke, but at least I was alone. With Rick waving and blowing kisses at me, I made the call.

"Soooo, Francescaaaa!"

I had fallen in love with the sound of Aurora's voice the first time I heard it, but it was never so reassuring to hear her smoky, knowing rasp as it was right now. I felt safe with her. Even so, I knew I couldn't tell her the truth. I had to protect Conception.

"Soooo, you have changed your mind? It does not really matter why, but you want to tell me?"

"Aurora, we are really not sure about Dolores. We have tried to speak to her recently, and she never replies. I guess you are right about her. We don't feel good about continuing with her and Beatriz… so…"

I took a deep breath hoping to God, Buddha, Allah, the Virgin of Guadalupe, and every other deity I could think of that she still had the baby girl for us.

"And… so I wondered if we could still speak about the little baby girl you have… you had…"

"Francescaaaa, I have her. I have *your* daughter."

Our daughter. This time, it sounded perfectly natural.

I waved at Rick as tears sprang to my eyes. In that filthy, noisy bus station I gave silent thanks that Conception's telling us of her sign from God had brought us together with the baby Aurora had promised us. It had taken innumerable twists and turns just to get here, but this time the fates had smiled upon us. It was as if they were saying, "You have passed the test and done enough. You deserve the reward now. You are ready."

With emotion welling up inside me I told Aurora that we would like to come and work out the adoption with her.

"Yes, yes, of course. But I am about to fly to Mexico City. I will be back on Thursday. You will come to my house at 9:00 pm. I text you the address. Bless you, Francesca."

No, bless you, Aurora.

🐾

Three days. Three more days. Anything could happen in three days. Where was the baby? Was she safe? When I told Rick what I was thinking, he hugged me and told me I was being silly.

"Fra, you have been so strong, so hopeful and so patient. This is your time to let go and feel what we—what you—have achieved."

I put my head on his knee and sobbed with relief and joy, and when I had finished I laughed and said, "Well, we have three days. What on earth do we do now?"

We had said goodbye to Tulum and the Caribbean, so there was no point returning; it would feel like going backwards. It also felt like a waste to spend three days in Guadalajara waiting for Aurora. We opened our travel guide, did a quick scan, and found the city of Merida, five hours away in the Yucatan, which sounded stunning.

First there were a few things we needed to do—and undo. We had to let go of the two one-bedroom flats we'd rented in Colima, and instead rent one two-bedroom flat in Guadalajara. We had to unravel our current travel plans and get tickets to Merida. So we headed for the internet café.

It was also time to call Pepe. His first reaction was one of relief. I didn't want to think about why; whether it was because he didn't like Dolores, or alternatively whether he'd been part of Alfonso and Dolores's plan to persuade us to buy a flat but was uncomfortable about it. Certainly a Vifac adoption was familiar territory for him, and I knew he was genuinely happy for us.

"You know what I am going to do?" he said. "I am going to ask Aurora to email me some pictures of the little girl, so Conception can send them to you and you can meet your daughter."

"Oh, my God, Pepe, are you serious?"

"Of course! Congratulations! I always knew this was the right thing for you!"

"Hang on a second." I had to tell Rick, who grinned from ear to ear. It was clear he was over the moon, but being Rick he had now adopted the confident demeanour of a man who had known this would happen all along.

In contrast to the bulk of our travels around Mexico, Merida would not be a holding post, a waiting room, somewhere to wander aimlessly while we contemplated what the next hour or day would bring: it would be a place to celebrate. As we sat on the bus, we finally talked about Beatriz.

"I am sad for her. She is the real victim in this whole big mess," said Rick.

"It's not even that Dolores is a bad woman. More like desperate and cunning," I added.

"Yes, but she was using her daughter as a bargaining chip. That's awful, no matter how desperate you are."

"She probably needed a family for herself, too, and was trying to find the best way to have Beatriz adopted while still maintaining her closeness. Either way, it's not my place to judge. Who knows what I would do in her position?"

Rick was unusually reflective for a moment.

"Look at us right now. God knows what we would have said about people like us had we not been in this position!"

"I wonder what she thought we would do if we did buy the flat? Come and see her, say once a year?"

"You know what, Fra, there are some things that we will probably never know about what happened behind the scenes, and it's probably better that way. We can choose to dwell on that or look forward. I know which one of the two I want to do. Let's get some rest now."

He put his cap on to shield himself from the sun and took my hand. For the first time in months I felt calm, deep calm. We were both exhausted. All that adrenalin coursing through our bodies wasn't needed now. We could sigh. We could sleep. We could throw anxiety out of the dusty bus window. I trusted Aurora as I would my own mother.

It seemed right to be in the beautiful city of Merida, the capital of the state of Yucatan. Their liberal use of limestone and white paint have given it the tag 'White City'. It's dominated by colonial architecture, with palatial mansions lining the Paseo de Montejo, a boulevard based on the Champs Elysees in Paris.

We tracked down a central hotel, left our bags there, and burst into the sunshine. We were both animated and smiling. People probably thought we were high on something. It felt good to be able to actually enjoy the city and explore its attractions, especially the craft markets for which Merida is famous.

We found one of the less touristy shops, which sold handmade wall hangings. Rick spied one, a burst of pink, red and orange embroidered with flowers, sunshine, and children. It would be an authentic piece of Mexican happiness for our as-yet-unseen daughter's bedroom.

"I feel like we're starting our journey all over again," I said to him.

"We are, Fra," he said. And he kissed me.

Merida is the most Mayan of Mexican states, and Yucateans are rather like Catalonians in that they are loyal to their state rather than their country. So much so that when they plan a trip to another part of Mexico, they will announce, "I'm going to Mexico next week." Ask them for directions and you will always get a helpful response, regardless of whether they are sure or not. Their manners are both curious and cute: when visiting, they will never leave until you ask them to. If it has been overlong, they will bolt only when given 'permission'.

After our shopping expedition, which also included a hammock for our as-yet-undeveloped garden, we tucked into my two favourite Mexican dishes: *sopa de lima*, a lime soup with a chicken broth base, accompanied by shredded chicken and crispy tortilla, and *cochinita pibil*, pork marinated in indigenous spices for several days.

At the end of the first day, a text came through on my phone. It was from Pepe.

PHOTOS SENT, LET ME KNOW WHEN YOU'VE GOT THEM

I grabbed Rick's hand and began to run. "Quick, there's an internet café in the main plaza."

"I need a beer," said Rick.

"No time. OK, get two. Quick." He veered off to a bar, bought two bottles of Dos Equis, and returned to the café where I sat waiting for the ancient computer to come to life. The noise it made reminded me of a gurgling Italian espresso maker, the kind you put on top of the stove. We held hands, willing Microsoft to hurry up. The email popped up with the subject:

FOTOS BEBE

Hand in sweaty hand, we opened the email. And there she was. Maria Guadalupe Cameron Torres, with her little chubby face and eyes peacefully shut, lying in a Moses basket on top of an anonymous kitchen counter. She was wearing a pink dress with elephants on it.

"The dress is too big for her," I cried. "My God, she's beautiful."

"That's our little girl," said Rick, tears running down his cheeks. "I don't believe it."

I called Pepe, who was in his office with Conception.

"Hola. Felicidades!" They said it together from the loudspeakers.

"Que linda bebe, no?"

They probably talked about it for days in that internet café: the gringos who came in and went from laughter, to cheering, to tears and back, again and again. Eventually the people sitting around us found out what was going on, and they too offered their congratulations, hugging us and singing as if we were their best friends.

"You realise when she is older we will have to tell her we met her in an internet café," said Rick.

After more beer and tears we emailed the pictures to both sets of parents, our brothers, sister-in-law, and my best friends and soul sisters, Lilly and Shannon. After we managed to pull ourselves away from our digital baby, the phone calls came thick and fast, from Europe, from Australia, from America.

"You know it's our turn to carry teddy bears and swig tequila now, don't you?" I said.

I called Aurora for reassurance.

"OK, Francesca, don't worry. This is your girl. You are going home with her, remember? I told you so. We will make this work and follow the necessary rules," Aurora insisted. "From here on, you will have no problems."

🐦

At 6:00 pm on April 5th we were on a plane from Cancun, back to Guadalajara. At the same time, Aurora was flying back from Mexico City. We were going to meet at her house to discuss how to proceed with the adoption.

It was faintly ridiculous to be in the same city as our baby and not be able to see her until people in various government departments had decided we could. It wasn't actually illegal, since private adoptions are indeed allowed in Hague countries. The problem was that the DCSF had decided they would not allow it. However, we were resigned to doing the right thing. After all we'd been through, waiting for a few more weeks would not be the end of the world. It would provide breathing space and allow us prepare for the biggest event of our lives. It was all good.

By the time the plane taxied to the gate, it was half an hour behind schedule. Emerging from the melee of the terminal, we ran for the cab rank, zigzagging between the other passengers, sand pouring from our rucksacks. I gave the cab driver the address Aurora had texted me.

"One more thing," I said to him. "We need to stop to buy some flowers."

"Sorry, but the shops are all shut now. Maybe at the gas station."

Here we were, thousands of miles from home, and there were still flowers to be bought from service stations. They were just as limp, neglected and unhappy as any you'd get back in the UK. We picked the best of a sad bunch and headed for our appointment.

We drew up outside a pristine white house surrounded by manicured gardens. Four expensive late-model cars were parked outside, but I couldn't see Aurora's beloved Mercedes. Aurora was very wealthy. Her husband owned a number of profitable businesses, although she'd always pointed out how the only thing she really enjoyed doing was working voluntarily for Vifac.

"Uau! Que hermosa casa, senores!" Even the taxi driver was impressed.

We pressed the buzzer on the carved wooden door. A large, barefoot Mayan maid in a white cotton apron, her hair in a large bun, opened the door and showed us through a marble-floored hallway. The woman gestured for us to follow her through the kitchen, fragrant with the smell of fried food. There were pans everywhere, dishes piled up on a sink, and the inevitable rows of multi-coloured habañero chillies. A little man sat in a corner, busily peeling avocados.

I did a double-take: the counter looked familiar. Where had I seen it before? Was it where the picture of the baby in the Moses basket had been taken? It couldn't be; the baby girl was at the Vifac casa.

We were shown into an enormous living room. I could feel Aurora's presence. Each wall was hung with paintings, including, unsurprisingly, the Virgin of Guadalupe. Coloured ceramic lamps sat on glass tables, polished to within an inch of their lives. Despite the show, and the European-style elegance, the house had a warm feel. We sat on one of the huge white leather sofas, feeling less than appropriate in our beach clothes.

"Una cerveza?" offered the maid.

Regardless of the time of day, Mexicans will always offer you a beer. I, in turn, offered our thoroughly distressed-looking flowers, which given our surroundings seemed even more pathetic now. Showing appropriately minimal interest, the maid placed them on a side table. The house was quiet, and Aurora herself did not seem to be in evidence. Eventually, a teenaged girl came into the room. I guessed she was one of Aurora's four teenage children.

"Hello, I've heard a lot about you!" she said in English. She shook our hands warmly and sat down with us on the edge of the sofa, eager to chat and make sure we felt at home. Like Aurora, she looked more European than Mexican. She was very tall and slim, with straight blond hair, and she carried herself very much as her mother did. She apologised for Aurora's absence, explaining she would be here soon. By now we were well versed in the Mexican practice of keeping late hours. Nonetheless it felt slightly awkward to be sitting here with the time getting on towards 10:00 pm.

We started chatting about Europe, Mexico, and our travels, and because Carla spoke English I let Rick do most of the talking for a change. Meanwhile, I thought about what we needed to do to make sure this baby was ours.

Details sent to DCSF from DIF Colima. DCSF sends these to our local council. Our council emails us—not with the details but just to tell us they have a 'referral'. We arrange a call with the council and only then we see details. We discuss details with social worker.

Normally it would only be at this point that you book your flight ticket and go and meet the baby. Only then do you get to see what the baby actually looks like in real life. But we were there already, so it would be more like: *One more call with council to say we like the baby and she seems healthy. Then we can visit the baby but not take custody till DCSF and DIF have ratified article 17c. Voila! I know it by heart now!*

Suddenly, the house came to life.

"Francescaaa. Riiiiiiiiiiiickk!" The voice. The lady herself. I looked up to see Aurora descending the white staircase like an imperious duchess. But what was that she was carrying in her arms? *Oh, my God.*

OH MY GOD.

It was the baby. Our baby, wrapped in a yellow cotton blanket. The way in which Aurora bore that child down the stairs suggested we were about to meet a royal progeny.

I think Rick squealed, or as close as a normally cool, distant Englishman can get to squealing. It certainly was a sound I'd never heard from him before.

And then he said: "Wow." Not the kind of 'wow' that men apply to cars or women or gadgets but a tender, gentle whisper.

"Ciao angelo, eccoti finalmente." *There you are at last, my angel.* I had reverted to my mother tongue without even thinking about it. Aurora handed me the bundle, and feeling the child's warm heartbeat against my body I had no doubt this was my daughter. I just knew this was why we had come here.

"Thank you for finding us," I whispered.

Barely four days old, Maria Guadalupe Cameron Torres did not have the slightly squashed appearance of a baby that age. She had the gaze of one who already knew the world. I was convinced she was one of those old souls who had been here before. Babies can't really see at this stage in their life; they only view the world in shades. Even I knew that much. But the way she looked up suggested she was pleased to be here. She had light brown hair, amazing almond eyes, and perfectly-formed full lips. She appeared to be long for her age, and she also had long, slim hands.

"Sei bellissima!" I said to her.

"I told you, I only have beautiful babies in Guadalajara!" Aurora's infectious laugh resounded around the room. "So, what do you think, ha? Always trust Aurora!"

What was I supposed to think, beyond that this indeed was a beautiful baby? It occurred to me that I was supposed to be checking her. But checking for what exactly? Aside from her well-formed face, she had two arms and two legs. Aurora had told me she was in good health, and it appeared to be so.

Rick was hovering over me, wanting his turn and pulling silly faces, so I handed her to him. I knew he had never picked up a baby this small before, but he was confident as he held her and then laid her on his legs. The sight of him melting as he gazed at her and held her tiny little fingers in his was enough to turn me into grains of sand. This was a side to him I had never seen. He was truly besotted.

"She is so beautiful, so sweet. Chu chu!" Was that my Mancunian husband cooing over a baby?

"I told you!" Aurora insisted, laughing again.

I laughed, too.

"Right now this little one needs feeding and changing."

And with that Aurora summoned another maid and our audience with our daughter was over after all of five minutes. She briskly dismissed everyone else in the room, including Carla, and became suddenly businesslike. We all sat on the sofas again.

"OK, here's the thing," she said. "We cannot keep a newborn baby in the casa. That's why she has been staying here with us."

"I know you are not really equipped for it at Vifac. You are there for the birthmothers," I said.

"Exactly, and we want to minimise their distress, as they are grappling with their own decision about whether to keep their baby or not. She's been great here. You know Sabina, who let you in, has raised all four of my children?!"

We knew children were normally given in custody to their new parents within the space of a couple of days. But we were not ready for what Aurora said next.

"Soooo... if you want this child you have to come and pick her up tomorrow. Or I will have to give her to someone else."

I knew Aurora wasn't threatening us; she was just doing what she had to do. But she'd put us right in the thick of it. Never mind Hague—that had gone out the window already. We were not prepared in the slightest.

One might ask how after wanting something so much I could have mixed feelings, but the fact was that *we were not ready*. As a matter of fact, we were *shell-shocked*. This was a huge responsibility, and we were totally underprepared. Emotionally, logistically, legally... no matter which angle you looked at it from, we had, well, stuff to do.

How could we be ready for a newborn when merely twenty-four hours earlier we were organising our lives to adopt a two-year-old? Normally a parent-to-be would be prepared. Books would have been read about newborns, courses would have been attended, family and friends would have been consulted, and if there wasn't family there was always family centres, midwives, and others. Pregnant women and expectant fathers will have had several months to adjust to the idea of a newborn coming into their lives. It wasn't so much that they would already have a nursery kitted out in pink or blue, but rather the psychological preparation and general knowledge they would have taken on board by this point. Feeding, sleeping patterns, colic, belly buttons, milk temperature, bathing time. Plus, they would have a support network of sorts; even if their parents were miles away they would have friends, neighbours and health visitors. Our unpreparedness had nothing to do with not being biological parents, as even adoptive parents who knew from the start that they would be adopting a newborn baby would have had much longer than we did to get ready. Much, much longer than twelve hours.

In effect it was like suddenly being told: *you're pregnant, you're due tomorrow and you're on your own in the middle of Mexico and don't know anyone other than a kind but very busy woman.*

"Tomorrow?"

"Yes. Tomorrow. I can't keep her here. I am out all day for work, and I'm an old woman. I am done with babies, you know! She has nowhere else to go, unless we give her to another family. I can arrange that in twenty-four hours too… but… this is your baby. I have known it all the time."

"But… Hague…"

"Stop this Hague. We will make it work, Francesca. Trust me. But you have to decide if you can take this girl, now," she said, placing her hand on my arm and looking at Rick.

My mind was racing.

"By what time?" asked Rick without missing a beat.

"We can do the entrega at 1:00 pm tomorrow," said Aurora. "I must apologise, as I won't be there. I am flying to Monterrey early in the morning. But I can arrange for someone to meet you at the Vifac offices at 11:00 am to sign the custody papers beforehand."

"Fine," said Rick. I nodded.

"Felicidades!" We hugged each other. Aurora's sincerity and her happiness for us shone through. She had made it happen for us. Just like she had promised.

We thanked her with endless hugs and left. Someone from DCSF who had never met us would look at a passport picture of Gaia and decide if she was right for us. Beyond belief. We as adoptive parents are asked to entrust our local councils and the DCSF with our most private and intimate details. They know everything about our lives, sexual relationships, fertility or lack of it, ex-partners and family history, bank accounts and work references. And yet we supply all this information only to find we are not trusted enough to meet our future child until someone has sent our social worker a tiny picture. It isn't just inhumane; it's insane. And it becomes more so when you are on the ground and can see with your own eyes what is going on and meet the people involved, yet you are not allowed to.

Aurora's son, Renato, had offered to drive us back to the sublimely titled European Lifestyle Apartments. We knew the place well already; it was where we'd stayed when we thought we might be able to adopt from Istituto Cabañas. It was also our home when Rick's father had his heart attack. The inhabitants were primarily Japanese or European businessmen, which made us an anomaly, but it seemed to endear us to the security guards, who always had a smile for us, the gringos with the rucksacks. Unfortunately Renato, like many young Mexicans, wanted to chat about football (Manchester United) and music. And naturally he was oblivious to our state of mind. To be sitting in that car answering questions about David Beckham and Noel Gallagher was rather like being high on drugs at your parents' dinner table, talking about your schoolwork.

As we neared our apartment, we realised we needed food. We hadn't eaten anything since breakfast, so we stopped for tacos and beer. The security guards greeted us like old friends, even bringing us up a drum of tap water. We dumped our rucksacks in the hallway and sat on one of the anonymous white, cold leather sofas in the living room shovelling our food down. Rick drained the last of his beer.

"We need to tell our parents."

"Before or after?"

"What?"

"Before or after the entrega."

"Before, as after…"

"…She will be ours."

"Our baby."

"*Our* baby."

"We have to get stuff tomorrow."

"Stuff for babies."

"What time does the supermarket open? We will need to get there early."

"Yep, we'll need a list."

"I'll get a pen."

Exactly what do you talk about when you have just found out you're going to become parents in under twelve hours?

15

Do Newborns Eat This?

"Do you realise that our baby daughter has kept me awake all night already?" yawned Rick, taking me in his arms.

We were lying facing each other.

"Our *daughter*."

"*Our* daughter."

"Yes, we *do* have children. A daughter. Can you imagine saying that?"

"Oh my God, Rick! Can you believe this? Today? Is this a dream?"

"Mmm."

He kissed me slowly. Our lips unlocked and he whispered, "No, this is very real. And now we have to go the supermarket to buy things for OUR girl."

We'd had no opportunity to think about what having a baby actually entailed. We didn't even have a list. We'd managed to get as far as thinking she would need clothes, bottles, nappies and a dummy, but that was it.

"What do babies eat?" Rick had asked the previous evening when, shell-shocked, we had tried to organise today's shopping expedition.

"Milk, silly."

"Oh, that's easy."

"No, special milk. You have to mix it up."

The fact was I had no idea what that special milk looked like or how to mix it up. My friends had all breastfed. Meanwhile I was going through my own version of 'baby brain', where I was floating in some kind of sweet ether with visions of our beautiful daughter in my head. So far on this trip I'd been able to think straight in the most demanding of situations. I'd known what to do and what to say. I'd been decisive, forthright and resourceful.

But why should I have been prepared for this? Back in the UK we'd been to training classes, talked to social workers and psychologists about what it would have been like to *raise an adopted child*, examining our motivations so we could all be sure we understood what we were in for. It was a process light-years away from the emotion that had suddenly invaded our lives: we were about to *have a baby*.

"It's going to be so much better," everyone had been telling us, "Just as if it was your child."

But this is going to be our child! I wanted to scream at them. A gift from a woman who could not take on this responsibility herself. Just that thought was enough to send me metaphorically flying and bring tears to my eyes.

Rick brought me back to earth with a thud. He was dressed and ready to go the supermarket.

"What on earth are you wearing?"

He was sporting thin cotton trousers, his old Adidas top, a woollen hat, a scarf, and a pair of Birkenstocks.

"You'll be freezing in those trousers. And no socks."

"We don't have any clean clothes. I can't bear to put dirty stuff on. And you know what it's like here; it's freezing now, and it will be boiling hot in an hour, so best to be dressed for both."

He was right. We had rucksacks full of dirty washing. My one set of dress-up clothes had been wrapped in a plastic bag to prevent them getting infected by the rest. I'd taken them out the previous night, hoping they would be OK for the entrega.

I threw a pashmina over a cotton dress and slipped on my battered Crocs. We really did look the part. We wanted to be at the supermarket early so we could have as much time as possible before going to Vifac to sign the papers at 11:00 am. So at 8:00 we presented ourselves at the mall, home to Wal-Mart. Nobody else appeared to be there.

"We're first," I said.

"It's not open," said Rick. As we got close up to the doors we could see that it was in fact firmly shut—for another two hours.

"Mexico. You have to love it," I said.

"We'd better grab a coffee."

Where else but Starbucks? It was the same branch we'd waited in for news of Rick's father's heart attack. Things had come full circle since then. After fearing for Jack's life, we were now about to welcome a new one. We found ourselves sharing our exciting news with the staff, who offered free coffee and muffins until we were well and truly stuffed.

At ten minutes to ten, we stood at the doors of the supermarket, our noses almost pressed against the glass. The doors opened and we grabbed a trolley each. Then we bolted like contestants in Supermarket Sweep until we found the right aisle. We paused, clueless, as we looked at shelves filled with packages featuring photographs and illustrations of happy babies at various stages.

"So what does a baby need?" Rick looked completely lost.

I picked up a packet of nappies.

"These," I said.

The nappies had a size chart on them indicating they were for a 5-10 kg baby. I realised I didn't even know how much our daughter weighed but figured 'Stage 1' nappies for a slightly lighter child would be best.

"Newborns!" I called out to Rick.

"What?

"It has to be stuff for newborns."

"Do you think she'll need this?" He was brandishing a jar of baby food.

"They don't eat that, Rick. Not yet." I knew that much.

"I'll get some just in case. She might want it in a few days."

Meanwhile I had discovered that a bottle was not a bottle: there were different sizes here, too. Even baby dummies were a different shape from toddler dummies. And when I wasn't sure, I threw in everything I could find. A padded suit for her to sleep in, though it seemed to be far too warm even for the cooler night temperatures; four kinds of milk; baby clothes in three sizes, all various hues of pink.

"Don't they do any other colours?" asked Rick, picking up another rosy package.

"Nope. Unless you want blue."

"I guess not." Even the blankets were pink or blue.

Rick had procured every toy in the store, most of which were really rather ugly. I packed in bottles, a steriliser, a kettle, and a bath. Then I looked at my watch.

"We're going to be SO late. Stop now! Come on!"

We sprinted towards the checkout, past employees who seemed reluctant to allow their shelf-stacking to disrupt their animated conversation. The woman at the checkout looked understandably confused at our haul. She couldn't see a baby either in my arms or my stomach.

"Ah! Did you see there is a two-for-one offer on bibs?" is all the lady at the counter could master.

Our trolleys were heavy and there was no way we'd get this monster haul home on foot, even if we'd had two extra pairs of hands. We paid, loaded the bags into the trolleys, and went outside to find a taxi. But Mexicans are not morning people, and the chances of a random taxi passing by in our slim time-frame were remote.

"We'll just have to walk," said Rick.

Theoretically, the walk was no distance. However, what lay between the mall and our temporary home was not a road but a motorway, where the pavement was minimal. And our heavy trolleys would have to be pushed up the road; 'up' being the operative word, as it was hilly. As the cars and trucks whizzed close by, tooting their horns at us, we put our heads down and pushed those trolleys with grim determination.

Breathless with our booty in tow, the looks on the faces of the security guards at our apartments were priceless. You could just see them thinking, "Truly these gringos are mad, perhaps even mentally ill." Again, this only seemed to endear us even more to them. Our request for help in taking everything upstairs was met with an immediate response. We asked them to order us a taxi in ten minutes.

The mobile rang just as we'd got in.

"Buenoooo." It was Aurora. My heart missed a beat. *This is it. There has been a mistake and it's all off.*

But Aurora was bubbling.

"I was at the airport and decided that my trip could wait. I cannot miss your entrega for anything in the world. I will be at Vifac waiting for you."

I told her we were running late. I showered and got ready.

I wore a silk black dress with tiny white dots. My hair was tied at the back, but some of my curls were cascading down my face. I wore tights I had picked up at the supermarket (my mum always told me you are not supposed to show skin in a Catholic church) and a pair of black shoes also bought at the Wal-Mart. I wanted to look good for the spiritual birth of my daughter. I threw a short black cotton top on so that my arms wouldn't show, and I made sure that my tattoo was covered. I didn't want to unnerve Aurora or the priest. I took a deep breath and went into the bedroom where Rick was ironing his brand new pale blue shirt.

"You always said that this colour goes well with my eyes."

"What trousers are you wearing?"

"The old-timer linen cream ones? Will they go well with these?"

It was the same cream suit he'd worn to our original council interview back in London. All that seemed a million years ago and a million miles away now. He picked up his new £10 black 'formal' shoes.

"Yes, perfect. Socks?"

"Shit, I forgot to buy them. I'll have to wear them without. Hopefully I won't get blisters. Should I put gel in my hair? How do women always know what to wear and how? I am lost, and you took five seconds to get ready!"

"Put this on and let's go. I'll prepare the baby room."

I wanted to make the baby's room look welcoming, so we put up the wall hanging I'd bought in Merida and scattered the strange supermarket toys on the bed. I filmed everything.

We were combed and brushed and there was just a final touch: we wanted to wear some jewellery we had bought for each other while in Merida. I asked Rick to help me put on the Mayan heart, a caracol necklace, he'd bought me. He'd requested a cross, which surprised me, as anything overtly religious normally makes him run a mile. Spiritual he may be, but the cross was a big step. Now, as we put our amulets on, I felt we were entering a new phase of our lives. We picked up the Moses basket, ran downstairs to the waiting cab, and jumped in.

I was calling on everything I'd ever learned in meditation to stay calm. Rick was sitting up very straight, as if he felt he had to show some outward symbol of the new responsibility we'd be taking on.

You and I are never going to be like this again. No more just us.
It was both a beautiful and terrifying thought.

Aurora was at Vifac to meet us. She had changed her mind about her trip out of town; she would not miss this day for anything, she said, and she was glowing. We were given papers that effectively said the baby had been relinquished to Vifac. That meant the birth mother had relinquished any rights. In the cool and quiet of her office, we signed.

"Felicidades, papa!" said Aurora as Rick's eyes filled with tears.

"Tell her she's made me the happiest man in the world," he said. I relayed the emotion to her.

And then it was time to go to the church. Our baby had already been taken to the church by Sabina, the maid. We were driven by

Aurora to the same church where we had attended the entrega on St Joseph's day. It looked even more beautiful in the sunshine. Aurora disappeared and left us to read our notes sat on the wooden benches.

The core of the ceremony required Rick and I to recite our commitment to our baby and to ask God to protect our daughter. It had to be done in Spanish. It was already prepared and printed on tiny bits of paper, which portrayed the Virgin of Guadalupe on one side and the words on the reverse. I coached Rick, as we would have to speak the words at the same time. We practised on the steps outside in the sunshine, then walked in holding hands. It was like getting married, but the emotion today was on a level far above what I'd felt back then.

Today, Aurora was our only audience. We didn't know anyone in Guadalajara. She asked me how the camera worked, as she wanted to film the ceremony so that we could show our families in Europe when we got back. As she fiddled with the camera, we sat on the pews and continued to rehearse quietly. Then I turned the little paper over and kissed the image of the Virgin of Guadalupe. I smiled, thinking of how appropriate it was that this country's protector is a woman. The women of Mexico had made a miracle happen. And a little Mexican woman was about to enter my life forever.

Aurora suddenly stood up and told us to do the same as the priest entered the church from the back, the baby in his arms. It is a moment that will remain carved in my memory forever. He handed her to me, this adorable bundle wearing a pink dress with a strawberry motif, and the tiniest of hair clips on her hairy head.

As I told my mother later, you had to be there. I could try to describe how I felt, but it all comes down to one thing: God had decided. There really is not much you can say when you are blessed with a new soul for the first time. It's probably why natural mothers give the stock answer of "it was the most beautiful moment of my life." We were giving birth, albeit in a different way, a spiritual birth, as Vifac say.

"Ciao, Gaia," I said, kissing her on her forehead.

"Yes, Gaia," said Rick. We had to name her, but we had not had much time to think about that. Because she would already have a multi-cultural background, we wanted a name that would work in Italian and English, but also in her native Spanish. When we thought we were adopting Beatriz, we felt that it would have been wrong to change the name of a two-year-old. In this instance, however, her birthmother had explicitly asked for her baby to be given a name by her new parents. We'd been considering Maya—for obvious reasons—as well as Sara, Claudia, or Gaia. But Gaia seemed right; like Mother Earth, she was here as a result of primordial chaos.

The priest was most generous, using his understanding of Latin to include some Italian in the ceremony. Rick and I managed to keep it together long enough to read our blessing. The priest then said a few more words while I held her, after which we all prayed. The ceremony was over. Rick shook the priest's hand so hard I thought he'd break it. When he was satisfied he'd let God know how grateful he was, I handed Gaia to him, and he didn't give her back for two days. I knew I loved my husband, but watching him with Gaia ignited something much stronger. It was love, yes, but far more profound than what had brought us together. He had turned my dream into ours. We had expanded. This was what it was all about.

Aurora had offered to give us a lift back. "Do you want me to wait while you feed her?"

"We were going to do it at home. We have no milk with us…"

"Dios mio, Francescaaa! Don't you know she needs feeding every three hours? It's already been two and half. We'd better go via my house."

Sabina, whom we'd met barely twelve hours earlier, was there to help. She showed us the correct milk powder and explained how much we needed to use and how to mix it with sterilised water.

"She will also need these," Aurora said, handing over a white paper bag full of medicines.

"What are they for?" I asked.

"The baby had an umbilical cord infection. She also has a throat infection, so she will need to take antibiotics. You must use this syringe to put the liquid into her mouth. The cream is for her belly button."

Panic swept me. Suddenly we had a four-day-old baby who was also unwell.

"How many times a day? When do we stop using medicine?"

"I don't know. Read the instructions or call the doctor on the label," said Aurora, hurrying us to the car.

That was it. Our induction into parenthood was over. As we got back into the car, I couldn't help asking the question that had been bothering me for days:

"What about the birth mother?"

I wasn't kidding myself. None of this was remotely 'natural'. We weren't going home from the hospital beaming with pleasure at our effort, to meet a crowd of parents, friends and nurses with balloons, 'It's a girl!' cards, and soft toys. Gaia was in the back of the car in her basket being comforted by Rick, while somewhere else, another woman was heading back home without her baby. Who was she? How did she feel?

There was not much to tell, according to Aurora. She was thirty-four. She was also called Maria, or maybe not. Often women leave a false name in order not to be traced, and this could have been the case with Gaia's birth mother, since she had given an identical name for both herself and her daughter. That was why she had requested that the baby's name be changed by her new parents.

She had three daughters, aged 17, 15 and 13. She was separated from her husband and lived with her grandparents in a small village. At some point she'd had an affair with a married man. The details of whether he was local or possibly from the US were blurred.

She found out she was pregnant and, like all the other women here, knew that to let this become public would have meant not just being judged, but cast out. Furthermore, her ex-husband, who was giving her money for their children, would have had nothing to do with her if he'd found out. Her position was untenable, and she had to act, as she couldn't afford to be seen to be pregnant even by her daughters.

'Maria' had been working as a security guard at a supermarket in her village. When she left for Guadalajara, she announced she had a chance to do better paid work for a friend. Everyone seemed to accept this, although it was not hard to imagine, either, that everyone knew it was a pretence. As long as appearances were kept up, everyone was satisfied.

Unlike 80% of the women at Vifac who change their mind about giving up their child, Aurora said Maria was adamant she was not going to take her baby with her when she left. There was no way she could go back to the village with a newborn baby. After the birth, Maria had asked to spend the first night with her. Aurora thought she had changed her mind. But no, she had not. If she took this baby home, she would lose everything she ever had, including her other daughters. Nonetheless, Aurora wondered if she would show at the notary's office the next day in Colima. She did, her eyes swollen with tears. She had been crying all night.

"I just need to know where to sign," she'd said. After she gave her baby one last hug, she disappeared. That was the moment Conception looked into the baby's eyes and decided it was a sign from God that she needed to tell us the truth, making the phone call that changed all our lives.

And that is all I was told about my daughter's life before we met her. I don't even know if her mother breastfed her when she was born.

❦

We returned, exhausted, to our apartment, and this time I thought our security guards were going to have heart attacks. When they saw us with the baby they were beside themselves. We explained, and they were effusive in their congratulations. I'll bet my last dollar that we gave them something to talk about for some time afterwards.

We took Gaia upstairs and introduced her to her room. Then it was time to introduce our daughter to our families; she was a truly modern baby who would meet her grandparents and uncles for the first time via Skype and webcam. After this, bed. As the three of us lay together, I looked up at the ceiling and prayed.

Tonight, Maria, mother of Gaia, I wish I knew you. I wish you were here and we were getting drunk on tequila together. We would be laughing and crying as we abused this sexist world that has made you do this, shouting who the real hero is and swearing loyalty to each other forever. We'd take it out on religion, politics, and the system.

But you are not here. Where are you? Are you on a bus back to your little village, your eyes swollen with tears, your hormones confused, your tummy barren again? Are you wondering what people will say when you get back? Will they know what really happened? Will anyone guess? Will you be able to look in the eyes of your children?

She was not an awful person. She was a good person in an awful situation, who did what women all over the world do every day. She searched for a way to give her baby a better life than she thought she could offer. For that brave act alone, she deserves more than a second thought.

16

Red Wine, Green Poo

I recall a friend having her first baby, a career woman who for nine months wondered if she would know what to do with a newborn. The first day she came out of hospital, I went to visit her, and she looked in her element. There was a complete air of confidence and calm about her. And it evidently translated to the child, who seemed utterly content.

"How," I asked her, "do you already know what to do with a baby?"

"You just do, and it's really rather easy," she answered while deftly picking her baby up, propping him at her breast. "You know, I surprised myself. When the midwives handed him to me my first reaction was, 'I can do this.'"

She could indeed, but I've met natural mothers who admit they have no idea how to deal with a newborn, and also heard of many others who found the bonding process hard. That latter part wasn't an issue for me: I loved this little girl and wanted to do my best for her. However as Rick and I prepared for our first night as parents, I felt inadequate and maternally underprepared. Not surprisingly, I'd buried my uncertainties in a series of functional and somewhat military preparations for the first night with our new baby.

We had our bottles prepared for the three-hour feeds. We had nappies and baby clothes organised. Nappy rash cream. Baby wipes. We even had the bath out just in case. It was now about 7:00 pm, but it could have been 2:00 am. For the past forty-eight hours my adrenalin had been running on code red, with the result that now I was over-hyped and over tired. Whenever I thought about sitting down, I worried I might be missing something.

"Is there something else we should be doing?" I asked Rick.

"Well, we should go to bed, so we can sleep until she wakes up. But how about I order us some takeaway first, Fra? You need food."

My last meal was lost in time somewhere, and I realised I was actually very hungry. I also needed to calm down. So while Rick went downstairs to order us some Thai takeaway, I opened a bottle of red wine and poured myself a glass.

I heard Gaia begin to cry, so I went in and picked her up. I felt stupidly clumsy as I took my daughter in my arms. *My daughter.* What was she crying about? It wasn't feeding time yet. I had no idea if this was a normal amount of crying. Was there such a thing? I blamed my inexperience for her discomfort. Even though she'd barely been on this earth a few days, this little creature had gone through a lot, and I felt that she just didn't seem right with me.

And yet when Rick took her it was different; she seemed to relax with him and fall asleep on his chest. At the time, I suspected it had something to do with the fact that she knew I wasn't her birthmother.

Finally, she stopped crying. I kissed her and laid her back in her basket on the bed while I sipped my wine. I knew Rick would be a while since Mexicans don't really do 'fast food', even when they say they do.

❦

"I know this is all very confusing, little one. You don't know me. I am not the woman who carried you for nine months, who kept you safe and warm. Now you are outside and it is very strange."

My mother had told me not to take her outdoors in her first few days.

"That's not what you do with newborns. Think about it. They have been in the womb for nine months. It's traumatic enough to be out of it, let alone outdoors."

But it was too late for that. This tiny angel had spent the first night of her life in her birthmother's arms, where the smell and rhythm were all familiar to her. And then she had to leave that natural and reassuring place, but not, like so many babies, to go home to a joyful welcome. Instead, she had boarded a rickety, noisy bus to Colima, her birthmother probably clutching her close to her heart, trying not to think about the desperate action she was about to take.

Did your mother cry on the bus? Did you realise she was crying because it was the last journey you would ever take together? Is she crying now, deep down inside where nobody else can see?

"Your mother signed those papers because she loved you. She loved you so much she wanted you to have a shot at a proper life. She had to save you. And herself."

And then in Colima her brave, wretched mother signed and handed her own baby over to Aurora. There would be another journey, this time in the padded seats of Aurora's luxurious car to Guadalajara and into the arms of someone else, an experienced maid. Another new smell, a different heartbeat, another unrecognisable set of voices. All inside the space of forty-eight hours.

"Then you came to the church. There was the incense and the priest and you were finally passed to us. And amidst more new smells and voices and new languages you had to trust us. You poor little girl. No wonder you have developed infections. You were not brought softly and gently into this world; you were thrown into it. I wish I knew how to make this better. I promise you I am going to give it my best shot, even though I suspect there are some things I won't understand until you get older. You are the best thing that has ever happened to me, to us, and I can only hope that you grow up knowing that you are loved and that our love can not only help you grow and flourish but also justify the courageous actions of your brave mother. Sono la tua mamma per sempre sai."

I told her I was her 'forever mum'. "I will never leave you, ever, not ever..."

I remember her breathing getting deeper and her eyes closing as she went to sleep. I had another sip of wine, and suddenly I felt heavy. And after that, apparently I fell into the arms of Morpheus. According to Rick I stirred slightly when he came back, but was unable to move or talk. He pulled me up and dragged me into the bedroom where I did not move until well into the morning. When I did, I had no idea where I was.

"What is that noise? "

"It's the baby crying, you nutter."

"What baby?" I asked.

I had fallen asleep and forgotten everything! Drugged by the drama and emotion of the past forty-eight hours, I had blanked out completely. I had barely drunk the glass of wine, but even so I had gone down spectacularly. Meanwhile, Rick informed me he had done all the night feeds, changed Gaia twice, and it was time to feed her again.

"Now, I think the best thing for you is to get up and do your bit."

I got up to find Gaia wearing clothes that looked all wrong to me, but a bottle was ready for her. I fed her, successfully produced a burp, and changed her. The colour of her poo ensured I was well and truly awake by now. It was bright green. Babies do not have green poo on a good day. Something was wrong.

I needed to talk to someone quickly. I got on the computer and saw that Fulvia, my primary school friend and single mother to my godson, was on Skype. She would know what to do.

"Bright green poo," I typed. "Help."

"What on earth did you give her?" replied Fulvia.

"Milk! What else should I been giving her? Pasta? It's the right dose. I read it on the jar and I have personally prepared the bottles with sterilized water before putting them in the fridge."

"WTF. Are you insane? Tell me you didn't give it to her straight from the fridge!"

"Whhhyyyyy…?"

"You idiot. It's common sense. The temperature of the milk has to resemble as much as possible being fed by a breast, so really we're talking lukewarm. Look, it's nothing you can't fix, but you'll need medicine for colic."

"Shit."

"Yeah, seriously, shit. Look, go and get some colic drops now, quick, and tell me how you get on. Quick. Ciao."

"Rick, we have screwed up…"

He didn't panic, but he didn't hesitate either. Even though he'd been up all night, there was not a word as I told him what we needed and how to say it in Spanish.

"I'll run." And I knew he would.

I needed more reassurance. I contacted my French friend Aurelie.

"OK, Francesca, so every three hours you feed her and make sure you burp her properly. You have to prepare the milk just before you give it to her, not beforehand, or it will go rotten. Then wait until it's lukewarm. Run the bottle under cold water to make it cooler, but don't add new water. Give her mint tea now—make sure it is lukewarm—and don't bathe her till she is better. Wipe the umbilical cord – but not with fluffy stuff! And leave her unclothed so it can get fresh air for a while. D'accord?"

I understood what to do, but I was terrified. I didn't want to make mistakes. I wanted to do this right and already I had failed. Suddenly this little creature's life was in my hands, and short of falling asleep on her basket, I hadn't really done very much. I had fought every step of the way for this child—and there was still much to be done—and yet I had already let her down. I was annoyed at myself. It was the first of many moments when I have questioned whether I am being a good mother, and indeed the very notion of what a good mother is.

🐟

We weren't even halfway home yet. We had Gaia but, according to Hague, we were not allowed to sleep with her so we had to take her back to the Vifac casa every evening only to return at the crack of dawn to take care of her again. There was much paperwork to be done before DIF and DCSF agreed that we could officially be her permanent guardians.

Meanwhile, DIF Colima wanted us to meet their psychologist. Mañana, they said. It would be routine, whatever that meant. It came completely out of the blue, and it presented real problems for us as we had to embark on the five hour trip with our newborn baby and leave her with Cristy, Alfonso's teenaged assistant who was charged with her first experience of nappy changing and bottle feeding.

A word to the wise: when Mexicans say mañana (tomorrow) you can never be sure they mean it. But just in case they do, you have to turn up. When we arrived in Colima, the psychologist said she was too busy.

"You have to go. Come back mañana." She actually came out from her office to tell us that.

"No, we are here now. We can't go back to Guadalajara and come back again."

"Well, I don't really have time for this."

Jesus. It was her job, and yet she acted like she was doing us a favour. We hadn't asked to come here.

"OK, we will sit on this bench and wait till you are finished, even if it means waiting until tomorrow," I said, sitting down and pulling Rick down too.

"All right, come in."

This was never going to be a chat: it was an inquisition. She didn't even get chairs for us. We stood in front of her desk.

"Can't you have your own baby?" The question was delivered with the warmth of a winter's day in Moscow.

Oh God, not this again. I looked at Rick, who understood what she'd said.

"We want to help one…" It sounded lame when it came out, even if it was true.

She glared, first at Rick, then at me, tapping her biro on the desk.

"We in Mexico don't need your help. And why take one of our babies away when you can have your own?"

I tried to explain that we meant it from the heart and had spent a long time in Mexico risking our jobs, and in fact our lives, to find the right child. I told her we turned down illegal requests, hoping it would help.

"Leaving your jobs was irresponsible, and I am not interested in your life story, or supposedly charitable efforts. I want to know why I should let you take this baby away from her country."

After talking to so many wonderful women at DIF and Vifac, we were in shock. Nothing we said seemed to move her. She'd effectively killed the conversation before we had a chance. Ten minutes later we were out of there, a harsh report no doubt trailing in our wake.

"What the fuck was that all about?" said Rick.

"About reminding us that we are not Mexican and we have no right to be here, I think," I replied.

It was, of course, about power. And games. In Mexico those games were never far away, even with so-called friends. Conception had tried it on two days after we were given custody of Gaia. While I was getting ready for Tulum, I received an emotional phone call from her.

"Hello, Francesca."

"Conception. How are you?" She was crying.

"I have broken my arm and it is very bad. I don't trust the doctor in Colima, so I need five hundred dollars to see the doctor in Guadalajara, who will fix me. I need an X-ray."

Five hundred dollars is a lot of money in Mexico. An X-ray probably costs $5.00. I knew what she was doing: she had saved us from adopting Beatriz and brought us Gaia, and now she was calling in her debt. It wasn't malice—it was just the way things were done here.

I put the phone down and told Rick.

"Offer her fifty. That should more than cover it."

I called her back. "Conception, I can give you fifty dollars and buy you the bus ticket, OK? And you can stay with us here at the lifestyle flats, so no worries about accommodation."

Suddenly she didn't need a ticket or a trip to Guadalajara.

"Thank you, Francesca, but I now don't need to come. I will take the fifty dollars when you come to Colima for your next meeting with Pepe and Alfonso."

By a strange coincidence—or not—around that time Pepe had also asked for money. His reasoning was that he needed a thousand pesos for all the work he had done (not a lot so far) and for petrol.

When you're in a foreign country, you have to go with the flow. At the same time you don't want to be taken for a sucker, so it's a careful balance. I was now wondering if Pepe knew Conception had a broken arm, or even if he was in league with her. When we turned up at their offices, Conception was wearing some kind of bandage, which she could have put on herself for all I knew. I found myself slipping $50.00 into the bandage as I said hello and hugged her. As an Italian, secret exchanges of money are all part of the deal. For Rick, however, it was all a bit surreal.

Meanwhile, we received news that the mythical Alfonso had returned from his sojourn. It was the 18th of April, and he wanted us to join him the next day while he attended a big Vifac meeting at Ajijic, a place that already had memories for Rick and I. It would, he said, be an ideal time to discuss the best route forward in terms of paperwork.

Alfonso's attitude on the phone suggested that the entire Dolores episode had not happened. He sounded genuinely friendly, happy to get to meet us, and overjoyed that we had Gaia. He did, however, mention that we needed to discuss money. I phoned Aurora, who had not planned to be at the meeting because she was unwell. Immediately she changed her mind and decided to come.

"I want to see how much he charges. I need to have words with him. I expect him to charge you our standard fee, but I bet he will try and charge you more because you are foreigners."

The conference hotel could have been anywhere in the world, except for the stunning view of the lake. Because it was Vifac, Gaia could be present. We walked in and looked at the table settings. There were the usual pads and pencils of course and up front there was a white board. But it was the huge bottles of tequila on each table that caught our eyes.

"Told you," I said. "They don't move a muscle without it."

Aurora came towards us, accompanied by a man who was short but whose face and head shape suggested he should have been a foot taller. It was Alfonso.

"Hola, amigos!" he hugged us both.

"Alfonso, mucho gusto."

Along came Pepe, Anna and Chita. Our entire Vifac family was all there.

Aurora sidled up to me. "I have told him not to fuck with you, OK?"

I smiled, and so did Rick when I told him. God, I loved that woman.

The rest of the day went well. Vifac had asked me to join some of their visioning sessions. Rick swam and read and looked after Gaia. Later we went to the village to have a look around, then joined everyone else for dinner and tequila. Alfonso seemed OK. The chat with Aurora seemed to have sorted a few things out.

But the fact remained that we were in limbo. We had a baby but we didn't fully have a baby. The psychologist's report, predictably bad, coupled with the fact that DCSF had gone into radio silence with DIF had made it such that DIF's procuradora didn't trust us. It was all going to get very hard and very messy until DCSF and DIF agreed. And right now nobody was moving.

🐷

There are far easier, less harrowing ways to find out how much patience and faith you possess than sweating on the details of your baby's adoption in Mexico. Rick had definitely lost his cool, and was increasingly agitated. He'd figured we'd done the deal and somehow this should be sorted by now. The heat was getting to him, as was our confinement. I seemed to be dealing with it a lot better, having consciously or subconsciously adopted the Mexican 'mañana' approach. I wasn't exactly ecstatic, but I was coping. He, on the other hand, had a major attack of cabin fever, both literally and figuratively, and there wasn't a great deal we could do to alleviate it. The heat was utterly oppressive, so taking Gaia out for a long time was out of the question. As a result, our walks tended to be back and forth to the mall, trying to pass the time between meals when we would return 'home' with our baby. Except that we didn't have a home and, theoretically, we really didn't have a baby.

"An email exchange between DIF and DCSF that's all we need, that's all, this is unreal," Rick blew up

"The mere fact that we have to follow this charade despite being right here with our baby entrusted to us by Vifac is insane," I had to agree.

"After all the information they require about us, the months of investigation into our lives and everything else surely they could send an email and put us out of our misery?" and on and on we went, stuck in a rut.

An email exchange should really have not been an issue. But because Mexican broadband is not always what it should be, DIF had used Hotmail, and as a result it appeared that DCSF did not believe it was an official email at first, so they decided not to reply and 'investigate' instead. For days. Meanwhile, we were sitting there with Gaia, the baby who was ours, but who seemed to belong to everyone else right now, or ironically nobody.

Back in the world of Mexican bureaucrats, things were not going well either. The procuradora at DIF in Colima had decided she didn't trust DCSF either since the gringos had not been returning her emails, so was not happy with the idea of foreigners adopting her Mexican child. Whether this had been fuelled by her psychologist's instant and frankly irrational dislike of us, we did not know, but she was not going to work with the DCSF until we found the birthmother and brought her to speak to her, a sudden requirement that came out of nowhere. We had more chance of seeing God in person, since nobody even knew her real name, and she knew that.

Alfonso had suggested that if we kept having trouble with DIF and DCSF we should dump the idea of a Hague adoption and go the private route. We would go to court privately, adopt Gaia in Mexico, and then have her readopted in the UK. It seemed a great idea, and the easiest way to proceed, but we were determined to stick to the Hague process all the way, plus DCSF weren't having it. They had introduced their own rule of not allowing private adoptions in Hague countries, even thought it is perfectly legal, and that was that.

Rick often commented that we couldn't really enjoy our first few weeks with Gaia because we were so terrified we would lose her. I was doing my very best to live in the moment, and I think I managed a pretty good job of it. However Rick was not faring well. He was constantly worrying Gaia would be taken away, and this only served to make him more agitated in the repellent heat. And so, in typical Rick style, he decided something—anything—had to happen. While various lawyers and governments were dragging their feet, we had to get our little family out of the confinement of the European Lifestyle Apartments.

We, that is Rick, decided that we would all go to Manzanillo.

"It's by the ocean, and also much closer to Colima. And Aurora would be close by," he reasoned. She had a house there where she was spending some time, as did Pepe's friends whom he often visited, so we would be among friends, and hopefully that would give us some reassurance.

We booked an apartment via the internet at 'Las Hasadas' club, perennial hangout of rich and famous Mexicans and Americans. It was the hotel made famous by Bo Derek in the movie *10*. We couldn't believe how cheap it was and the pictures looked fantastic.

On arrival we realised that Bo had left and taken all the charm, luxury and indeed people with her. Our flat was another serviced apartment, on the ninth floor of the building. Though it had a jacuzzi it was broken and smelly, and it was pretty useless in every other respect. There was no air circulating, which made it even hotter than Guadalajara. The view from the balcony was breathtaking, but instead of whales, we saw oil tankers going by twice a day. The freezing dirty waters of the ocean meant that we couldn't swim. It was too hot to enjoy the jacuzzi. The town itself was rather uninspiring, just a long road full of supermarkets and shops, and a small market in the old part of town. Still, it wasn't the highway in Guadalajara, and we had a sea view, which made us feel cooler even though we weren't.

✦

"Arrrhh! Rick! Quick!"

It was the 30th of April, our second morning in Manzanillo, when I opened Gaia's nappy and found blood. Rick ran in. His face went white, but he immediately rang the paediatrician in Guadalajara on his mobile, who said the first thing we needed to do was find a lab and get some tests done. Then we were to ring him with the results. A lab. Hmm. We wrapped the smelly nappy and drove to town to find one.

We saw signs for the lab, but couldn't find it because it didn't look like one, more like some illegal shop front. There were curtains instead of doors, and the man who greeted us was wearing a white cowboy hat, which didn't inspire confidence.

"It's OK," I said. "Look, he has certificates on the wall."

"Oh yeah," said Rick. "Where did he buy those from?"

The man told us he couldn't test 'old poo', so we had to throw the dirty smelly nappy we had been carrying away, and wait for Gaia to fill a new one. He took a stool sample from it and told us to come back in an hour for the results. We received them and then read them out to our paediatrician on the phone from the lab itself.

"Ahh, I see, parasites. That is what it is. You will need to get the medicine and start giving it to her straight away."

Barely a month old, our child was already on her fourth course of antibiotics.

"You have to act girl, you can't keep on going like this," were Aurora's precious words. "You need to take this girl home and we can't keep on looking after her in the evening, it just doesn't work. Listen to Alfonso and step out of Hague, it's the best thing you can do now."

Even Anne from London seemed to agree that was our best course of action, especially since she knew that DCSF had no intention in moving.

Next task would be to get our dossier back from DIF so that we could go to court. And that was when I decided I needed to do something to shake them into action since they were hanging on to our documents, refusing to release them to us so that our decision to proceed privately could not go ahead.

"This really feels like a personal vendetta," Rick had remarked.

"They just keep shifting the goalposts."

"It's Mexico, darling. They don't just shift the goalposts, they steal them and burn them."

He was right. It did feel like the procuradora at DIF was using us as an example; it was as if we were the foreigners she had chosen to put through hell just to show that though adoptions were possible, they were not going to give up their Mexican kids that easily.

Alfonso and Pepe were really trying hard to make them see reason. Alfonso, in particular, had turned out to be a loving and caring human being who would not hesitate to reassure us. But Rick's anger was palpable. I rang DIF in Colima again and spoke to one of the procuradora's assistant, who said:

"Sure, we have finished with your papers. You can pick them up." Except when we rang him to say we were coming in to do so, he had disappeared. The only thing to do was to contact the Mexican Ministry of Foreign Affairs.

"Yes, they are your papers now and you should have them," they told us.

But how were we going to get our papers out of the procuradura's vice-like grip? I sat down to write a letter to her. Aware that in Mexico the kind of businesslike directness we employ in the UK would not go down well, I did my best to keep the letter as diplomatic as possible. Or so I thought. To check my Spanish, I emailed it to my friend Oscar.

"Híjole! Eres completamente loca!"

In other words, Oscar was horrified. I had overstepped the mark big time.

"Truly, Francesca, I can understand your frustration, but this letter is mad. It's like setting fire to DIF. We must speak."

I suppose I had wanted the letter to be somewhat incendiary, though I understood what Oscar meant. Speaking to him was problematic, given our flat's location and the time difference with Argentina. We couldn't get any internet signal in our flat. The access to email and the web had been our lifeline for this whole trip, and without it we were desolate. The only place where the computer would pick up broadband was downstairs, outside the office. It was, in effect, the car park.

And that is how I came to be in a garage at 5:00 am on the 4th of May. I had asked the superintendent of the building to keep the broadband on. He'd also thoughtfully kept a light on, one that had attracted a swarm of wasps. I am allergic to wasp stings, to the point where I keep the adrenaline antidote with me in case I am stung, as they can be fatal . Except the medicine was upstairs. Given my other problems, the possibility of dying that morning had slipped my mind. OK, here goes, I thought.

"Where the hell are you? I can only see cars behind you. Where are you sitting, in a garage?" asked Oscar on Skype.

"Sure," I replied. "Where else should I be at 5:00 am? You look much more cosy in your bed!"

He laughed, and then his tone changed abruptly.

"OK, Francesca, we have a problem, sweetie. This letter you have written—and I understand where you are coming from—will blow the roof off the house and get you nowhere. These people will hate you and you will be in serious trouble. I mean it."

"Why?"

"You have used language that has touched their pride and questioned their power. Frankly, I wouldn't be surprised if they sent someone to kill you. They murder people for less in Mexico."

"Crikey."

"Look, you cannot confront them. No way, OK? So what I have done for you is toned it down and taken out anything I think will upset them too much."

"So now it won't get me killed?" I laughed, meanwhile crouching to avoid a wasp.

"Well, it's a lawless land," he said, "so we can never be sure."

Despite Oscar's attempts to nullify my excesses, the letter caused a furor, not least because I had cc'd the Ministry of Foreign Affairs. The procuradora immediately wanted to meet me, and even before doing so she agreed she would release the papers to Alfonso's office, which she duly did. That meant Pepe, since Alfonso was missing in action somewhere as usual.

Gaia was improving on the medicine, though I couldn't help thinking about what all those antibiotics were doing to her tiny little digestive system. Still, the objective was to make my baby well, and this was the way to do it. Meanwhile, Rick's boss, understandably anxious at his absence, wanted to know when he would be coming back. The worldwide credit crunch was starting to impact everything, and as he worked for a financial services company, they needed him back in action. Rick assured him that he would be back in the office by June 1st, which suddenly seemed impossibly close.

The pressure cooker was filling up with ingredients. Whether the lid would blow off was up to us.

♠

Eventually the procuradora had no choice but to release our papers. We had to go to collect them in Colima, and we had to do it without Gaia, who still did not officially exist. Not as our daughter anyway. This time, Alfonso's sister's secretary was happy to look after her. When we arrived to drop Gaia off, I couldn't help noticing the woman's own toddler had lush, shiny hair. I was eager to know how the Mexicans did it; no matter who they were, they all seemed to have such lovely thick hair.

It was apparently very simple. "Oh, we shave their heads when they're young. Everyone does it, and it means the hair grows back very quickly."

I was very impressed, though Rick didn't seem to think anything of it. He was in discussion with Alfonso regarding what to say to the procuradora. Alfonso looked tense.

The four of us, Alfonso, Pepe, Rick and I, enjoyed a huge lunch with a few beers while we waited for the phone call summoning us to the procuradora's office. It was all very casual, but this was the way they did things here. I was tense at the thought of seeing the procuradora, so I struggled to eat. Even the guys joking about Mexican politics and their plan to make a movie out of our little adventure—with Danny De Vito starring as Alfonso and Harry Potter as Pepe—didn't help too much.

Alfonso's mobile rang.

"It's her," he announced. We all stopped talking.

"Bueno, si que gusto, licenciada." Alfonso was speaking with deference. He was, as we say in the UK, sucking up to her big time.

"Yes, well, I am so sorry. I know about the letter, yes. You see, they are Europeans, and they are different from us, strange. When you tell them you will do something by a certain time, they kind of expect it to happen, so they got a bit upset when things were held up at your end. Really, they are very nice people, and they are very sorry for any misunderstanding. I pass along their apologies."

I gestured to Alfonso that this was enough, and he should stop apologising.

"Hey, Francesca, you have caused enough trouble with the letter. Of course we will get the papers now, thanks to you, but shhhhhh, OK?"

It was Pepe whispering, and perhaps he was right. There's no doubt we found the cultural gulf difficult at times; for us tomorrow morning is tomorrow morning, preferably with a determined time. For Mexicans, and indeed many other Latins, it means some point in the future, but not necessarily pre-determined. But it was their country, so officially we were the strange ones.

Rick and I went to DIF with Alfonso, leaving the jovencito to go back to the office. En route he'd suggested that it would be best if only he went in. I could see that he was literally shaking with fear.

"Do you think she'll eat him?" I said to Rick.

"Nah, not meaty enough."

Finally, he remerged with our precious folder in his hands.

"She has asked to speak to you, Francesca."

Rick took my hand.

"No, just you," she said, appearing at the door. I went in, my back straight and my shoulders square, determined to show her I was not intimidated. I knew I had challenged her power with my letter and in some ways I had probably humiliated her. But it wouldn't have happened if she hadn't played the power card first. She looked at me coldly, gestured at the chair so I'd sit down, and she did the same.

"I have asked to see you because there are a few things you need to understand. You challenged me with your letter, without knowing why I was doing what I was doing. Here at DIF we need to protect children, and we believe that no matter what, they are better off with their birth families, even when they are beaten by their parents."

That's a bit flawed, surely.

I had to keep quiet. The previous night on the phone Oscar had said, "Remember, Francesca, respect. It's all about that. Keep your pride for yourself."

"So… you can have your papers now, and I wish you the best of luck with it all and your girl, and I truly hope we can work together again in the future."

Hmm sure.

I had to say something.

"Thank you, licenciada, that's very kind. As you know, we cannot wait any longer, and her birthmother isn't to be found anywhere. We love this child, and if she were to go back into the system to wait for her birthmother to be interviewed by you, she would never leave it. And I think that would be a tragedy."

"You may say so, but our institutes are extremely well run, and if she were to remain there she would still have very happy life."

Happier than with a loving family?

I knew two things. Adopting Gaia was the only chance to give our little girl the future she deserved, not the one the procuradora felt was right. I also understood that there was little point in arguing with this woman.

"You are right. I have seen DIF's homes, and everyone was wonderful. Thanks so much again for helping us. It means a lot to us."

She got up and shook my hand.

"All the best."

I nodded, and with my back as straight as an army officer's I walked out to meet Rick and Alfonso. As soon as we got round a corner, Alfonso shouted.

"You did it, Francesca! We have got them!" We all hugged each other and jumped around with joy. We were one little step closer to getting our little baby girl home.

Back in Manzanillo, Rick took an afternoon nap while I took Gaia for a walk. I passed a hairdresser and my curiosity got the better of me. I decided to go in and ask about this business of thicker hair.

"Oh, yes," she said confidently. "Everyone does it. I can do it for you now."

I had no idea what I was expecting. I certainly didn't envision someone taking a cheap plastic man's razor to my daughter's head. The result was horrifying. My beautiful daughter did not look so pretty now. Her large baby's head stood out even more, like a boiled egg. I knew straight away I'd done the wrong thing. Noting my reaction, the hairdresser reassured me:

"It's going to take two weeks, and it will be back at the length it was a few minutes ago, you will see! And thicker!"

As I headed back to our apartment, I did my best to persuade myself she was right, but deep down I didn't believe it. Rick was having a beer when I got back. Before I could say a word, he looked down into the pram.

"Oh my God, what have you done?" Rick was staring down at Gaia, clasping his hands to his head.

"Well, you know how that lady told us they shave their heads. I thought I would try it with Gaia…"

"Fra, that is the most stupid thing you have ever done. She looks terrible."

"It will grow back soon. I'm sure, in two weeks apparently, or less," I said. "And you'll see, it will be thicker and lovelier than ever."

"What were you thinking? I mean, I know you're bored, but this takes the cake." He took another sip of his beer and shook his head at me.

All the talk of lush hair growth had proved to be the urban myth it probably was, at least in our case. It actually took eight months for Gaia's hair to return to the length it was before what became known as That Haircut. The next day was Mother's Day in Mexico, my first one. We sat and had a picnic on the beach with our bald, not-yet-fully-legal baby.

17

Have You Met Our New Old Friends?

The next morning, we were both irritable. We had been out with some American acquaintances until the wee hours. Rick had a hangover. The heat was making him testy. Last night, during conversation, it had become clear how much of nothing we were actually doing right now, and it was getting on Rick's nerves in a big way.

"I want to sort this out now," said Rick.

When we'd notified DCSF of our desire to proceed with the adoption, DCSF had inquired as to our status regarding nationality. My reply was this:

Dear Mr Kimberley,

So many thanks for your help and support at this stage. We have now discussed the details with Anne and have been meeting our girl every day since. As per your request these are our details:

Rick John Bailey born in Glasgow, Scotland on 06-02-71

Francesca Polini born in Rome, Italy on 11-10-1969

Rick holds a UK passport, Francesca an Italian one. Under EU regulations Francesca does not need a visa or any immigration permit to live and work in the UK. She has been living and working in the UK for 14 years to date.

Prior to leaving for Mexico, I'd sat through the British Citizenship test "Life in the UK" in order to get a British passport. However the Home Office in the UK had advised it would not be necessary, as I was a member of the EU and married to an Englishman. Our local council and various social workers had confirmed that only one of us needed to be British to adopt a child internationally. And then, suddenly, out of the blue, an email arrived from our council team leader, Anne. Apparently to adopt Gaia, I would need 'settled' status.

"What are they talking about?" said Rick. "You are bloody well settled."

"I have to prove I have been resident in the UK."

"How many times?" Rick was getting angry. "They already know that from all the work they've done on us at the beginning. How else could you have worked there for all that time?"

"Apparently I needed to prove to the Home Office that I have been resident all this time, and that would have given me a residency card. We need it."

"Oh, Jesus, what do we have to do now?" Rick was well and truly at the end of his tether. I wasn't too happy either, but I didn't let it show. It would just create more bad energy, and we didn't need it.

It seemed that DCSF and the Home Office wanted me to front up in Mexico City with my passport. I had to show it to the Italian Embassy, who would verify that it was legal and write a letter to confirm this to the British Embassy. Only a fool could have made this procedure up, but as I'd learned by now, government departments did apparently hire a large number of people whose job was to construct unworkable and ridiculous rules.

Speaking of jobs, it also seemed I had to ask my current employer and previous employers to say I had worked for them in the UK. More bureaucracy. And then, just to make it even more fun, my boss Thomas emailed, asking to meet in Mexico City. He had business there, and he needed to see me urgently. This did not feel good at all.

"At least I can see Thomas and the various embassies in one trip," I said.

"Fra, you amaze me. Only you would see a positive in this nightmare."

Both Rick and I agreed with Alfonso that getting DIF and DCSF to concur was going to be hard work, and so a Hague adoption was now out of the question. Moreover, the residency card would not have arrived on time. If we were going to get things done, we would have to take the more roundabout route.

We would have to go to court in Mexico, adopt Gaia, and then return to the UK and re-adopt her. That itself was fraught with problems, but right now the inability of DIF and DCSF to see eye to eye left us no alternative. And now that we had our papers, we could do it. We formally notified DCSF of our intention to step out of Hague, letting them know that if we waited any longer we would lose the baby, and so we were officially putting it in the hands of Mexican lawyers.

We'd actually booked our court hearing to adopt Gaia two weeks earlier. It would be happening in two days time, on the 14th of May. There was one small problem, however.

"You need two Mexicans who have known you for five years as witnesses," said Alfonso.

"I feel like I'm in a computer game where they just keep adding more levels," said Rick.

With Alfonso and Pepe we figured out our first witness. It would be Pepe's girlfriend, Isabel. She had spent time in Europe, and had worked for an NGO that was affiliated with mine. It was conceivable that we could have known each other over that time.

Then there was Renato, who worked for the Red Cross. He had spent time in America when Rick was doing a business degree there. Tenuous? You bet. But it was all we had, and like many things in Mexico, we had the feeling that this was more about appearances than anything else. Or so we hoped.

The hearing would take place early the next morning in Colima.

That night, we arrived at Alfonso and Pepe's office at 8:00 pm for our briefing. We were very touched that Alfonso had also invited us to stay over at his house. In effect this was his parent's house, since Mexicans tend to live with their parents unless they have a good reason not to, like getting married, and even then they don't always move out.

As always, Pepe and Alfonso had been somewhat cavalier with the details of what would happen in court. They'd neglected to tell us that Rick and I would do none of the talking, while our witnesses—who had known us very well for five years—would be doing all the talking on our behalf. So we were invited to rehearse the questions in their tiny office at 9:00 pm.

Pepe opened the proceedings.

"There will," he announced in a solemn tone to his audience, "be seven questions. There are always SEVEN questions."

With the utmost seriousness, he then proceeded to detail what those would be.

"First. Do you know these two people, Francesca and Rick?"

The witnesses looked at him intently.

"You will answer YES."

Both Isabel and Renato were assiduously taking notes. Pepe continued.

"Are they responsible parents?"

Isabel and Renato looked up from their note-taking.

"You will answer YES."

It transpired that the first six questions all required an emphatic yes. Pepe could have cut this bit short, but he was enjoying his moment.

"Then," he continued, "the complex part. You will each be asked if you would like to add something."

"Oh dear," muttered Rick under his breath. "Here is where it all goes pear-shaped."

By now, Pepe had acquired the demeanour of a military general addressing his troops before their final push. He paced the room, stopping in front of Isabel and Renato.

"YOU will say how you met each other, blah, blah, blah, and how you think this is a wonderful match."

And that was pretty much it. We went out for dinner and drank tequila to cement our relationship as true amigos. Then Rick and I accompanied Alfonso back to his home. The front door was opened by a diminutive old man, obviously Alfonso's father. There was no need for him to be up this late, but he had stayed up specifically to greet us with the Mexican mantra, "Mi casa, es tu casa." *My home is your home.*

As with every Mexican we had stayed with, we were shown incredible kindness. Alfonso gave us his room while he slept on the sofa. The next morning we woke up to a table laden with the most wonderful, tantalizing array of food.

"You need to eat properly today," said Alfonso. It transpired he had been up early to go the markets himself. I got ready in his room while Gaia sat in her car seat. As I was putting on makeup, I chatted to her about what an important day it was. When I finished, I picked her up and laughed.

"There is no way back now, girl! Let's make you look even prettier for the judge." She wore a pink hat that concealed her boiled-egg head, and a pink dress. We had our gorgeous breakfast and met Alfonso's mum. She was a tall, confident, well-groomed woman who clearly had her husband right where she wanted him.

"It's so good to meet you. Alfonso has told me so much about you; he refers to you as the European heroes."

I thanked her. "We are not heroes, just people who have love to give." The notion of doing something special or heroic via adoption did not sit well with me. After all, we were getting something out of it, too. While we were eating, Alfonso's sisters also arrived to wish us good luck, followed closely by Pepe.

"¡Buenos dias! ¿Como esta la pequeña Buda?"

Gaia had become the 'little Buddha.' Her bald head and her perfect posture in her chair made it inevitable.

We left early to meet our witnesses, or 'very good friends', as

Rick called them. Renato was wearing his doctor's uniform, as he was on call. Both he and Isabel were intently revising their notes from the night before. Rick took the opportunity to feed Gaia so that we wouldn't have to do it in court, while I spoke to Pepe about the proceedings.

"Where is Conception?" She hadn't been present for our last couple of meetings with Pepe.

"Oh, she has gone," Pepe said, in a tone which meant 'I say no more'. Had she been fired for telling us the truth? I made a mental note to ring her after the hearing.

The court hearing went well. It took place not in a courtroom, but the tiniest office room, with two desks and one little bench. On one desk, a heavily pregnant woman was typing away the answers of our witnesses on an ancient typewriter. On the bench next to her was the judge, Pepe, and Cristy, Alfonso's intern. We stood in a corner, holding Gaia.

The other desk was occupied by a woman who was buried under piles of papers and didn't seem to have anything to do with us. Every now and again someone would come in, squeezing past the three of us, and dump yet another pile of papers on her desk, then share a coffee, a cigarette, or a chat with her. It was about as informal as things got.

I couldn't help wondering if it was all a charade. Did the judge really expect that we'd known each other for so long? Isabel and Renato were wonderful, and as well as their six perfect 'yeses', they said some wonderful things about us that they seemed to have picked up the previous night. Moreover, the fact that Isabel was doing a doctorate, and Renato had turned up in a Red Cross ambulance, imbued the proceedings with a certain status. At the end of the questions, the pregnant typist insisted on hugging Gaia . She was due in two weeks and was expecting a baby girl, so she wanted to see what it felt like to hold her. Gaia looked lovely. None of this seemed very professional, but there was a great deal of goodwill, and a strong desire to help us.

We came out and hugged each other. It would be two weeks before the results were known, but Alfonso assured us that this was simply routine. Still, it was sometimes hard to know what to believe and what not to believe, and generally we still didn't feel 'safe'.

While everyone went off for lunch, I had to board a bus in the heat of the afternoon for my sojourn to Mexico City. Gaia had recovered from her most recent infection, but Rick assured me if there was any problem he would call the paediatrician.

I arrived late at night. Mexico City was an incredible place of fables and secrets, which at first didn't seem to be as dangerous as I'd imagined. It definitely had a different 'speed' from the rest of the country, though. My taxi driver who honked and buzzed around in a green Volkswagen Beetle drove me to the hotel that Cetty had booked for me. It was in the Delegación Benito Juárez, not far from her office.

The next morning, as I looked in the mirror, I saw a mother who was about to be unemployed. It didn't feel right, but my priority was to get our daughter home, so I wore my jeans, sandals, and white cotton shirt. I pulled my hair up so I wouldn't get too hot, put my sunglasses on my head, picked up my diary with all the addresses and phone numbers, and headed for breakfast. I sat at a table by the window, watching the Distrito Federal morning life, and had toast, jam and tea, before heading for my first stop, the Italian Embassy.

After a wait of about half an hour amongst loud Italians who were talking over each other, the clerk looked at my passport as if she had never seen one before, then gave me a letter I could take the British Embassy. There I met with Rob, a guy I had been speaking to on the phone. He gave the passport the overly-long scrutiny that you often get from border police at checkpoints, then plonked a few stamps in it that apparently made everything OK. Along with the evidence from various employers, this would all be sent to the Home Office, who would issue the residency card 'as quickly as possible', though they couldn't guarantee a timeframe.

Then it was off to do something nice. I had a lunchtime

interlude with Cetty, my colleague and friend who'd been helping us with translation and anything else we needed in Mexico City. I told her I was nervous about meeting Thomas.

"I bet he wants to tell me not to go back."

"No, I'm sure he wants you to come back... the guy who is replacing you is leaving early."

"No, he went funny on me a couple of months ago. I think he wants to get rid of me."

"Oh, Fran, like he would make you travel all day and night do that to you on the day of your court hearing, and while you are on maternity leave. He's bad, but not that mean. Anyway, he could have already written you a letter or email if that was the case."

He could have. But he didn't. When I met with Thomas later that day, he told me that he wanted to replace me with someone else, and had removed my job.

13

The Countdown Begins

I was upset and tired. But mostly, I was scared. While not in the league of Ciudad Juarez, which drug gangs have turned into one of the most senselessly violent cities in the world, Mexico City is up there among the world's most dangerous places. The city, despite its stunning architecture, was starting to feel intimidating. I nervously wound my way through speeding cars to get to the bus station.

At the ticket desk I found myself next to an American man who didn't speak Spanish, so I helped him with the translation.

"Tell your gringo friend that I don't like his eyes," said the man at the desk. They were blue. Not good. "Where the fuck is his money? I won't give him the ticket till he has paid. *Chingada madre*."

This was no place for a foreign woman on her own, not even a well-travelled one.

Certainly my vulnerability hadn't been helped by my encounter with Thomas. He'd played the 'how are you and the baby' card for about a minute and then given me my marching orders. Though my taxi journey to the station was a non-event, I'd found myself shaking in the car. Everyone I'd spoken to warned against taking taxis in Mexico City; the taxi drivers themselves had warned me against fake drivers who hijack tourists or stab them for a bit of cash or their suitcase. I had been lucky so far, but this driver seemed different.

Alfonso and Pepe had insisted I did not go alone, and the wonderful Aurora had offered to drive me, but I felt I had to do this alone.

The portly men in cowboy hats who seemed amusing when I was with Rick, had tonight distorted into more sinister, shady figures, as my imagination worked overtime. I boarded the bus at 10:00 pm and shrank into my seat, wrapping my scarf around my head and doing my best to look as unapproachable as possible. Glancing around, I wondered who would come to my aid if I were attacked; it wasn't going to be the frail old lady in the next seat.

I was totally spent. I leaned against the window, desperately wanting to close my eyes, yet fearful that something would happen if I dozed off. It was an arduous fourteen-hour trip, and at some point sleep claimed me for several hours. I woke up, happy to be alive, as the bus pulled into Colima.

I hopped out to get some food for myself and some of the tamales—rice-stuffed banana leaves—that Rick loved. Another four hours on the bus, but now I felt on familiar territory. I reached Manzanillo and jumped into a cab. At that moment nothing mattered more than being with my husband and baby.

"Ah, good, so you managed not to become a statistic then," joked Rick. He was happy to see tamales for breakfast. But he wasn't really in the mood for much more.

I'd texted him to let him know I was boarding the bus in case I never came back, but also to relay what had happened with Thomas. He wasn't surprised, but that didn't make it any better for either of us. I loved my job, and even though I knew it would have been difficult to return to the same position with a baby, particularly as a large amount of travel was involved, I was truly sad. It was the way Thomas had announced he didn't think it was a good idea for me to go back, and he was actively looking for someone else. It was not just tactless; it was downright cruel. I was hurt by the way a lot of my team appeared to have removed the sword from its scabbard the day I left, even the ones I trusted the most.

Rick's apparent lack of empathy for my situation annoyed me

too. On one hand, it was understandable, as he had his own concerns with his employer. Things were moving at pace with the banking crisis and he needed to get back. They had sorted out a new job for him in the reshuffle. However, there was a provison that left no room to maneuvere: he had to be back by June 10th. It was now the 23rd of May, and it was looking increasingly unlikely he would be back by then.

Rick was businesslike enough to know that the world moved on, and though his employer wanted him, they couldn't wait forever. The air was thick with tension. I was living with a man who now felt he had no control over anything, and that was probably the worst thing that could happen to someone like him. Here was someone who had always run his own show, who looked after budgets in the tens of millions, and had run departments of hundreds of people. Initially, leaving that behind had been liberating, but now the lack of action was eating away at his soul. Seeing me cry about losing my job made him blow his top.

"How on earth can you possibly still care about your bloody job? You've already spent enough tears over Thomas and his lack of emotional intelligence. That is gone, OK? But we are stuck here. Stuck, stuck!"

"Well, sorry, it's been a long journey and it's all a bit too much to take in."

"I am going mad, Fra. I've had enough. I'm going stir crazy in this stinking hot flat with no connection to the world, not even the internet. I have spent the past five months speaking *through you,* as I cannot master enough Spanish. Do you know what it feels like for me? And now we have this girl we call our daughter, but we don't really have her, not yet. Do you get it, Fra? She's not ours. It's crazy. Meanwhile we're in the hands of two lawyers who are lazy even by Mexican standards, who never return our calls. Let's see, what else can be bothering me? Oh, my brother is getting married in two weeks and I am supposed to be his best man, and I haven't seen my dad since he nearly died. But you want me to sit here and hold your hand and wipe your tears because Thomas hurt your feelings? Piss off!"

"Rick, this is so typical you. You just never really care when it comes to *my* feelings, that's all. You are selfish."

"You're the one who is self obsessed. You and your belief in the bloody Universe doing the right thing for us. It's not delivering. Do you get that?"

I didn't reply. There was no point when he was like this. Marking time wasn't exactly fun for me either, but Rick was on the edge. He exiled himself to the terrace. I picked up the laptop and took advantage of Gaia sleeping to write some emails. When I opened the computer I saw a message that Rick had sent to a group of his friends.

Hey guys,

Writing from stinking hot Manzanillo. And then I will have to go downstairs with three lifts to even be able to send this to you. I feel trapped. The little girl is sleeping in her pram next to me. I love her. She is my daughter but apart from Fra and the two mad lawyers nobody seems to think so quite yet. We're on permanent trial. It's harrowing. I wake up at night thinking that someone will come and take her away, and by law they probably could. I wanna come home and have had enough of this. Hopefully I can fly back the day Sven Eriksson arrives to coach the Mexico team so I can kick his ass before I go. Mexican beer is not bad though. Sorry for being such a misery but that's the way it is. I'll survive. Maybe.

This was a man who rarely let it all out cutting loose. I felt for him, but I was hurting too. I decided to take a nap. I woke up as Gaia was wailing. What was Rick doing? I jumped out of bed and ran to the terrace to shout at him. He could at least attend to her after I'd been travelling all night. I found him with his head in his hands, crying over the speech he was trying to draft for his brother's wedding.

He looked up at me.

"Fra, I will never forgive myself if I miss the wedding, and it's been too long since dad had his heart attack. I wasn't there, and now I have to be there. I can't not be there."

I put my arms around him.

"You will be there, even if it means us staying behind. Now, we better feed that little girl." I was being functional and pragmatic, but it was all we had. That and hope, although Rick didn't have too much of the latter left in him right now.

Much hinged on the outcome of the court hearing. A successful court order would mean that we could immediately apply for Gaia's new birth certificate and her passport. The birth certificate situation was an interesting one, to say the least. If you do a domestic adoption in the UK, for example, the records of the baby's life exist forever and are traceable. Instead of a new birth certificate, you receive an 'adoption certificate', which is legally the same thing. However, it also contains details of the child's name as well as the birthparents.

In contrast, adoption of a child in Mexico takes him or her right back to year zero. The Mexican way of doing things would mean Gaia would never have to know she was adopted if I chose not to tell her. This fits in very well with the strong Catholic culture where people do not want to admit an inability to have their own children. Just like the woman disappearing to 'work' when she is pregnant, it is a pretence that everyone tacitly agrees to.

The isolation and frustration that Rick was feeling so intensely was exacerbated by the fact that our only contacts at this point were with Pepe, Alfonso, and assorted helpers. In addition to being the facilitators of our adoption, they were our friends, and they cared about us. This was a double-edged sword. Their natural desire to just take the day as it came—mañana—meant that perhaps things were not happening for us as fast as they could have. On top of that, they would say they were going to do things but you were never sure if they meant it or if it was just talk. Our need for urgency was something that was alien to them and their culture.

I remember when I told them we were in danger of losing our jobs if things didn't move on quickly.

'That's OK," they replied. "You can stay here with us."

Their chief concern at present seemed to be the need for us all to celebrate the court hearing, despite the fact we had no result. A gathering had been arranged prior to my leaving for Mexico City, but Rick and I felt no desire to celebrate. What if the court rejected us or didn't believe our witnesses? We needed reassurance, but every time I called Alfonso, either he wasn't there or he just wanted to chat about preparations for the party. Rick would mutter about him having disappeared, and I'd have to remind him that Alfonso also had other clients and other things to do. And he did have our interests at heart.

I got hold of Pepe, whose response would have been infuriating if I wasn't so used to it by now.

"Maybe a week more. Maybe three days. Maybe I will see the judge and ask him?"

Maybe. Maybe.

Sticky days rolled into sleepless nights in a life that was seemingly on autopilot. We worked out that there was about an hour's window in the late afternoon where we could sit on the balcony and get a breeze before the mosquitoes turned up for their evening bite fest.

Meanwhile, partly to make Rick feel something was happening, but also because I wanted to be sure I had clarity on what happened once the court order was issued, I called the Mexican Passport Office.

"You will need her new birth certificate, plus the original copy of her old birth certificate, plus your identification papers of course. You will also require the court order and the Spanish version of your certificate of eligibility, plus a letter from your lawyer and a paediatrician's report."

I was confused. Alfonso had said nothing about needing a copy of her old birth certificate, which I had never seen. I called Pepe.

"Well, if he says you don't need it, then I guess you don't need it."

"But the man at the office said I did need it."

"Don't worry, Alfonso knows what he is talking about."

The next day was the 24th of May. The phone rang. It was Alfonso.

"So you will be getting the court order on the 29th of May. I have it for sure."

"You're absolutely sure of that, Alfonso?" I asked.

"Yes, I am. The judge has told me." I relayed the news to Rick, who reacted quietly. He wasn't ready to put his money on anything yet, I could tell.

However, now we knew the date to pick up the court order, we could plan our departure from Mexico. We had to assume the outcome would be positive; there was no point in assuming anything else. The timings would be tight. It would go like this:

May 29th: Leave Manzanillo for Colima

May 30th: Pick up court order and new birth certificate. Head to Guadalajara

June 1st: Travel to Mexico City

June 2nd: Apply for Gaia's passport at Mexican Passport Office

June 3rd: Go to British Embassy for final entry papers

June 4th: Fly back to London.

<hr />

With the exception of the flight tickets, which could be done in English by Rick, I booked the necessary appointments. The countdown was officially starting, and it had renewed Rick's energy.

"Alfonso wants me to go and celebrate. There is a party at his parent's rancho. Do you mind if I go?" What he was really saying was he wanted to get pissed with the boys on his own. I was glad to see him opening up again.

"Let's at least have prawn pasta before you head off. I bought fresh fish at the market this morning. It will be good to have something in your stomach. You know they never eat before midnight."

Half an hour after he left, he sent me a text.

ON THE BUS, SICK AS A DOG – YOU OK?

I felt a bit strange, but more uncomfortable than sick. However, my digestive system took longer than Rick's, and pretty soon we figured we had food poisoning. I could feel my temperature rising, so I knew it was bad. I lay in bed with Gaia right next to me so I didn't have to move far to feed or change her, and put a bucket on the other side so I could throw up without getting out of bed. Rick didn't last the night out. He texted to say he was on his way back and feeling very, very ill. The security lady saw him on his return.

"Virgin de Guadalupe, you look awful."

He told her we both had food poisoning and that I was trying to look after Gaia so she offered to come up and help.

"You are both so pale. What the hell did you eat?"

"Prawns, but they were fresh straight from the sea, so maybe it's a stomach bug?"

"You silly woman! Have you seen the state of the sea here? Petrol ships going back and forth fives times a day and no sewage system! That's why we eat the farmed ones."

I should have thought there was a reason why farmed prawns were heavily advertised and much more expensive; how very sad.

Her name was Ester, and she was adorable. Gaia took to her instantly, which was a relief. It was clear Ester knew what she was doing, and in her arms Gaia seemed peaceful and happy. I was not feeling as ill as Rick, and after Ester had been with us for a few hours I told her it was OK, I could manage. She insisted she would come if I needed her, but while Ester was wonderful, I wanted to hold my daughter close, even if it meant putting her down occasionally to run to the toilet.

Gaia was growing rapidly, even though her hair wasn't. In spite of her many infections, she was much calmer and had started to smile. I used to think that when people told me their baby's first smile was their biggest joy, it was a cliché. But they are right; it was the most precious gift I'd ever had. Despite the waiting and the tension, we were enjoying her. Rick had already watched football with her and insisted that he personally give her her evening bath, something he still tries to do every night. When it got cooler at night we carried her down to the beach and showed her the birds.

"What do you think of these huge strange creatures, Gaia?" I would ask her. "We do not have them where we are going. Or this sun. Soon we will fly away to somewhere much colder, so being Latin women we must make the most of it."

It had taken a month before I felt that she knew me, knew my smell, and wanted to be held close by me. With Rick, it hadn't been nearly as difficult. I realised that the swapping of mothers must have been strange for her. It was amazing to see how she responded differently to each of us. She knew who was who. The only way she would keep still in bed was when Rick stroked her back—and that remains the case to this day. At first, I was a bit envious, but once we had gotten over the initial adjustment period I realised it was a good thing. After all, we were not in competition. We were in this together.

I was overjoyed at how much love I felt for Gaia. I didn't have to try. It felt perfectly natural, and it came from my heart, not my head. I had heard parents say that the moment they see their baby they instantly know they love them more than life itself. But this love grows more each day. Bonding is the most incredibly intense feeling, but it has no start, middle, or end. It just keeps happening. That's what makes it so special. I loved everything about her. I even rejoiced in the smell of rancid milk stuck in between the folds of her chubby, Buddha-like neck.

And now, as we contemplated packing up our Mexican life, I looked at her, this precious creature in my arms. I would fight for her, not just now, but forever.

Rick and I had to jettison pretty much everything we'd bought for her in anticipation of our travels.

"We won't be needing any of this," he said, gesturing at Gaia's pram, carry basket, and car seat. "And look, she's grown out of all of her clothes."

"We can't take all those toys, either."

"You mean our Wal-Mart collection? Oh, I am disappointed."

I already knew what I wanted to do with all the stuff. I would give the pram, carry cot, and seat to Vifac so they could be given to a new mother who had decided to keep her baby and couldn't afford much.

For the rest, we would go and see our old friend, the director of Istituto Cabañas, the home that did such a wonderful job of looking after five hundred children. This was the woman who couldn't help us because we hadn't been married for five years, and who, probably because she didn't want to engage in any more emotion, had cut us off rather coldly. But now, when I rang to tell her our news, she was delighted.

"Oh, I am so happy for you Francesca. Of course I would love to see your little girl. It's so wonderful that you want to see us again and that you remembered us."

We had left some of ourselves behind at that orphanage, just as we had done everywhere on our travels. We were explorers who had reached our destination. And now, as we prepared to leave Mexico, we were retracing those early steps. While we would keep in touch with people, there was undeniably closure in the air. The excitement of going home as a family to the UK was imbued with sadness at leaving this beautiful, chaotic country. While our stubborn perseverance was what had kept us going, we knew we had only reached our summit because of a strange and wonderful group of people who had shown us a level of humanity and friendship beyond anything we'd imagined, people whose natural kindness was truly humbling. And now we were leaving them.

Leaving Manzanillo itself was not so hard. It had the least

emotional resonance for us, much like an airport waiting room. Except it was now where Aurora would be coming to say goodbye, as she would be travelling later. Rick had to stay in the flat, as Gaia was asleep and Aurora didn't have time to stop. I went downstairs where she was waiting next to two male security guards, who seemed very impressed by her.

"Are you ready to go?"

"Yes, we have a tight schedule, but we should be back on time for the wedding."

"That's my girl! I had no doubt you would succeed. I am never wrong."

"Aurora, what can I say to thank you? There is nothing that would be enough. What you have done is incredible."

"Well, you don't have to say anything, as I am not the one to thank," she said, pointing at the sky. "God has been watching you, and so have your grandparents. Now hurry up and go. Remember, you are too blessed to be stressed!"

No Aurora, I am blessed to have met you, I thought as she kissed and hugged me through my tears. With no more words, like the duchess she was, she stepped into her shiny Mercedes and drove off. The security guards looked at me sobbing, uncontrollable tears streaming down my face.

"Nice car," said one.

The other one nodded.

❦

Our next step was to drive to Colima, where the court order allowing us to pick up Gaia's birth certificate had come through earlier than expected. Our Mexican contingent had already organised the important stuff: the farewell party. It would be held at Alfonso's sister's flat, with witnesses, lawyers, friends and friends of friends all in attendance. Aurora, bless her, rang us and sent a few boxes of beer, perhaps thinking the tequila might run out. But it didn't. It flowed continuously as the toasts and speeches became ever more lavish and ridiculous. Rick was much weakened from food poisoning, and on any other night he would have been in bed, but he wouldn't have missed this for anything. As a result, he was getting drunk very quickly. I held back, since Gaia needed at least one sober parent.

"I am honoured to have met such people like you. The little Buddha is more blessed than the real Buddha!" Pepe raised his glass.

Not to be outdone, Alfonso stood up, raising himself as majestically as his lack of height would allow.

"This was not a process or a coincidence. You were meant to succeed, and we were meant to meet. God bless you. We will always be here for you. Mi casa es tu casa!"

"So what was the best part of Mexico you visited?" enquired one of the guests.

"Cuba!" I joked.

"Oh, I love Cuba too. Pepe and I loved it when we went," said Pepe's girlfriend.

"You went? I thought Pepe said he had never been!"

"Oh yes, we went at Easter!" she said, not knowing that was actually the time Pepe told us he was having an operation and had disappeared, leaving us with Dolores and Conception.

"You little bastard!" Pepe tried to duck as Rick smacked him on the head.

We cheered everything we could think of, and then raised our bottles all over again, while Gaia slept peacefully in the car seat in the bedroom. I think she was accustomed to the level of noise of her country; she always seemed to find it easier to sleep in chaos than silence.

By 11:00 pm, nobody had thought to fire up the barbeque, but of course it was still early in Mexico. Finally, at 5:30 am, after dancing, shouting, laughing, crying and singing at the top of our voices, the party broke up. We'd asked Alfonso to book us a hotel. Unsurprisingly, he'd not done it. Not because he had forgotten, but because we were amigos, and amigos don't stay in hotels. But he'd neglected to figure out where the amigos would stay tonight.

"No problem," said his sister. "You two will sleep here in my flat. I will go to my friend's house."

And with that, she gathered up her pyjamas and went off to knock on her friend's door at 5:30 am, where presumably her presence would be seen as a completely normal occurrence.

Pepe was to join us at the office to pick up the court order in three hours. Mindful that he was drunk, and not terribly good at timekeeping even when he wasn't, Rick waved him off with the words, "Pepe, if you don't wake up on time, I will fucking kill you."

At 8:00 am, half an hour before we were due to pick up the court order, our mobile rang. It was Pepe. Up until now, his English had been limited to his passion for the Chemical Brothers.

"Pepe," said Rick, who was also still drunk.

"Andale. Rick. I am waked." He pronounced it way-ked. It was funny. And sweet.

In life, the moments you build up in your head as momentous events frequently become quite the opposite. At 8:30 am Pepe, his eyes hidden by dark sunglasses, waved to us from the steps of the office. Rick, too, was heavily hung over. It was one of the 350 sunny days Colima gets each year, but today it was positively luminous.

Gaia wore her best dress. It was white, with little yellow hand-sewn ducks. I wore jeans and a smart white top, and I felt great. With the fragrant aroma of tequila emanating from Pepe and Rick, our daughter officially became Gaia Ruby Polini.

Gaia had to sign her birth certificate with a fingerprint. I picked her up and leaned her over so that the large lady could press her little finger on the inkpad and then the certificate.

And then suddenly we were outside again. We celebrated at a fruit stall with guavas and mangoes with lime juice and, of course, chilli, and drank copious amounts of water. Suddenly everything that had happened in the past few months tumbled through my head like an emotional express train.

And now Pepe was ready to say goodbye.

"Promise you will come and see us, Pepe?" It felt lame to say such a thing. In such moments the words never work. Plus it all felt so hurried.

"Of course! Don't worry." And then some English out of nowhere. "I'll miss you guys. Say hello to the Chemical Brothers for me," he said. He tried to hug Rick who, despite his time in this Latin country, couldn't quite get his head around hugging men tightly. So he hugged me twice as hard.

"Remember to contact Danny de Vito so he can play Alfonso in the movie about all this. OK?"

"Yeah! I have already contacted Harry Potter to be you," I joked. We waved as we stepped into our respective cars. We drove alongside each other for a while, but suddenly Pepe was frantically gesturing to us, something in his hand.

"Stop, stop," I said to Rick. "He wants us to pull over."

We stopped next to him.

"Here," he said handing us the court order, "you might need this."

Between Colima and Mexico City we would stop in Guadalajara to obtain some necessary papers from the paediatrician. That meant one last stay with our old friends at the European Lifestyle flats, so we could also visit Istituto Cabañas. We had dropped the pram at Vifac, but kept the car seat so that we could use it for Gaia to sleep in. I had clothes and toys for the home, but desperately wanted to do something more.

"Oh, this girl is lovely," said the director. She thanked us for the clothes and toys.

"We need all the help we can get, as you know."

"Look," I said to the directora, "we are both so touched by what you do here and impressed with how you do it. So we want to help you by raising money."

"Oh, thank you so much, that's very kind."

"But here's the thing," I said. "I want you to tell me what you need. What would make a big difference to you?"

"A washing machine."

"No, a BIG difference. We're talking about getting Europeans to raise money here. Aim higher."

"Francesca, do you have any idea what an industrial washing machine that serves five hundred children costs?"

"Aha, I am with you now. How much?"

It turned out that the sum required was equivalent to around £7000. It was a big commitment, but I promised her that no matter how long it took I would send money each month. It would not be easy, but I was determined to do it.

More grateful hugs at the paediatrician's, and then it was time to call Conception to say goodbye. She had been good to us, but had gone strangely silent.

"Oh, Fracesca, how is everything?"

"Great, we are on our way back. I couldn't leave without saying goodbye."

"Oh, that is such wonderful news."

"What happened, Conception? Why are you not at the office any longer?"

"I was fired. I think it's because I broke my arm, and Alfonso can't afford to have me around without working, but it's fine. I'll find something else. I am at my sister's rancho now, helping her out with the animals."

Even though she didn't seem too disappointed, I wondered if she'd made up the reason for getting fired to protect my feelings. That's what these people were like. I would probably never know.

After tonight, Rick, Gaia and I would be making the most important journey of our lives. But tonight we would celebrate with a last meal in Guadalajara. It could so easily have been Rick's last meal. I had no idea what it was, but that night he became ill, erupting with another violent bout of food poisoning. Perhaps it was recurring? Or maybe it was the stress? He was vomiting and had diarrhoea, but we still had to catch the bus to Mexico City the next day.

With Gaia in my arms, one sick husband, and four massive suitcases we said goodbye to the European Lifestyle Apartments and left to board the day bus to Mexico City. Gaia slept quite nicely in between feeds and dirty nappies. Thankfully she wasn't affected by any food poisoning, but poor Rick was throwing up periodically out of the window and racing for a toilet at every stop.

We'd asked Alfonso to come to the Mexican Passport Office with us. Though my Spanish was good, I felt at this point I didn't want to put a foot wrong. We also both felt that we needed moral support, and Alfonso had become a great friend.

"But, my friends, you don't need me! You could do my job with your eyes shut by now! And all you have to do is hand over the documents and twenty-four hours later you will get the passport. I have done this so many times, it's dead simple," he said.

"Gaia said she needs Uncle Al."

"OK, guys, I am catching the overnight bus so I can be there in the morning."

Arriving in Mexico City, we were less triumphant conquerors than wounded army. Rick had to lie down as soon as possible and take on lots of fluids. Gaia had done well, but she too was tired and a little confused. I was loath to leave Gaia with Rick in the state he was in; in the UK, they would have probably hospitalised him for at least twenty-four hours, but we had things to do. We'd booked a furnished apartment, as we needed to sterilise bottles for Gaia, internet access, and a cot. Rick slept from the moment we arrived. I bathed Gaia, and then we both went to bed.

Alfonso arrived early in the morning, looking somewhat dishevelled from the journey.

"I have my suit in my bag. Do you mind if I get changed?"

"Do you want to shower? Please, mi casa es tu casa!"

I was so pleased I could finally say it back! Rick waited until the last minute to get out of bed. He was so weak and uncoordinated I had to button his shirt. Alfonso had said appearances mattered. I wore my one smart dress I had worn for the entrega and meticulously prepared Gaia. I plonked her in the baby sling, and off we went.

"I have never seen you guys so stressed. Stay calm. It's all going to be OK. I promise you, this is the easy bit. You have done the hard work now," said Alfonso.

"Where is the original birth certificate?" demanded the passport office clerk. I looked at Alfonso. He was as ghostly as Rick. I decided to play dumb.

"Oh dear," I said, "I thought you said we didn't need it."

"No, no, I told you on the phone. You understood."

"Normally that is kept on file at court. I am their lawyer, I know this," insisted Alfonso.

"That's ridiculous. I do this every day sir, and people come with the right documents, or a better excuse for not having them. And anyway, you can't have the passport for five days."

My heart sank.

"But you didn't tell me that."

"It takes twenty-four hours when it's a natural baby. With adoptions it's longer, as the documents need to be looked at by a few different departments. It's the rule. I am sorry. Come back when you have all the documents and allow for five working days, OK?"

We were flying in two days. But that wasn't going to happen now. We had no idea what to do.

"I'll think of something, guys. Even if it takes me going back to Colima to get the papers by plane, we will do this." As lovely as he was, we knew Alfonso couldn't snatch victory from the jaws of defeat at this point.

And then, divine intervention. To this day I really, honestly believe someone was watching over us. Because, at that very moment, Aurora called.

"Buenooo. Todo bien?"

I explained what had happened.

She muttered something about Alfonso being incompetent and then told me to go to reception and ask for Maria Gloria.

"Call me back if she is in."

It turned out that Maria Gloria was indeed in the building.

"OK," said Aurora. "You give me half an hour, OK?"

I sat on the steps of the office to feed Gaia. They wanted special passport pictures of her, and these could conveniently be obtained from what looked like a fast food van outside. It was funny, as the picture specifications required me to hold her up but not so my hands were visible.

True to her word, Aurora called.

"Okay, I have spoken to Maria Gloria, and she will do me a favour and let me send the original birth certificate later. So you can get your passport."

"Oh, Aurora, thank you, thank you."

"Not so fast. She cannot do anything about the five days. You will be waiting, I am afraid."

For the moment it didn't matter, as I delighted in watching my baby daughter 'sign' her passport. She had to dip her finger in ink and fingerprint it.

"OK," said the clerk. "I will call you in five days to tell you when to pick it up."

There was nothing to do but accept it. We would have to change the flights, but first Alfonso wanted to celebrate with steak and wine. Rick would not be celebrating; he would be going back to bed. However, as it was Gaia's day, she would be the star guest. We put her in the car seat next to us at the table. Alfonso sat there looking at her affectionately and playing with her non-stop.

"God, Alfonso, I cannot believe we have nearly made it, but now we'll be cutting it fine for Rick's brother's wedding and I couldn't bear to see him disappointed."

" Relax. You have ten days still. You'll be fine!"

"Alfonso, I am an optimistic person, but honestly, how can you always be so positive?"

"Aha, well, that is about being Mexican and believing in God, and of course the Virgin of Guadalupe. It's been a tough time for me, too. I am glad I have found you guys. I tell you I will never go away for so long again. It was a mess."

"What do you mean?"

"Well, Aurora was really cross with me because I let Dolores stay at the Vifac home, and she had been causing trouble. I pretty much only work with Vifac, so you can imagine how important they are to me. Without them, no clients."

"So you do worry."

"Well, worry is a bit negative, but let's say it wasn't easy at a time when Pepe wasn't so helpful."

"Who told you that?" I wondered how all this information had come together, because it just didn't sound right.

"Dolores. And Conception was bitching behind my back with my clients."

Did he know what she'd said to us?

"What do you mean?"

"Dolores told me that that Conception was taking the opportunity to stab me in he back. I felt so disconnected, but it was all so nasty I didn't want to come back."

"Alfonso, can't you see what was really happening?"

"What do you mean?"

"The people you speak of are really lovely and good hearted, except for one, and she is the link between all the problems. Dolores should be your worry."

"I feel for her."

"You know, I don't like to judge, but you take being non-judgmental to another level!"

"She is a lost soul."

"Who was manipulating everyone, including her little girl, for her own interests. Holy Virgin of Guadalupe, Alfonso, are you blind?"

"I think I am the only one who actually understands her."

It was worrying to hear him spout this stuff. Where had his judgment gone?

"I think you are the only one who doesn't see her true colours. Maybe you fancy her?"

"Don't be silly, Francesca! I am still looking for my soul mate, and my mum would kill me if I dated someone with a kid! Let's toast to Gaia!"

Matriarchal women and their eternal little boys! I couldn't get over just how naïve Alfonso was.

We toasted Gaia and then I fed her. Alfonso was leaving and wanted to say goodbye to Rick. We found him stumbling around. He handed Alfonso the baby car seat.

"Will you take this to Aurora? It goes with the pram we left."

"Of course, my friend. You guys have a safe trip, but if you need to wait longer than five days, you know we are here for you."

Despite his frustrating manner of working, Alfonso really was a good soul, albeit one who didn't always see the big picture.

It had occurred to me that once home we would not have anything for Gaia. Whilst in Manzanillo, I emailed my friends, asking them to start gathering anything they thought we might need for a nursery. Now I opened my laptop to find an email from my dear friend Fulvia.

"They are already in Gaia's room."

Apparently she and another friend, Alex, my friend whose son's birthday party I had gone to such a long time ago now, had been in and already set up the room. As I was reading my other emails, my phone rang. It was Maria Gloria, the woman from the passport office.

"Are you available to come and pick your passport up at 4:00 pm?"

"Whaaaat!" I shrieked so loudly that I scared Gaia, who was on my lap. Rick came out of the bedroom.

"Are you OK?"

"We can pick up the passport. Oh, my God."

To this day, I will never know if it was Aurora who kept pushing. I did ask her once, but she dismissed the question.

"I'm coming too," said Rick, scrambling into some clothes.

I recognised Maria Gloria straight away. In fact, I felt her as I walked in. Special people have a brighter aura.

"Oh, my God, thank you so much. You don't know what this means to us." I honestly was ready to go down on my knees at that point.

"Look, I have huge respect for you and your husband and the work of Vifac. I live in this city, where there are two million street children who will never have a shot at life, and most likely a short life to boot. And you, you have given this little girl a life and love. You are good people."

I honestly didn't think Rick and I did anything special, and I still don't believe we have. Maria Gloria came around from behind the desk and hugged me. I burst into tears, but someone else had done so first. It was Rick, in a display of emotion I had never seen. How he had the energy left for those tears, I'll never know.

"God bless you," she said, kissing Gaia on her head.

"God has already blessed us."

How different the world looks when things start to go your way. Rick was still horribly ill and had lost loads of weight, but we were literally twenty-four hours away from finishing the process we'd begun almost five months ago. Tomorrow we had an appointment with the British Embassy at 8:00 am. It was actually with the same person I'd met when I had to prove residency. All we needed was a stamp in Gaia's Mexican passport allowing her to stay in the UK until we could apply for her British one.

"I will come too," said Rick. He didn't want to miss any moments, even if he had to crawl to get there.

🐷

The next morning, our little family fronted up at the embassy, ready to put the final piece in the jigsaw. The Scottish man I'd dealt with previously waved me over. He looked through the documents and said: "OK, you leave it all here and then pick up the visa in ten to twelve weeks."

I actually didn't think he was speaking to us at first. Maybe he was talking to a colleague about someone else. But no, he was looking directly at me.

"Sorry?" I got closer to the glass.

"Come back in ten to twelve weeks."

"But on the phone you said it would take twenty-four hours. Don't you remember?"

"In twenty-four hours you can have all your documents back. But you won't have that stamp in the passport until the UK Home Office has approved it, and that takes time."

"But we have our flight tickets booked."

I couldn't believe this was happening. It seemed like all the goodwill everyone else had shown us was being wiped out in one fell swoop.

He paused and looked at me sympathetically.

"Listen," he said, "there is a technicality, and it's perfectly legal. Mexico is a non-visa country, which means Mexicans don't need a visa for the UK if they enter as tourists. You can take her in that way and apply for the visa when you are there."

I was dubious about this instant solution. It seemed too easy.

"Are you sure?"

"I gave the same advice to another couple a few days ago. It will take a lot less time, too, as you won't be sending documents back and forth. Once you are back in the UK you can go straight to the Home Office."

He seemed to know what he was talking about. He was an immigration official, after all. Rick nodded, and we decided to take his advice.

That night, Rick managed some dinner before throwing half of it up. It was a positive development, all things considered. We raised our glasses.

"We did it," he said.

"We busted through."

"Jesus, I can't believe it Fra. I really can't."

"I love you," I said, and I kissed him.

He kissed me back passionately.

I didn't sleep at all that night. I was watching a complete replay of the past five months in my head. Tomorrow we would head for the airport, our Mexican adventure would end, and we would return to the UK a family.

"What a tiny baby you have," said the lady at the check-in counter the next morning.

"Yes. We just adopted her. We are taking her home," I said proudly.

I really think Aurora was behind the check-in desk or hovering above, because the check-in attendant suddenly handed us two first-class tickets.

"But we didn't book this. You've made a mistake."

"I'm upgrading you and your baby to First Class. Enjoy the flight."

We'd left London on a cheap charter flight in the depths of winter for an adventure that many said was stupid and ill-advised. We had no precedent; in fact we really had no idea what we were doing, and half the time we had no idea what the Mexicans were doing either. Now, five months to the day later, we were flying back with our precious baby to start a new life.

Epilogue

All during the flight home, I couldn't help reflecting on how much had changed in such a short time. In many ways, it had been the most trying period of my life, of our lives, of our marriage. We'd had our hopes raised countless times, only to see them dashed again and again. We'd seen a side of adoption that had scared both of us. Rick and I had our hearts broken repeatedly, each time worse than the last, until we'd retreated into ourselves, licking our wounds and wondering how much more we could take.

But there were things to be grateful for, too. We had not allowed the events of the past five months to tear us apart, even though there were times when we wondered if we could stand the strain. We'd learned more about ourselves, about how much punishment we could take. We'd discovered new sources of inner strength. We'd met wonderful people who opened their hearts and homes to us, treating us like family, reminding us that we were part of something greater: a human family, with a bond that transcends culture, language, and politics. We had sacrificed much, but for everything we'd given up, we'd gained something better.

And, of course, we had Gaia, who was the cause of, and the reward for, our epic quest. Looking down at her in my arms, I marvelled again and again at this tiny bundle. How could such a wee thing inspire such feeling in so many people? She was truly miraculous. I remembered how I'd felt myself beginning to expand as soon as I made room for her in my heart, even before I knew her. Now she was really here, on her way back to the country that would become the only home she'd ever remember. I had trusted in the Universe, and Rick had, too, and because of our leap of faith we had made our dream a reality. We had a baby. We were a family. We were complete.

And then we landed in customs, and learned that our struggle was not over yet. Not even close.

🐟

In comparison to the immigration official who'd pulled us out of line and locked us in an interrogation room, people like Miguel the shady lawyer, or the vicious procuradora who had resented us for not being Mexican, seemed like angels. As soon as she left the room, I burst into tears. Rick and I were both exhausted, he was still feeling the effects of food poisoning and now, after the long flight home, during which we had dared to let ourselves believe that we had succeeded, our hopes had been dashed once again. Our very future as a family was in jeopardy. My maternal instinct had kicked in, and I was in fight-or-flight mode. Adrenalin was coursing through me. But who did I fight? What could I do that would not further jeopardise us? Nothing. And so we waited, and waited, and waited, until we felt that we were going to explode.

Finally, after several hours, another official, also a woman, appeared. She had with her some of the documents we'd spent months gathering and safeguarding, but she told us Gaia's passport had been confiscated, and the other papers were being used to verify that we were telling the truth. This woman seemed somewhat more rational than the first one, at least. Once again, we went through the whole story, explaining about DCSF, about DIF, about Vifac, and at the end of it she said, "Frankly, I don't understand why you were pulled aside."

Finally! A ray of sunshine in the clouds! Maybe now she would admit that the whole thing had been one big mistake. Rick and I looked at each other hopefully. He reached out and squeezed my hand, reassurance in his eyes.

"But it's too late," the woman continued. "You've already been referred to a case worker. Please understand there is nothing I can do now. The wheels have been set in motion, and you will have to go through the system."

"Case worker?" I said. This phrase conjured up horrible images in my mind. You only ever hear this term in association with abusive parents, with Children's Services, with people who had their kids taken away from them because they were unfit. I clutched Gaia close. She was able to sense my fear and panic, and she began to cry. Now I knew only one thing: if someone tried to take my baby out of my arms, I would fight tooth and nail. Consequences be damned. I was a mother, and this was my child.

Rick, no doubt, was having similar thoughts. But he managed to stay calm. Once again, he was my rock, my rational left brain.

"So what happens now?" he asked. I was amazed at how reasonable he sounded.

The woman explained: Gaia would be given a temporary visa that allowed her to stay in the country for a week. We could go home with her now. But there was every possibility that we would have to return to Mexico with her if the visa could not be renewed, which it would have to be, on a weekly basis.

"For how long do we continue this?" Rick asked.

"Until it's decided that you legally adopted her and that she can stay," said the woman.

Finally, we were turned loose. Our jubilation had been smashed to smithereens. We were suspects now, the government having decided that we had brought Gaia into the country illegally. The old fear I was foolish enough to think we'd left behind in Mexico had followed us across the ocean, and it weighed like a thousand-pound gorilla on our backs.

But, for the moment, we were back home. And it was wonderful to cross the threshold of our place with Gaia in our arms. We walked her around the house, showing her this and that, delighting in how she already seemed to transform the place we had left as a couple and returned to as parents. We thought with wonder of the journey she had made. She would never remember it, but it had altered the course of her life forever. And ours, too.

🐾

The next months were, unfortunately, fraught with the same uncertainty that had plagued our last weeks in Mexico. We were subjected to yet another Home Invasion by a case worker. We had to submit to weekly interviews, during which we were asked what Gaia had been doing—as if she was capable of anything other than eating, sleeping, and pooping. We also received a letter informing us that Gaia was forbidden to marry, seek employment, or change her address.

"You hear that?" Rick told Gaia, in stern, mocking tones. "No getting married. Actually, that's the only part of this I agree with. I absolutely forbid you to get married, young lady."

Eventually her passport was returned to us, stamped with a three-month visa. This was progress, but it still meant that Gaia could not leave the country. This meant no visits to Italy to introduce her to our families. Some of our family members were able to come to England, and gradually she began to meet her uncles, aunts, grandparents, and of course Lily from Australia, all of whom welcomed her with tears of genuine, heartfelt love.

In the meantime, I began a letter-writing campaign. I was determined to inform every single person who could possibly matter about what had happened to us and how ridiculous it was. I wrote to our Member of Parliament, the then Foreign Secretary David Miliband and the Home Office. We hired an immigration lawyer and an adoption lawyer. Slowly, the tide began to shift in our favour. Our local council could have prosecuted us, as it turned out, but instead they were wonderfully supportive, and I believe this too had an effect. As weeks turned into months, and months became a year, finally Gaia was granted a British passport, with no travel restrictions placed upon it. Then we took her to Rome, and only then did I feel as if we were well and truly home.

Today, Gaia is a beautiful, bubbly two-year-old. She is tri-lingual, equally comfortable speaking English, Italian, and Spanish. She even translates for her daddy whenever he becomes hopelessly lost in the mishmash of languages. She is a wonderful swimmer, able to dive to the bottom of a pool and retrieve toys all by herself. I was a great swimmer as a child, and tears of pride spring to my eyes as I watch her cavort in the water like a little dolphin. I am still amazed on a daily basis at how this little Mayan soul has ended up in our European lives.

Our struggle to adopt Gaia has inspired me to fight for the cause of making international adoption smoother for everyone. To this end, I have founded Adoption with Humanity (AdoptionWithHumanity.com), a non-profit organisation that exists for the purpose of helping people who find themselves in the same situation we were in. We exist to support parents who, like us, feel called to share their blessings with a child who has no parents and no home, and we exist also to fight for the rights of abused, neglected, and abandoned children everywhere. With the wealth of the world so unequally distributed, we feel that a child without a home should be free to find one anywhere, regardless of citizenship.

The bonds we formed during our search for Gaia are stronger than ever. Out of respect for Vifac, we had her christened Catholic, and Alfonso and Cristy, his intern, travelled to Rome for the ceremony, during which they became her godparents.

Michelle, who we met at our first council meeting, is today the mother of three adopted siblings, ages five, three, and two, who had suffered through years of neglect and placement in various foster homes. Michelle is exhausted, but happy. She is also an inspiration to me whenever I feel overwhelmed by the burdens of one child.

Dolores is still trying to get Beatriz adopted. Most recently, as I heard from Pepe, she found a US family who was willing to take Beatriz—as long as they took Dolores, too. But Dolores was refused entry into the US, and so she and her daughter continue to exist in a hell of her own making. I think of poor Dolores often, but even more often I think of Beatriz, praying that she finds somewhere stable and secure to land in this confusing and frightening life.

I am still raising money for the Istituto Cabañas which I send regularly.

We are in touch with Pepe on a regular basis, partly because we have decided to adopt a second Mexican child. This means that we are beginning the whole process again. We had an email exchange with DCSF (now DfE, Department for Education) not long ago… during which the same case worker from our last adoption told us he was not sure we are allowed to adopt a child from Mexico! After being told we had to choose a different country to adopt from, I began another letter-writing campaign to various politicians, including Ed Balls, and finally we were approved to go back and do it all over again. This time, we expect things to run more smoothly, although we are prepared for anything. Somewhere out there, a second little soul is waiting to join our family, and we have already begun to make room for him in our hearts.

Every night, as I put Gaia to sleep, I tell her the story of how we found her all over again. She loves to hear the tale of how she came from a magical land called Mexico, how she was brought to us by an angel named Aurora, and how we will soon be going back to find a little brother for her. Gaia is well aware that most babies come from their mother's tummies, but whenever anyone asks where she came from, she says with pride, "I came from a plane!"

Because we plan on doing our second adoption through Vifac as well, we are in touch with Aurora about once a month. Just last week, in fact, we received a call from her.

"Fracescaaaaaaa," came that wonderful, smoky voice, as deep as a man's. "I have some news for you. Get your bags ready. Your second baby is going to be here by the end of the year."

And as we all know, when Aurora says something. . .